Jade Winters

Faking It

by Jade Winters

Published by Wicked Winters Books

WICKEDWINTERS

Copyright © 2014 Jade Winters

www.jade-winters.com

Edited by Lisa Frederickson

ISBN: 978-1-500-36035-1

Other titles by Jade Winters

Novels

143
A Walk Into Darkness
Caught By Love
Guilty Hearts
Say Something

Novellas

Talk Me Down From The Edge

Short Stories

The Makeover
The Love Letter
Love On The Cards
A Story Of You

Acknowledgements

Though my name is solely on the cover of this book, it would not have been possible but for two people: Lisa Frederickson and my partner, Ali. I was incredibly lucky that Lisa took on the task of editing this book and guiding me through the previously uncharted territory of humour. Thanks for your invaluable creative input and great wit.

I also owe a huge debt to Ali for the tireless work she does on every book I write. This one was no exception. Without her, none of it would have been possible. I am eternally grateful.

For Ali, as always

Chapter One

"You're fired!"

Danni's smoky, emerald green eyes glared at her boss. Who did Pete think he was, *Donald Trump?*

"You're kidding me!" she retorted, shaking her head from side to side, her butterscotch blonde ponytail swishing midway down her back.

"Do I look like I'm *kidding?*"

To be fair, he didn't. He looked pretty stressed. His balloon-like face was crimson with a quivering bulge pulsating at his temple. As much as she would have loved to tell the jumped-up squirt where to stick his job, she couldn't – her rent was due at the end of the month and without her wages, she would be out on the streets.

She scanned the Mediterranean style restaurant, desperate to avoid further eye contact with Pete. As Danni's gaze finally rested on the rustic pizza oven, her delicately sculptured face grew even more lost and forlorn knowing she didn't have long to plead her case. The evening shift started in fifteen minutes. "Come on Pete, give me a break! I've only been working here three weeks."

"That's the problem. In three weeks you've smashed more plates than a whole season of weddings in Greece!"

"That's not fair," she immediately protested, watching as he used the back of his hand to wipe the sweat from his greasy forehead. *Yuck.* She dreaded to think how many of those salty droplets made their way into the coq au vin of unsuspecting diners as he prepared their tasty casserole. "Chef's special" indeed.

Pete threw down the T-towel he was holding in his large veiny hands. "Not fair, Danni?" he asked, raising his eyebrows. "Follow me."

Heart pounding, she followed Pete to the kitchen, the scene of her latest disaster. There, he revealed a pile of broken dishes she had "hidden" beneath scraps of tiramisu in the bin. A pretty sorry effort, she had to confess. Evidently her attempts at a cover-up were about as effective as a chocolate teapot.

She glanced around the familiar kitchen nervously. Stainless steel pots and pans dangled from a silver rack above the ten-ring hob. Jimmy, a dark haired, wannabe chef, stopped wiping down the surfaces, made a quick dash past them and headed to the back door.

"Well, I can explain what happened there," she said, grappling for words she knew wouldn't come.

Pete moved to stand in front of her and held her gaze; there was a strange melancholic expression on his face. "Look, Danni, you're a great girl. The customers love you, but love isn't going to pay the bills. You're too much of a liability." With that, he turned on his heels and strutted purposefully towards the door.

Danni gasped at Pete's final insult. *Liability!* How rude! She stood dumbstruck, watching him retreat from the kitchen, his head bowed down as if he was looking for something. *Manners perhaps?*

Resting her hip against the worktop, she absent-mindedly picked up a raw carrot from a white chopping board and angrily bit the tip off. "Fan. Fucking. Tastic," she muttered between crunches as she ripped the white apron from around her waist. Twenty-four and unemployed again.

***

"It's going to be all right!" Danni told herself as she began the drawn-out ascent to her flat on the sixth floor. She had to put things into perspective. It was only a job and a crap one at that. It wasn't as if she'd lost a limb or that waiting tables was ever going to make her a millionaire. All that thankless job had ever given her was minimum wage and chronic lumbago. By the time she reached her floor, she was fighting to catch her breath. She was secretly convinced the air was thinner up there. Why she'd ever agreed to rent a flat in a building without a lift she'd never know. It was just another one of those decisions she made without thinking – she seemed to be doing more and more of that lately.

Normal breathing resumed, she crossed the small landing and slipped the key into the lock on her rickety front door. Before she could make the triumphant step over the threshold she heard a shuffling of feet behind the door opposite and then a creak. Danni turned to look and saw a swirling cloud of smoke filter through the small crack in the doorway. Her pot-loving neighbour's head appeared through the gap, scanning the hallway nervously.

"Danni – you want some ganja?" he whispered in a pseudo-Caribbean accent, his pupils the size of saucers.

Mick was a tall, anaemic looking, twenty-something from Reading. The nearest he had ever come to the Caribbean was a portion of rice and peas at the Notting Hill Carnival in 2004.

Her evening marred by her "unexpected" sacking, she would just about take a hit of anything if it promised her a few minutes of amnesia. "Thanks Mick."

"Bad day?" he asked, opening the door a fraction more and leaning forward to pass her the joint.

Danni took the roll-up and dragged on it deeply before exhaling a plume of smoke. "You could say that," she said passing it back to him.

He let out a small giggle. "You wanna come in and play Grand Theft Auto?"

Her head drooped dejectedly – the last thing she needed was company. "No thanks. Maybe some other time."

Mick nodded and without a word, ran his tongue over his dry lips and closed his door. She had been living next door to him for over a year and didn't think she had ever seen him when he wasn't stoned. He had offered her "da herb" most days during that time. Though dabbling in illegal substances wasn't a habit of hers, she occasionally took him up on his offer, though not very often – she liked her brain cells firing on all cylinders. Now, had he been offering a daily supply of chocolate chip muffins, it might have been a different story.

The brief interaction over, she stepped into the hallway of the shabby two-bedroom flat she shared with best friend Josh and stopped suddenly in her tracks. She stood as if paralysed, staring at a single self addressed envelope resting innocently on the mat beneath her. Her heart was thumping uncontrollably. Could this be it? Her ticket to the fabulously glam lifestyle she so desired? She truly believed every living soul had a pre-destined path in life and that everything happened for a reason. Maybe just maybe, there was good cause for her losing her job so suddenly.

Nervously, tentatively, she knelt down and scooped up the cream coloured envelope between her fingers. Mercilessly, she tore at the envelope with the tip of her nail – today was not the day to be afraid of paper cuts. Heart in her mouth, she withdrew the crisp white paper, the bold lettering – Desti Publishing – flashing before her eyes. This was one of the best publishing houses in the UK. Surely the fact that they had taken the time out of their busy schedule to reply meant it was good news.

Excitement bubbled up inside of her as she scanned the page below. "*Dear Danielle*". Danni's free hand clapped over her open mouth. Oooh, they had addressed her by her first name! That had to be a good sign. She read on. Her wide eyes began to shrink. Why was she finding it so difficult to swallow? As the words floated across the page, she blinked to dislodge the tears welling in her eyes. Her fate was sealed.

She knew she should be used to receiving these letters by now. Rejection letters. *"You're no good"* letters. *"Don't-give-up-the-day-job-that-you–just-got-sacked-from"* letters. This was number fifteen. Instead of becoming stronger with each damning blow, the insult struck harder, taking another part of her poetic soul every time. Not bad for a piece of work that had taken her two years to write! Twoooo whoooole years. Seven hundred and thirty days of creative toil all dismissed in a single sheet of A4.

Danni flicked on the hallway light, kicking the door shut behind her with her foot. Right, where was the vodka? Had she polished it off with rejection letter fourteen? No, that night it was the Babysham and Red Bull combo. Another bad decision.

Five minutes later, she was reclined in the cramped box they called a living room, sipping on a glass of flat Fosters she'd found behind the numerous take-away cartons in the fridge. That was the funny thing, no matter how poor she was, she always seemed to have money for a take-away.

"What the hell am I going to do now?" she asked herself, eying the pile of laundry balanced on top of the TV. She didn't have anything left to sell – everything of any value was either in Cash Converters or the pawnshop. Her life was pathetic. She had always thought by the time she had hit twenty-four she would have her life sorted. She'd be settled down with the woman of her dreams – smart, brunette, part-time cake-baker (preferably muffins, though willing to compromise). She would be on her second bestselling novel and the toast of literary circles.

In her fantasy, she saw herself as the female Oscar Wilde, full of sardonic wit, a celebrated storyteller. She and her beautiful lover luxuriating in a moderate sized house in Islington (she wasn't a showy sort of gal) with four bedrooms and a terrier named Sparky. Her days would be spent writing and replying to the thousands of messages she'd received from fans from around the world. Her evenings filled with charity events and dinner parties with other successful writers, where they would debate the huge pressures of being a successful international author.

Danni grimaced as the fantasy disappeared along with the last few drops of flat lager. Maybe she was getting ahead of herself; she did only write chick-lit after all.

There was only one course of action – first thing tomorrow, she'd scour the papers for a way out.

Chapter Two

Brooke removed her black-rimmed glasses and eyed the time on her mobile phone. She let out a long sigh. *Ten o'clock.* Megan had promised she would be there by six at the latest. What would her defence be this time? A drunk passenger? A delayed departure? A flat tyre on an Airbus A380? No, surely she wouldn't use those ones again. If there was one thing that Megan was good at, it was making up elaborate excuses. As an air hostess, Megan had a lot of material to work with.

Loosening her thick cocoa coloured tresses from a hair band, she clicked save on the Word document – she was done with the manuscript she was editing. Trying to concentrate on *"Think Yourself Happy in Four Days - Volume Fifteen"* was all she needed tonight. *But what did she need?* Even she didn't know anymore. She rested her head against the back of the seat, her blue eyes half circles of fatigue. Eight months ago, things had seemed a whole lot clearer. The classic tale of "girl meets girl, girl has lots of sex and girl lives happily ever after", was not quite running to plan. The sex was good, really good, but Brooke wanted, *needed*, something more.

She rose to her feet upon hearing the familiar sound of the front door slamming shut. She could just imagine Megan standing in the hallway rehearsing one of her ridiculous stories. Megan always went into a little too much detail, making the tale seem all the less plausible.

Tonight was one night too many. She didn't know how much longer she was going to be able to put up with living under a cloud of uncertainty. Although Megan told her she loved her, her actions said otherwise.

Brooke remained motionless, anxiously waiting for her lover's entrance and the familiar "confrontation scene". She stood gazing at the study door a few moments longer, before realising Megan wasn't coming to look for her at all. Instead, she heard footsteps heading in the other direction, towards the bathroom. Could she really be bothered questioning Megan yet again? Would it really do any good?

Against her better judgement, she made her way along the corridor to the bathroom and stood "casually" in the doorway, just as Megan was fixing her long dark hair into a ponytail. Though Brooke had seen her naked a million times before, she couldn't suppress the wave of desire that rose within her. She ran her eyes over Megan's slender form; her strong shoulders, her pert breasts, her wonderfully firm thighs. She really was something.

Megan jumped as she caught sight of Brooke. "Won't be a sec," she said as she quickly stepped into the bath and dragged the shower curtain across, symbolically dividing the two even further.

No apology then? No "How are you? How has your day been? Were you worried I was in a plane crash?" *Nothing.* Brooke eyed the pile of discarded clothes strewn across the floor and was tempted to scoop them up and throw them into the wash bin. It was as if she had been programmed to pick up after Megan despite the fact they didn't even live together. *Why couldn't things be like they were at the beginning?*

With that, Brooke was suddenly plunged back in time, reliving every detail of their first night together. It had been during a weekend away in an old cottage in Norfolk. Brooke was there with friends and had asked Megan to join them. Respecting Megan's wishes to take things slowly, Brooke had reassured her they'd have separate rooms. She had wanted Megan so much, yearned for her even. There had been weeks of flirting, texting, teasing, all leading to that one moment when everyone else had gone to bed. That one moment when Megan had knocked on her door. Brooke opened it and not believing Megan had come, just grabbed her, kissing her with aching passion, tearing her clothes off almost as though she was afraid she might never have this moment again. She remembered how Megan's lips felt; soft, warm, so sensual that every nerve ending in Brooke's body tingled. She remembered the first time she felt her beautiful breasts, her nipples standing erect, so inviting that Brooke felt as though she might explode if she didn't have her. She recalled the feel of her silky skin, her smell, the way she tasted, the moment she climaxed in her arms. Brooke remembered it all, she *felt* it all; it had been one of her favourite nights on earth.

The sound of the gushing shower jolted Brooke back into the present. The rose-tinted glasses of the past were gone. She turned away and walked to the bedroom to wait.

As she sat on her bed and looked around the room she saw traces of Megan everywhere. Her shoes on the floor by the chest of drawers, her jewellery on the bedside table, a solitary trainer sock in the centre of the room. But nothing permanent – none of her clothes hung in the wardrobe, none of the books on the shelf were hers. She didn't even leave her toothbrush.

"What are you still doing up?" Megan smiled, entering the room wearing nothing but a fluffy yellow towel.

Brooke frowned. "I've been worried. You could've had the decency to call."

Megan opened a drawer and withdrew one of Brooke's T-shirts. She never used to wear anything to bed except perfume. Another sign that things were different.

"Don't you think I tried? Your phone was switched off," Megan retorted casually.

Brooke looked puzzled for a few seconds. "Really? Funny how nobody else had trouble getting through."

Megan let the towel drop to the floor and pulled the T-shirt over her head. "Lucky them."

Brooke stripped down naked and lowered herself into bed, waiting until Megan turned around to face her before speaking again. "So, are you going to tell me where you've been? What was more important than spending time with me?"

Megan's eyes flickered momentarily. "If you must

know, a new girl started today. We took her out for a quick drink. I couldn't get out of it. Is that all right with you?" She slid into bed, lying on her side facing Brooke.

Brooke narrowed her eyes. "I don't call four hours a quick drink. And don't you think it's kind of late to have someone new out on their first day at work?"

"Not everyone's like you Brooke. Some people actually live in the moment and don't obsess about tomorrow."

Brooke snorted. "Are you saying I'm a stick in the mud?"

"Slightly …"

"I'm boring, is that it?"

Megan turned to face away from her and let out a sigh. "No, just that some people are impulsive and we both know you're not. Nothing wrong with that but it's the truth."

"The truth, huh?" Brooke said, deliberately taking a deep breath to control her temper. "If we're being so truthful tonight why don't you just tell me why you're still with me? My sister said–"

"–Oh God, what's Mandy said now?"

"That you're a commitment-phobe and–"

Megan let out a laugh. "A what? I seriously don't know why you listen to that woman. You know she doesn't like me. She's just jealous 'cause you've got a partner now and don't spend all your time being used as a dumping ground for her pathetic life."

Brooke's mouth dropped open. "I don't think her having a disabled child is pathetic, Megan. I try to give her moral support, that's what you do when you love someone. All she wants is for me to be happy with someone who treats me with a bit of respect."

Megan rolled over to face her again, stifling a yawn. "Whatever."

"Megan, I just think you treat this place like a hotel. I didn't give you a key so you could come and go as you please with no consideration for me or my feelings."

"Do we really have to do this right now?" she asked, her hand snaking its way between Brooke's legs. "I can think of much better things we could be doing."

Brooke's temper cooled as desire overtook her senses. Megan looked up at her, hungry and lustful.

"Let's not fight, baby," Megan said. With a lazy, sensuous movement she reached up and planted a lingering kiss on Brooke's mouth before ducking beneath the covers.

Brooke tossed her head back and arched her hips as Megan's tongue gently teased her centre.

Maybe the argument could wait.

Chapter Three

"Wakey, wakey, sleepy head!"

The deep, melodic voice permeated Danni's hazy brain, kick-starting it back to life with a jolt. "Who? What? Where am I?" She jerked bolt upright, glancing around her bedroom through squinted eyes before settling her gaze on the buff form of her handsome, six foot room-mate, Josh. Dressed in dark blue jeans and a tight fitted white T-shirt, he had the good looks of a young Brad Pitt, circa Thelma and Louise.

"What time is it?" she croaked, flopping back on the pillow in sorry defeat. Her head was pounding, her mouth so dry that it was a miracle a Bedouin tribe hadn't set up camp inside. Jeeeeesus, what on earth had she drunk?

Josh glanced down at his watch. "It's ten o'clock. I thought you were working tonight?"

"Well, *I* thought I'd be shacked up with Angelina Jolie by now, but that didn't happen either, now did it?" she retorted, rolling over onto her stomach and dragging the pillow over her head. A small groan escaped her lips as she felt the mattress depress beside her – Josh, like her hangover, wasn't going to go away that easily.

He wrenched the pillow from under her throbbing head and rested it on his lap. "Please don't tell me you've been sacked again."

"If I did, would it surprise you?" she asked,

peeking up at him from one half-open eye.

"Not really, but I thought this job was a keeper?"

"So did I - but you know what they say about counting your chickens."

Josh grinned. He had a wonderfully reassuring smile that made everything seem better – even though in reality, it wasn't.

"So what happened *this* time?" he asked, taking Danni's hand in his own.

Was it common for a man to have such amazingly soft hands, she wondered. She let out a long sigh, flipped over onto her back and stared up at the ceiling. "Let's just say I was smashing."

"Smashing?"

"Yeah, as in smashing plates – into lots of tiny bits!"

"Oh. I see." He laughed.

"And there's even more bad news," Danni continued.

"I know," he interrupted. "I saw the letter scrunched up on the coffee table." He leaned over and gave her shoulder a quick squeeze. "Don't give up, Danni. I think you're a fantastic writer. Look at all the rejections J. K Rowling got before–"

She rolled her eyes. "–if one more bloody person tells me about J. K sodding Rowling I'm going to scream."

Josh held his hands up. "Okay, okay I'm sorry."

"Seriously, Josh, look at what you said about that Amanda Hocking. Don't bother getting it traditionally published, just upload your book to Amazon you said. You'll be a millionaire you said. One year later and I've sold two copies; one of which was returned and the other was bought by my mum. And now, the traditional publishers don't want me either."

Josh stifled a laugh. "Maybe you just didn't promote it enough. You can't just sit on Facebook and Twitter all day making friends and hoping they will buy it."

"Josh, I couldn't even give the book away, I put it up for free for a week and had ten downloads – TEN!"

As much as she hated to admit it, Josh did have a point – promotion just wasn't her thing. When she first self-published her book she had spent the first week friending everyone she could on Facebook whilst posting about her book every ten minutes. Eventually, after religiously refreshing her Amazon sales report with the same frequency, she came to the sad realisation that no-one was actually going to buy it. So she had spent her days liking hilarious cat photos instead. A much better use of her time.

Josh rose to his feet. Peering down at her he said, "Babe, I can always have a word with my dad. You know he runs a publishing company. Like I said before, I know chick-lit's not his thing but I'd be happy to see if he knows anyone else who would consider publishing it."

"Thanks Josh, that's really sweet of you, but there's no point."

"So what are you going to do – mope about feeling sorry for yourself?"

"For tonight, that's exactly what I plan to do."

And tomorrow and the day after and the day after that, she mused. What did she have to get up for?

Josh cleared his throat. "Well I'm going to make you something to eat, my hangover special."

Danni gave a small shake of her head. "I don't think I could manage anything if I'm honest."

"Why doesn't that surprise me?" Josh laughed. "I see you've been necking that lager that's been in the fridge since we moved in."

Danni felt her stomach lurch, saliva welling up in her mouth – not a good sign. "Are you serious?"

"Deadly." He laughed, strolling over to the door.

"Oh my gawd. Do you think I should go to A and E? I think I might have alcohol poisoning," she said, suddenly clutching her stomach.

"A and E? AA more like. Nah, I think you'll live. Eating something will set you right though."

Danni covered her face with her hands. "Oh, Josh, I really am in the shit this time, I don't know how I'm going to cover the rent this month."

His tone was soft and reassuring, almost parental. "Don't worry about it – something will come up. If the worst comes to the worst, I'll cover it for you."

Danni leant up on her elbows, frowning. "Thanks, Josh. I think winning the lottery is my only hope – though there's fat chance of that happening seeing as I can't afford a bloody ticket."

Josh looked at her sympathetically. "Listen, I'll make extra food in case you change your mind." He smiled as he closed the door behind him.

At least she had Josh. He really was a guardian angel. *A guardian angel who makes a mean pasta. Is there any better kind?*

***

When Danni woke again an hour later, her bedroom was enshrouded in darkness. Low chatter from the TV leaked through her door. The faint scent of roasted tomatoes and oregano tickled her nose. Her stomach rumbled. The thought of food was now suddenly very appealing. Powered by her new-found hunger, she slid off the bed and shuffled cautiously towards the door. She was mindful not to trip over the discarded clothes that littered the carpet; her "floor-drobe" as she liked to call it.

Danni's bedroom was the biggest room in the flat – not that she needed the space. She knew sweet F. A about accessories and colours. It was still the same shade of pale blue it had been when she first moved in. The only furniture she owned was the double bed her mum had bought her and a desk she'd picked up in the bargain corner at IKEA.

She followed the intoxicating aroma like a woman possessed, her nose pointed out in front of her, inhaling every beautiful scent. Reaching the kitchen, which was the size of a postage stamp, the smell of garlic struck her nasal passages like a midwife slapping a newborn baby. Josh had made her favourite sauce, just what the doctor ordered. She couldn't help but salivate as her cardboard tongue began to tingle at the very thought of tasting that heaven-sent creation.

Within minutes, she had reheated the spaghetti and was sitting on the sofa with Josh who was quietly reading one of his many self-help manuals.

The low-ceilinged living room looked like a cross between a gym and a one-star hotel room. The wood chip magnolia walls didn't appear as if they had been repainted by the landlord for a good ten years. On the far side of the room, an aging bench press sat with a rack of weights beside it and a poster of a half-naked body builder tacked to the wall. Though Danni was as easy going as the next person she had drawn a line at Josh's plea to install floor to ceiling mirrors next to it. All in all, with its brown patterned sofa, black leather recliner (courtesy of Josh's dad) and a faded wooden coffee table, the room was a disaster.

She twirled the spaghetti on her fork and shovelled it into her grateful mouth. It was so good. She chewed for a few seconds before a feeling of intense queasiness crept up on her. She lurched forward to grab a glass of water from the coffee table, and gulped it down in a vain attempt to keep her food from popping back up to say hello. Realising this method wasn't going to work, she placed the bowl and glass onto the table and sprinted to the bathroom.

"Are you okay?" she heard Josh call from behind the door as she slumped over the toilet bowl and released the contents of her stomach. "Uh huh," was all she could manage, as she vowed to herself that she would never drink again.

After several minutes she groaned and pulled herself up from the floor. Grabbing her toothbrush, she fastidiously cleaned her entire mouth before turning and opening the bathroom door. Josh was still standing there.

"I'm okay, Josh," she whispered, passing by him and returning to her place on the sofa. Noticing the bowl of pasta still sitting there she retched and motioned to Josh. "Oh God, please take it away."

He smiled then grabbed the bowl. "Okay, okay. It's gone. Do you want some Alka Seltzer?"

"No, it's okay. I don't think I'll be able to keep anything down."

When Josh returned from the kitchen he sat back next to her and resumed reading his book.

Her nausea subsiding, she turned to him and read the cover – *"Life Transformations : One Magic Month"*.

"So who's promising to change your life in thirty days this time?"

Josh looked up with a scowl and returned to his reading. He drank in every word of self-help books. Plus he got them all free courtesy of his publisher father.

"Well?" she urged.

"Don't pretend to be interested, D, you always take the piss."

"I'm not. I swear. I'm interested."

"No, you're not."

"I am," she protested through a smirk.

Josh let out a heavy sigh. "Maybe it would do you some good to actually read some of these books, instead of–"

"–Instead of what?"

"Instead of being so judgmental."

If she had been drinking at that given moment she would have spurted out the contents with the force of an Orca's blowhole. Fortunately, her mouth was empty so she could do nothing but give an exaggerated gasp. *She* was judgemental? She was the least judgey person she knew – "live and let live" all the way. She just thought all of these books on spiritual enlightenment were a bit clichéd. A great big cynical money-making con.

"Josh," she said finally finding her voice. "I appreciate you believing in all this mumb–" She stopped mid-sentence. She wasn't going to win an argument by insulting him. "–stuff, but I don't buy it. All they seem to do is repeat the same old rubbish with a new spin. If these books actually worked, the self-help industry would be bankrupt not earning millions a year. Anybody could write them and the worst thing is the books bloody sell." Unlike my own, she refrained from adding.

Josh put the book on his lap and turned in his seat to look at her with all the innocence of a gullible child. "If that's the case, why don't you put your money where your mouth is and write one, Ms Guru?"

She stared at him blankly.

He rolled his eyes at her lack of response adding, "Why don't *you* write a self-help book?"

Danni shuddered at the thought. Though she could turn her hand to any piece of writing with a good dollop of research, she didn't like the idea of someone in a vulnerable state of mind taking her words as gospel. "Ah, I didn't say *I* could write one … I … uh."

Josh turned back to his book. "Like I thought, all talk."

"Hang on a big gay second," she said laying a hand on his forearm. "I didn't say I *couldn't* write one. I simply mean I don't have the time to dedicate to such a … uh … life-changing work. Some of us have bills to pay."

Josh turned at stared at her. "So are you saying you could do it if you had the time to?"

"Of course I could. It's not exactly rocket science."

"Ok, then do it. You have the time now, prove me wrong."

"Oh yeah, and how am I supposed to support myself while I write my seminal masterpiece? With chocolate buttons? Correct me if I'm wrong, but last time I checked the currency in this country was pounds and pence. We don't all have a rich daddy to fall back on."

Josh's face suddenly looked troubled. "D, we need to talk."

He snapped his book shut and put it down on the coffee table. Josh never stopped reading halfway through a book. Her gut began performing somersaults. Was this the end – had Josh had enough of her being unreliable and broke? Oh God she knew it – she had known her days were numbered. Though who could blame him? Who wanted to carry a useless heavy load? Well, actually she was quite slim, but that was immaterial. God she would miss him. She loved this man like a brother.

Her face was bleak with sorrow as she said, "It's okay Josh. I know what you're going to say. And it's okay. I totally understand. Believe me when I say this, nothing will change between us. I'll always be your friend." Fighting back the tears, she put her feet on the floor and attempted to stand. Josh gripped her hand and looked at her with a confused expression.

"What the hell are you talking about, D?"

"I'll go tomorrow."

"Go where?" he asked, a mask of uncertainty on his features.

"Back to my mum's. Only until I get a job. Then I'll–"

Josh pulled her back down onto the seat. "D, why are you talking about moving out?"

Danni's eyes widened. "I thought you wanted to talk?"

"I do but it's not about you moving out. Why on earth would you think something like that?"

Danni shrugged her shoulders. "Dunno. You just

look so serious."

Josh ran his hand over the top of his head, his features twisting in frustration. "This is nothing to do with you – well not directly anyway."

"What is it Josh? Has something bad happened?" Danni was on tenterhooks as she waited patiently for him to speak.

He took a deep breath and slowly released it. "Yes and no."

Only one thing truly bugged her about Josh – he could never get straight to the point. "Well ... which one is it?"

"It's my dad."

Danni's hand flew to her mouth. "Oh God, Josh, I'm so sorry. Here I am talking about–"

Josh held his hands up in the air. "He's not dead, Danni."

Danni's mouth dropped open. "Oh, sorry. I mean, good."

"He's turning sixty on Saturday."

Danni grinned. "Oh, well that's good isn't it? I mean, him being alive and all at sixty." Her words were not coming out quite as she wanted.

Josh rubbed his chin. "Depends how you look at it."

"Oh, Josh, you're driving me insane. Just tell me what the problem is."

"My dad doesn't know I'm gay," he mumbled.

"Ooookaaaay." This news wasn't surprising to her. Josh wasn't exactly an "easy spot". Yes he was well-groomed and dashingly handsome but he didn't work in fashion, PR, or any other of those stereotypical professions that set the alarm bells ringing. He was a builder; a builder devoid of any design sense and one with zero affection for either Barbra Streisand or Judy Garland. In fact, *how could he be gay?*

"My dad thinks I have a fiancée," he said sheepishly.

Danni's eyes widened. "What? Why on earth would he think such a ridiculous thing?"

"Because, that's what I told him."

She clapped her hand to her mouth. "*You* told him. Why?"

"I don't want him to disown me. You know I told you we had a falling out last year."

Danni nodded.

"Well, I wasn't exactly honest about what we fell out over."

Danni frowned. "I'm confused. You said it was over money."

"It was. Well sort of. My dad was going to loan me money for a deposit on a house, until he found out who I was going to be sharing it with," he said angrily as he shot up from the sofa and paced the floor back and forth.

Danni watched him pace, the pieces of the puzzle began to fall into place. "Adam? Big camp Adam?"

His expression momentarily took on a look of disgust. "Yes. I told my dad about Adam being gay and let's just say he was less than kind about the idea of us buying together."

"But you weren't even shagging Adam, he's just a friend."

"I know, D, and that's my point. He didn't want me sharing a house with him in case everyone thought *I* was gay."

"But you are Josh."

"I'm well aware of that Danni."

"Did he actually say that to you? That it was because he was gay. I mean, I doubt anyone would want their son sharing a place with camp Adam."

"Not in so many words but it was obvious that was the reason."

Danni looked doubtful. "Okay, if you say so."

"Look, after his reaction to me sharing with Adam, there was no way I was going to tell him about myself. Especially with my mum being ill, I didn't want to add to the stress." Letting out a sigh of annoyance he said, "The point is, however screwed up it all is, I don't want to lose him now we're on good terms again. He's all I've got left now my mum's gone."

Danni sat motionless, staring at Josh with pity. "I wish you would have told me the truth, Josh."

"I'm sorry. But I was ashamed to tell you my own dad had behaved like that."

"It's not your fault he's a bloody bigot," she said in a half-grunt. Tapping her temple with the tip of her finger she continued, "Just give me a minute to get my thoughts together and I'll come up with a plan of action."

He came to an abrupt halt and looked at her with a dazzling smile. "I was hoping you'd say that."

"Say what?" she asked hesitantly, a frown creasing her otherwise smooth forehead.

"That you'd help me of course."

"Oh, you know I will. Anything you need, just name it."

He was by her side in seconds, on his knees, looking up at her with his blue pleading eyes. *Oh God, is he going to propose?*

"D, will you … pretend to be my fiancée at my dad's birthday party?"

Danni jerked back as if she'd been tasered in her lady parts. "What! I … I," she spluttered unable to get the words out.

"Come on. It's one party. You're witty and great with people, you'll easily pull it off. And if you help me, I'll help you. Like I said, my dad's a publisher, you're an aspiring writer. I know you want to make it on your own and I admire that, but he could really help."

"Josh, I don't know. And why your fiancée? Why not just your girlfriend?" Could she really go through with such a charade, pretend to be Josh's fiancée? She hated deception and was a terrible liar. Surely his dad would be able to see it in her eyes.

Josh's shoulders sagged, "Every time I talk to him he asks me about my love life – when I'm getting married and having kids. Last time I spoke to him I just caved in and it slipped out. Now I don't know how to backtrack."

"Just tell him you split up or something. Tell him she ran off to a convent. Tell him anything, Josh. You don't have to put yourself through this."

He looked at her with puppy dog eyes. "But he was so happy, Danni. I haven't seen him so happy since my mum died."

"How long are you going to lie to him? The truth will come out eventually and won't that be much worse?" she said sighing loudly.

"Look, I know this all seems crazy but I know what I'm doing. Yes, eventually I'll say we split up or something but for now this is how I want it."

Danni frowned. "Okay, but how will this crazy masquerade help me? For starters, your dad specialises in non-fiction, all those self-help books you love. I can't say I have too many words of wisdom to share with the world at this stage in my life."

He grabbed her hand and looked doubtful for a second. "Oh come on, Danni, I'm sure you could think of something. You're a brilliant author, what have you got to lose? At least you would get to write. Maybe not the kind of book you'd like at first, but it's a start. Impress him with a book *he* wants and who knows what it could lead to?"

It was a good offer all right. And he was talking sense. Perhaps she should try something new, but a self-help book? What on earth did she know about it? She would feel like a fraud. Still unsure, she sighed. "Josh, this is a lot to take in. I appreciate the offer and everything but …"

He pushed himself to his feet, walked over to the window and leaned his back against it. "I get what you're saying, but just give it some thought." He smiled sweetly at her. "And I promise not to sulk if you decide not to do it."

Danni remained silent, pondering the situation further. She couldn't believe that in the year 2014, when gay marriage was legal and Ellen was every granny's favourite lesbian, Josh was still hiding his sexuality. She was torn. On one hand, she hated the thought of lying, more importantly she resented *having* to lie, but on the other, wanted to help her friend. Hmmm, it was all swirling around in her hung-over swamp of a brain.

"Oh sod it. If it means helping my best friend, of course I'll do it."

Josh crossed the floor and pulled her up into a bear hug that nearly crushed the life from her. "Thank you so much. I owe you big time for this. I knew you wouldn't let me down."

Laughing she drew back a little. "Okay, okay. This pretending lark is just for one night isn't it?"

"Cross my heart and hope to die," he said, leaning back and making the mark of a cross on his chest.

"Okay, it's a deal. We just have to draw up some house rules about what 'touching' is deemed acceptable. I don't want you getting all heterosexual on me after a few shandies."

Josh feigned disgust. "This isn't going to exactly be a heap of joy for me either, you know," he said pulling his shoulders back proudly. "We have five days to work out the finer details. In the meantime darling fiancée, you have to come up with an amazingly fresh angle that will blow the self-help sector away!"

"No pressure then, hubby dearest," she mumbled miserably. "Self-help books and heterosexuality all in one night. Now that's what I call faking it!"

Chapter Four

The atmosphere in the office at Reynolds Publishing was quietly industrious as Brooke sat at her desk pretending to be engrossed in her work. She had been working as an editor at the company for four years and had loved every minute of it. Even on days like today when she was finding it hard to focus on her work. Despite it being Monday, she was anything but refreshed from the weekend.

The large open plan room was stark white with windows overlooking the City of London. Her colleagues, mostly in their late thirties, with the exception of one or two, sat at their computers sombrely working away with little interaction with each other. Brooke minimized her Word document and clicked on the browser. She logged into Facebook and scanned her newsfeed. The usual "my cat looks like Hitler" and "lose two stone in a week" posts abounded. Nothing much piqued her interest.

"Hey, did you see the email from the Roy about tomorrow?" her fellow editor Ethan asked, grinning from the desk directly opposite hers. He brought his hands to rest behind his head, reclined back in his seat and began whistling.

Knowing she wasn't going to get a minute's peace if she didn't engage with her metro-sexual twenty-something colleague, she relented and looked up at him in his tailored black suit. "Tomorrow?"

Ethan was beaming. "We're going to his birthday party, remember?"

Brooke groaned. "Oh no. I completely forgot!"

He tugged on his multi-coloured tie. "How could you forget the boss' party? I can't wait; I'll finally get to meet his niece Helen. Roy showed me a picture of her today. She's soooo hot."

Rising, she walked around to his desk and perched on the edge.

"That's nice for you, Mr Lusty-Pants but I was looking forward to a quiet night in."

He flashed her a quick smile. "Again? When was the last time you went out?"

She twisted her lips to the side. "Hmm, it has been a while."

He looked at her thoughtfully. "And you really want *another* night in?"

Brooke brushed her long hair away from her face. "Okay, Ethan. No need to rub it in. I'll be there."

He raised his thick dark eyebrows. "Anyway, at least you can go shopping to buy yourself a nice new outfit."

She blew out a breath. "Yeah because buying clothes is every woman's favourite pastime."

"Shopping's in your blood – I know how you ladies get when the opportunity arises. Women were born to shop."

"Where on earth did you hear such rubbish?"

Ethan pointed to his computer screen. "Right here. This enlightened author claims to know the secret to making a woman happy."

Brooke snorted. "Really? And what's that then? I could really do with some tips myself."

"I'm hardly going to reveal the poor man's secrets. If you want to find out you'll have to buy the book."

"You're not serious are you?"

Ethan's cheeks flushed. "Of course I am. This is the *one* book any red-blooded male will ever need in this life."

Brooke let out a long groan and shook her head slightly. "No wonder publishing is going into the ground."

"Don't be such a buzzkill, Brooke. People are looking for a bit of light relief, a bit of fun to brighten up their dull miserable lives. The days of needing a dictionary to get through a book are long gone."

Brooke tilted her head and stared down at him. "The way things are going Mr Progressive, soon no-one will even know what a dictionary is."

Ethan frowned, his eyes following the new buxom blonde receptionist as she passed by. "Always the pessimist, that's your problem." He turned his attention back to Brooke when the receptionist disappeared from sight. "Anyway, back to tomorrow, I think we'll have a great night. You, me, vodka, the boss' niece. Perfect!"

Brooke let the idea wash over her for a minute. Megan would be out of town which meant another night in front of the TV watching re-runs on Netflix.

Besides, Ethan was right, she always had great fun when they went out. Having worked together for three years, Ethan and her boss, Roy, were the only true friends she had at work. The others were merely colleagues; people to share everyday pleasantries with but nothing of a personal nature.

"Anyway I'd better get back to work." She stood and made her way to her desk. Dropping down into her seat, she scrolled to the new stories on her newsfeed and was surprised when a post from Megan appeared at the top. *Flying high.* She clicked to view Megan's timeline and saw she had posted two minutes previously from Edinburgh. *Edinburgh?* She was supposed to be on her way to Australia. Confused, Brooke clicked on the chat button and wrote a quick message.

Almost immediately Brooke's mobile phone rang with a familiar ringtone – she knew exactly who it was.

"Are you playing detective this morning?" Megan asked, sarcasm dripping from every syllable.

"No. I just wondered why you were there."

Megan blew out a breath. "I have a stopover in Edinburgh before flying to Singapore." For a moment there was just silence on the other end of the line. "I told you that this morning." Megan's voice had the faintest American accent. She had been born in the US but her parents had brought her to the UK when she was fourteen years old.

"I'm sure you didn't Megan, I think I would have remembered."

"Brooke, I'm telling you I did. You must have still been asleep," she said in an impatient tone. "Anyway, I've got to get back to work. I take off in thirty minutes."

Brooke looked over at Ethan who was listening intently to her conversation. She swivelled around in her chair so her back was towards him, then lowered her voice. "Okay, I'm sorry. You know I'm a heavy sleeper. Have a safe trip. I love you."

The connection went dead. Brooke sat motionless, staring blankly ahead, the phone still clasped tightly in her hand. Were things ever going to be straightforward between them? Last night they had been so close in the afterglow of their love-making yet today they seemed as distant as two continents. Suddenly, fatigue crept up on her. If she laid off nagging Megan about the amount of travelling she did maybe things would stabilise between them. Did it really matter if they only saw each other a few times a month? Lots of people coped with long distance relationships. After all, it wasn't as if Megan was cheating on her – now that was something that didn't even bear thinking about.

Chapter Five

Danni stared at the screensaver on her laptop. Nothing. Nada. Zilch. Inspiration had deserted her. Where were those creative juices she thought she'd be drowning in? The only thoughts currently occupying her grey matter involved a McDonald's breakfast wrap and double shot latte. Two of her favourite guilty pleasures.

She sat on the sofa a little longer, the screen seeming to ridicule her lack of progress. Why oh why had she agreed to his insane idea? Oh yeah, because she was an idiot! Maybe the publishers were right – she just wasn't cut out to be a writer. She'd be better off saving herself any further embarrassment and just throw in the towel while she was still young enough to train for a more lucrative career. Accountant? Banker? Basket weaver? All she had ever wanted to do was write – that's why she had spent three years at Kings College on a creative writing course. It was her passion, her calling. But then again, we all know what happens to young women with "callings". Just ask poor Joan of Arc.

The sound of her gurgling stomach brought her back to the moment. She was going to have to feed the ravenous beast within before she made any final decisions. Closing the lid of her laptop, she grabbed her coat and hurried towards the door.

The burger restaurant was busier than usual.

Young mums and their children were loitering near the play area filled with multi-coloured rubber balls. Danni ordered her wrap and instead of taking it home to devour it, she decided to eat in for a change. You only live once, she joked to herself. Push the boat out! She wasn't in any rush anyway – the only thing awaiting her back home was a blank screen. She spotted a quiet area and was just within reach when she felt a hand touch her leg. She jumped in the air, quickly looking to the owner of the arm. Her neighbour Mick. *Shit.* This was all she needed. His eyes were glazed as he looked up at her, still munching on his bacon and egg McMuffin. He nodded to the empty seat opposite him. Reluctantly she sank into the chair and they both ate in silence.

Danni glanced in the direction of the entrance as the glass door flung open. In stormed a short stocky man with a face like a slapped arse – an expression Josh was fond of. This man looked mean, the type you wouldn't want to meet down a dark ally. Or a light one at that. He passed by her like a whirlwind and headed to the counter. Seconds later, a petite woman with short spiky dark hair stood on tiptoes in the threshold of the doorway, frantically glancing from left to right, until her eyes finally settled on Mr Angry. The woman marched towards him and a hushed argument ensued. Minutes later they were both seated behind Danni. She was glad for the distraction seeing as Mick didn't look like he was going to speak anytime soon.

"You expect too much of me!" the man growled.

"Too much?" the woman fired back. "What have I ever asked of you other than to be a decent, caring partner?"

"Huh!" his voice rose in anger. "If only it was that bloody simple. You don't want me to be just any partner – you want me to be exactly what *you* want. Someone I'm not." The exasperation in his voice was clear.

"I just want us to be happy," the woman exclaimed, sounding tearful.

"Then stop bloody trying to change me – just let me be who I am!"

Danni heard the jarring scrape of the chair being pushed back on the tiled floor, before seeing the man rush past her table and make a quick exit, the woman close on his heels.

Slurping her lukewarm latte, Danni felt a touch of sadness for the pair – she fervently believed there were two sides to every argument but the man did seem to have the winning point.

Mick leaned forward. "That's why I'm single," he whispered.

"Really. Why's that then?" Danni whispered back.

"Too many expectations."

Danni pulled her face. "Aye?"

"Dem two, don't you see it?"

No, she couldn't. All she could see was Mick looking like he was on the brink of falling asleep in his McMuffin. "I'm afraid you've lost me Mick."

"Expectations ruin everything. Too many people

trying to be what their partner wants and they're surprised when it all goes wrong, I dunno ..." he said shaking his head slowly.

Danni sat back in shock. That was the longest sentence Mick had ever said to her. Not only was his word count impressive, he actually made sense. He was right. That was love in a nutshell – expectations, too many expectations. No wonder relationships were so hard. As Danni mulled over the idea further, the more profound it seemed to become. Was this her eureka moment? Had inspiration struck in the Golden Arches? She picked up both of their empty wrappers, walked to the bin and cheerfully tossed them in. *Hmm, unrealistic expectations of relationships. I think Mick could be onto something.*

***

The idea of a book about expectations was proving more fruitful than she could ever have imagined. The internet provided endless links and websites. The forums were the most interesting. There, people discussed their real life experiences and others offered their points of view. The general frustration of unlocking the door to love was everywhere. This might just be the theme she was looking for.

Danni glanced up at the door which creaked open like a haunted house in a Scooby Doo episode. It was Josh. What was he doing home so early? How had he showered and changed clothes without her even realising it? She looked at the screen and gasped – it was after six – she had been so captivated in her research that she'd lost track of time. Now that had to be a good sign, right?

"You look very industrious." Josh smiled, rubbing a towel over his wet hair and dropping heavily onto the sofa.

"I am, and I've been at it all day. Josh, I had an epiphany in McDonalds."

"An epiphany? Is that part of their new menu?" he said grinning.

"Seriously, Josh, I think I have my idea for the book. And I have Mick to thank for it."

Josh's forehead creased. "Mick?"

Danni nodded enthusiastically. "Yes, I bumped into him this morning and we – oh it doesn't matter how it happened it just did. I think I'm actually excited about it too. Let me get you a beer and something to eat my dear husband to be. Bangers and mash?" She winked, laughing as she planted her lips on the top of his head before flitting to the kitchen.

The sausage fest on the go, Danni returned to the lounge with two cold beers and sat on her knees in front of him. "Right, are you ready to hear my idea?"

He took a swig from his bottle. "Yep. Hit me with your genius. I'm all yours."

Danni took a minute to organise her thoughts, taking a long gulp of her own beer. "Okay so this is it. I'm going to call it *Unlocking the door to love.*"

For the next twenty minutes, Danni enthused and gesticulated with all the energy of an impassioned orator. She spoke of her ideas on relationships and how expectations invariably strangled them. Josh looked captivated, nodding and drinking it all in.

"I love it, Danni, ... *Unlocking the door to love.* It rings true. I knew you could come up with something interesting." He smiled, leaning over and squeezing her shoulder.

Perhaps he was right; her dreams of becoming an author were not so far-fetched after all. She'd won over the son; now all she had to do was pitch the idea to his father's publishing house. She could only hope Josh's father had the same impeccable taste.

Chapter Six

A solitary taxi weaved its way along the tranquil country lane, leaving the buzz of city life behind. The narrow road bordered by hedgerows seemed to reduce in width as tall oak trees towered overhead, darkening the dismal autumn afternoon further.

A sleep-heavy Megan was so lost in thought that she failed to realise the car had even stopped, until the cab driver tapped the glass window that separated them. Startled, she stared at him momentarily before diverting her attention to the world outside the vehicle: a small whitewashed thatched cottage partially hidden by a row of conifer trees, beckoned her. The well kept house showed no signs of its two hundred years, the only thing out of place in the landscaped grounds was a red moped parked near the wall.

The driver, a broad-shouldered hulk of a man, squeezed himself out of the cab, wandered around to her door and removed Megan's 30 kg case as if it was a flimsy pencil case. Exiting the taxi, she smiled and handed him a ten pound note. In a flash he was in his cab and disappearing back down the road.

All was still as she stood in the small lane. *Home sweet home.* She smiled, grabbing her case by the handle then strolling through the wooden archway and up the lavender-edged flagstone pathway; the familiar scent assailing her senses. Arriving at the cottage, she inserted her key, pushed open the heavy oak door and dropped her case victoriously on the parquet flooring. She'd better start dinner before it got too late.

She headed straight for the kitchen and opened the fridge door, her hand hovering over a pack of fresh salmon fillets. A frown creased her forehead – salmon fillets were Brooke's absolute favourite. Taking them from the shelf, she ran them hurriedly under the cold tap and wondered what Brooke would be doing at that very second. Driving herself insane, no doubt, trying to figure out how to "fix things" between them. The incident earlier on Facebook was a close call. She had forgotten to switch off the location on her phone, she wouldn't make that mistake again.

Megan's brow furrowed. She resented Brooke coming into her mind at that particular time. *Her* time. Brooke was too emotional for her own good. Everything had to be talked about, dissected and explored which Megan found all so very tiresome.

What had started off as some harmless flirting, had soon blossomed into an affair, a relationship from which she was unable to extricate herself.

Megan seasoned the fish with salt and pepper and slid them into the oven on a tray. Taking a mug from the cupboard she checked the kettle for water then pressed the on switch. Opening the coffee container on the worktop she heaped two teaspoonfuls into the cup and when the kettle had boiled, poured the water in and stirred. She took a quick sip, scalding her tongue, then sighed as she rested against the counter. The kitchen was large and rustic, with an Aga taking centre stage. As she glanced around she realised how much she loved being there, it was a stark contrast to Brooke's London flat.

Coffee in hand, she walked into the front room. *Someone's been tidying up.* It wasn't usually the tidiest of houses so it was clear an effort had been made just for Megan.

She moved to the wall cabinet, placed her coffee down and switched on the IPod dock, immediately starting to dance as if to celebrate her new-found freedom. Above the music, she heard the bang of the front door slamming shut, then a voice calling out, "Hello?"

She leaned over and muted the sound. "I'm in the living room," she called back, smiling as she heard the rush of footsteps heading towards the room.

"Mummy M, Mummy M." A small frizzy haired child with large brown eyes, beamed as she ran full pelt at Megan, almost knocking her off balance. Megan bent down and gathered the child up into her arms, squeezing her half-heartedly. "Ah, hello, Kelly. Have you missed me?"

The little girl nodded in response, still clinging to her leg as she stood up.

"We certainly have," a voice uttered from the door. A woman, the spitting image of Halle Berry, walked over and embraced her lovingly, planting a tender kiss full on her lips. "Especially me."

Chapter Seven

The big day had arrived.

Tonight was the night Danni would be outed as a raging heterosexual. The night she would publicly declare her undying love for her handsome beau, Josh. Dig deep and find the Meryl Streep within, she said to herself as she stood before her rather sorry looking wardrobe.

"So, Danni. What's it gonna be?" she said aloud, scanning the rows of black clothes before her.

Nine pairs of jeans – black, sixteen sexy vest tops – mostly black, and a cream woolly jumper given by her nan, Christmas 2006. "All is not lost," she muttered, she still had a secret weapon in her fashion arsenal – the killer white trouser suit. Elegant, sexy … diiiiiirrrrrrty? Noooooo! Her heart sank as a Shiraz stain the size of Wales screamed at her from the left lapel of an otherwise pristine white suit. Why oh why hadn't she taken it to the dry cleaners? Why had she not checked earlier? Why did she always feel the need to ask herself questions in sets of threes? Truth be told, this was the mother of all wardrobe disasters.

In the grip of blind panic, Danni could hear Josh's footsteps clomping ever closer along the hallway. Time seemed to slow down. His every step made her heart thump that bit harder. Every thud made her mouth a little drier so that her usually well-proportioned top lip disappeared, giving her a rather unfortunate gum to teeth ratio. What on earth would he say when he discovered this almighty fashion faux pas?

"Right girl, deep breath; time to face the music," Danni whispered, gathering herself.

Josh bounded into the room without knocking, wielding a large shopping bag in each hand. He was sporting a ridiculously wide smile that made his dimples erupt.

"Your shopping, madam."

"For me?" Danni enthused as she gratefully snapped up his offerings like a hungry spaniel at a dinner table. She peeked excitedly inside the first bag whereupon her jaw dropped abruptly to the floor. What lay within was just too hideous to imagine, too terrifying to contemplate. Had Josh gone mad? Surely he didn't expect her to wear a … a … SKIRT! She was a feminine girl, granted, but she had always been more of the tight trouser type than the classic skirt wearer. Frock-shocked, she fished out the offending teal coloured skirt and dangled it in the air as if she was wielding a veritable turd. Her facial expression said it all. "Oh Josh, you shouldn't have. No, you *really* shouldn't have!" She forced a grin so as not to seem ungrateful.

Josh stood by, a wicked smile appearing on his face. "Go on, take a look. There's more."

Was he serious? Summoning the Gods of Fashion, she sunk her hand back into the shopping bag, hoping for a more favourable result this time. She bit her lip, thought of England and grabbed what lay within. 1-2-3 'king hell! A blouse? *A blouse?* Really? The very word made her feel nauseous.

So this was Josh's idea of helping her – dressing her up in an outfit likely to induce convulsions. He gestured toward the second bag on the floor. "Look. I got you some shoes as well! See how much I love you!"

Oh sweet baby Jesus! Danni reluctantly walked over to her bed and laid the clothes down – not knowing whether to laugh, cry, or feign a coronary. A quick check of her watch confirmed her worst fear – the shops were now shut and her fate was sealed. Skirt and blouse it was.

Turning back to Josh, her eyes narrowed as she bravely fished the shoes from the final bag. Oh joy of joys – four inch stilettos! The heels were high all right, but not half as high as you would have to be to buy them! Now she knew Josh had gone raving gaga.

"Josh, I appreciate the effort, but in all the time you've known me when have I ever worn footwear like this?"

He looked at her sheepishly. "It's a night of firsts, Danni. Besides, you'll look amazing and my dad will be well impressed. He loves girls who, you know, look like ladies."

"And men who look like men? Good job he didn't see you at last Friday's Pricilla Queen of the Desert party, hey? I know what, why don't we give him a call and ask him what type of knickers I should wear too. A thong perhaps? I do love a nice floss."

Josh winced. "Yuk! Come on, D, you're being a bit dramatic aren't you. It's only a skirt and shoes."

"Only ... *only*," she choked on the words. "Have you seen the size of those heels? I'll need a Sherpa guide to get me into them!"

Josh laughed loudly. "You'll soon get used to them, D. Besides, you've got great legs and I think you should show them off. Right, enough chat. I've booked the cab to pick us up at seven."

"Seven? God, Josh, you bloody owe me big time. Now clear off while I work a miracle."

***

The door bell rang at seven o'clock on the dot.

"Come on, D – get a shake on," Josh called out.

Danni sprinted from her bedroom with the stability of a new-born Bambi, wobbling into the lounge where she collided with Josh head on. Despite the graceless entrance, Josh's face illuminated as he eyed her from head to toe.

"Wow! You look amazing, Danni," he gushed, holding her by her shoulders.

"Really?" Danni asked looking down at herself. "Well, I do feel rather sophisticated – and very, very tall. An inch higher and I'd need a pilot's licence."

The pair giggled for the entire taxi journey, partly through nerves and partly due to the taxi driver's lack of understanding of the Highway Code. Apparently, red lights did not mean stop after all. Within half an hour, they were at their destination. Electric gates opened onto a deep carriage driveway, giving way to an imposing double-fronted detached house bordered by impressive poplar trees.

"Deep breath my lovely fiancée. It's show time!" Josh grinned.

"Some house," Danni remarked, clearly impressed by the opulence before her. "You didn't tell me your family live at Downton Abbey."

"Not quite. Right, just relax, be yourself and everyone will love you." He winked, squeezing her hand as they stepped from their Ford Mondeo carriage.

"JOSHIIIIEEEE!"

An enthusiastic greeting interrupted the final pep-talk as a young woman in her early twenties bounded towards the pair, and flung herself against Josh's chest like an excited puppy.

"Hey, Helen. Wow – someone's looking good." He laughed with an obvious affection for the petite brunette.

"Ahh, thanks Josh. I'm so glad you came. I thought you were going to make up one of your excuses again."

"What, and miss partying with my cousin? No chance!"

Helen broke away from Josh and said to Danni with an excited tone, "And you must be the lovely Danni, we've heard so much about you."

"All good, I hope."

"Yes, of course. Well, Josh clearly has great taste in ladies," Helen said eyeing Danni up and down appreciatively. "Right, let's get inside and breathe some life into this party." Helen laughed, tossing her head back giddily as she slipped between Danni and Josh. "I just know this is going to be a great night!"

Danni struggled to keep her balance as she was dragged up the gravel path by Josh and his over-enthusiastic cousin. Helen had a lovely spirit, just like Josh. It must be in the blood. Surely Josh's dad couldn't be as bad as he made out. Whatever the reality, Danni was about to find out. She gulped as she tugged at her skirt and followed her giggling "fiancé" and his cousin into the laughter-filled house.

Chapter Eight

Brooke, wearing a black strapless dress, took a sip of her crisp white wine and scanned the room. Huge speaker sets accompanied by a mixing desk sat at the back of the room, with the DJ bobbing his head to the Little Richard music. A few of the elderly guests were dancing by a make shift bar situated near the large glass windows that overlooked an immaculate garden.

Ethan stood beside Brooke, swaying his head from side to side, a large neat scotch in his hand. That was the first time she had seen him drink spirits – she always took him for a beer sort of a guy. He was no doubt trying to make himself look more mature than his twenty eight years.

"So where's Ms Wonderful then?" Brooke teased between sips.

Ethan glanced around the room in an attempt to look casual. "I haven't seen her yet, but trust me, when she arrives, the whole room will know. I think even you'll have trouble taking your eyes off her."

"What do you mean *even me*. Are you trying to say something?"

"Well, you know what I mean. I know you only have eyes for Megan but when you get a look at this babe."

Brooke pulled her face. "Babe? You know Ethan, you have some pretty sad vocabulary when it comes to women."

Ethan didn't respond, instead he stared at the entrance. "Oh God, here she comes!" he stammered in an unusually unconfident manner. He quickly gathered himself. "Quick Brooke, look at me like I'm the most interesting man you've ever met," he said adjusting his tie and stretching his spine so as to appear taller.

"That will be hard," she teased, as she followed the direction of his eyes and locked upon Roy's son Josh and two women heading their way. Brooke was stunned. Everything in her body seem to freeze for a second. "Is that her?" she whispered softly, totally mesmerised by the presence of one of the female strangers.

Ethan nodded, his eyes still transfixed ahead.

For once Ethan hadn't been exaggerating; the woman was simply breath taking. "Wow!" Brooke mouthed, unable to tear her focus from the gorgeous blonde stranger. She felt almost shocked by her reaction. This wasn't the first time she had seen a beautiful woman. Hell, Megan turned heads wherever she went, but this time it was different. It felt almost surreal – an instant unexplainable connection.

Within seconds, Josh and his two companions came to a stop in front of them.

"Hi Ethan, hello there Brooke," Josh said, gripping Ethan's hand warmly then leaning in to kiss Brooke's cheek.

"So, this is my cousin Helen," he said motioning to the petite brunette beside him.

Ethan's cheeks flushed as he nodded at Helen.

He looked as if he might devour her at any second.

Josh turned to the blonde woman beside him and continued the introductions. "You haven't met my lovely fiancée Danni yet. Danni, this is Brooke and Ethan, they work at my dad's publishing house."

Ethan smiled and shook Danni's hand. Brooke stood transfixed, her face burning as she realised her mistake.

"Brooke is the best editor in the business," Josh enthused, patting her shoulder affectionately.

Brooke instinctively turned to Danni first, as if drawn to her. She held out her hand, mesmerised by the emerald coloured eyes that bore into her own.

"Nice to meet you Brooke," Danni said with an easy smile that looked as intimate as a kiss.

Was it in Brooke's imagination, or was there a moment between them?

She smiled, then reluctantly tore her gaze from Danni and held out a welcoming hand to Helen. "Hello there, lovely to meet you."

"You too." Helen smiled.

For the next few minutes, Brooke didn't take in a word that passed within the group; instead her eyes discreetly revisited Danni's face. She guessed her to be not much younger than herself, maybe early twenties. Her features were framed by long, blonde tresses that cascaded past her shoulders and draped across her back in fleeting golden waves. Brooke studied the curve of Danni's neck, with its luxuriant slope leading along her high, narrow shoulders. Every nerve in

Brooke's body was smouldering as she greedily drank in this stranger. She was struck with a sudden realisation that no-one had ever had that effect on her – not even Megan.

Josh's booming laugh suddenly jolted Brooke back to reality. She watched the pair, their ease around one another. She smiled as Josh brushed his fiancée's cheek with his lips, before gently encircling his arm around her back as if to shield her. Brooke felt a tightening in her stomach at the obvious affection they had for one another. Why couldn't her relationship with Megan be like that?

Josh gave Danni's shoulder a loving squeeze and smiled, "Right, I'm going to find my dad, Lord knows how much bubbly he's had by now. Ethan, do you want to get the ladies some drinks?"

Ethan beamed at Josh. "Sure. What are you drinking, Danni?" he asked.

"White wine will be great thanks."

"Same again for you, Brooke?"

Though she didn't really want another, she thought it might help to settle the butterflies partying in her stomach. "Yes please." Brooke smiled.

"I'll come with you," Helen said, grinning at Ethan in an unashamedly flirtatious way.

The small gathering dispersed. Left alone, the two newly acquainted women stood in a slightly awkward silence.

Brooke bit her lip as she took a steadying breath. "Nice party."

Danni glanced at her. "Yeah, looks like great fun."

Both women looked around the room at the rather ancient crowd, then back to each other where they burst out laughing.

Danni stepped closer, leaving little personal space between them and grabbed hold of Brooke's forearm. Leaning her head towards her ear she asked in a conspiratorial tone. "Do you think they're going to play any music from our generation? Or from the last three decades even?"

Brooke couldn't help but enjoy the sudden closeness between them. She closed her eyes briefly, wanting to make the moment last until an image of Megan flashed in her mind and she became engulfed in a haze of guilt. Brooke backed away slightly. "I doubt it, unless we slip the DJ something."

Danni gave her a mischievous look. "Hey, that might not be such a bad idea. Though it might give him flashbacks of 'Nam!"

Brooke held Danni's gaze for a few intense seconds; her magnetic, compelling eyes making Brooke's heart flip. What was causing her to have this reaction to a woman she had just met? She shouldn't be having feelings like this for anyone but Megan. The thought of betraying her even mentally made her feel uneasy. Infidelity was just not in her DNA.

She took another sip of her wine before holding out the glass to Danni. "Do you want some? I don't think they're going to be back any time soon. I think

Ethan's probably attempting to seduce the boss' niece with some very bad dancing."

"Thanks." Danni laughed. She took the glass from Brooke's hand, their fingers briefly brushing. "I'm gasping."

Ignoring the spasms her touch had elicited inside, Brooke gathered herself to speak. "So, have you set a date yet?"

Danni sipped on the wine slowly, then looked at Brooke, puzzled. "A date?"

She nodded towards Danni's ringless left hand. "You know, for your wedding?"

Danni looked down, shifting her weight from one ridiculously high shoe to the other. "Oh yes, uh no, not yet."

"You two look a great couple." Though she was sincere, the words were a struggle.

"We do?"

"I'm sure I'm not the first person to tell you that." There it was again. Another pang of jealously. *This is crazy!* A young couple with their whole lives ahead of them and here she was feeling envious.

"Well, Josh is a great guy, and pretty easy on the eye, too," Danni quipped.

Brooke smiled and looked anxiously towards the bar area to see if she could spot Ethan. She watched as the bartender skilfully manipulated three bottles in his hands, pouring what seemed to be a measured amount of liquid into the three glasses placed out on the counter. Not seeing Ethan anywhere, she turned back to Danni. The silence between them was broken as they caught sight of a senior citizen attempting a rather ambitious Michael Jackson move. They laughed like two schoolgirls. It had been a while since Brooke had giggled like that. She liked Danni and despite the intense feeling of physical attraction, she felt an immediate sense of friendship.

"So you and … Ethan is it? You seem like you get on well. Are you *just* colleagues?"

Brooke couldn't help but feast her eyes on Danni's mouth each time she spoke. Could she see the desire in her face? She glanced away. "Me and Ethan? Most definitely."

"Oh. I thought?"

She turned to face her. "No. Nooooo. There's nothing wrong with him, but well, he's not my type … I'm gay," Brooke blurted, thinking it best to just get it out there, however clumsy.

Danni's eyes widened. "No kidding so am …" She stopped suddenly, her mouth gaping open. "So am, is, Ricky Martin! Can you believe that man getting all those women worked up into a frenzy? What a tease."

Brooke laughed. She found Danni's reaction to the revelation both strange and charming. Perhaps Danni was just surprised to hear Brooke preferred women. She wouldn't be the first and she doubted she'd be the last.

Danni handed Brooke her wine glass.

"Yeah well, all the signs were there with Ricky.

He's an immaculate guy. He must take more time to get ready than I do. Mind you, your Josh is pretty well turned out too."

Brooke laughed again as her mind battled to find something else to say. Normally she found maintaining conversation as easy as breathing. She was a natural at it, which wasn't surprising considering the nature of her job, but she felt tongue tied with Danni.

After a few minutes silence Danni leaned in towards her. "So you're an editor? Must be an interesting job?"

"It can be," Ethan said interrupting the conversation from behind and handing them each a drink. "Brooke and I get to work with some great writers and I guess a few mediocre ones." He took a sip of his drink. "It can be amazing as we also get to read some great new manuscripts, you know from unknown authors hoping to get published."

"Sounds like great fun," Danni enthused.

Brooke practically sighed with relief as she placed the empty wine glass on a nearby table and took a sip of her full one. She had never been so grateful to see Ethan in her life. She felt back in control now, the runaway train was back on the rails and proceeding at a regular speed. "It can be. There are a lot of average authors out there though. We want to find something special, someone special," Brooke explained.

"Don't pay any attention to Brooke, she's a real perfectionist. She's an amazing editor with equally amazingly high standards. I reckon Shakespeare would have got a hard time from this one. *Romeo and Juliet* would have been sent back for a rewrite," he teased, nudging a giggling Brooke.

"So what do you do, Danni?" Brooke smiled, feeling more relaxed with her Ethan-shaped security blanket. Although she was adhering to etiquette, she was genuinely interested to know.

"Depends which answer you want. What do I do to make a living or what do I *want* to do?"

"What do you *want* to do?" Brooke asked.

"Well, it's all a bit embarrassing now because you must have heard this a million times, but ..." Danni paused as her eyes darted from Brooke to Ethan then back to Brooke again. "I'm a writer, or rather; I'd like to be a writer."

"Oh really? Then you might just be what I'm after." Brooke blushed at the somewhat Freudian slip. Danni glanced down.

"So, uh. What genre do you write?" Brooke recovered.

"Chick-lit, but at the moment I'm trying my hand at something completely different – you know, self-help, life philosophies. Josh thinks I might be good at it and apparently it's the kind of title that's selling. It seems we could all do with some help these days. Josh believes I have a good way of looking at the world. I'm not so sure."

"Well," Ethan said taking a business card from inside his jacket pocket. "We'd be happy to take a look at what you come up with."

Danni took the card and toyed with it playfully between her fingers. "Really? You don't have to feel obliged."

"I'm not. Besides, as Brooke said, you might be just what she's, I mean, *we're* looking for!"

Brooke blushed for a second time and sensing Danni's eyes upon her, offered her excuses and stepped out to call Megan. It was all too intense and she was beginning to think Danni was feeling awkward too. That was the last thing she wanted.

Chapter Nine

Danni didn't know how much longer she was going to be able to stand in those bloody shoes. Josh had lovingly dubbed them her "killer heels" – *Kilimanjaro* more like! A handful of humans and the odd mountain goat may be able to survive at such heights, not her. Her toes were numb and she was convinced if she didn't take the shoes off soon, she might lose her extremities for good.

She tilted her head as she watched Ethan's lips moving up and down, without actually digesting a single word. She wasn't being rude; it was just that her mind was infinitely more interested in the striking brunette that had left their circle a minute earlier – Brooke, whose face possessed a slight asymmetry that only enhanced her natural beauty. Not to mention the long, supple lashes that fluttered above her piercing blue eyes.

Danni couldn't believe her luck. What was the likelihood of her bumping into her ideal woman on her first date with her fake fiancé? What's more, she'd had to endure this life-changing encounter in full SSB - stilettos, skirt, and blouse. No mean feat for her. She didn't know how she had managed to maintain her composure when they were first introduced; all she had wanted to do was scoop Brooke up into her arms and run off to the nearest Premier Inn.

No, there was no getting away from it. Danni was

officially smitten. She had felt an instant attraction to the enigmatic editor. Brooke may have seemed the reserved type, but Danni knew there was much more lurking beneath that black strapless dress, and God, was she longing to discover it. Brooke had the most perfect lips she had ever seen. Luscious, plump and pink, those lips were made for one thing only – kissing her and her alone. Danni pondered all the adjectives she might use to describe them – sensual, delicious, divine. Was it her imagination, or had Brooke's sea-blue eyes been undressing her as they spoke? Could she really have found her attractive too? Danni replayed the moment their hands touched on the wine glass, how every nerve in her body had seemed to jolt to life. She suddenly felt deflated, coming to the sad realisation that none of that mattered. What could she feasibly do about her feelings – she couldn't ask for her number without blowing Josh's cover. *Damn you Josh Reynolds! Damn you and your homophobic caveman father!*

Waking from her daydream, Danni managed to catch the last few words of Ethan's story, enough to let out a perfectly timed chuckle right at the punch line. Danni peered over his impeccably tailored shoulder as she saw Josh and a tall handsome older man approaching. As the pair got closer, she grew increasingly intrigued by the older man's appearance – fake tan, dyed black hair, and he was, yes, he was actually mincing. His white skin-tight trousers and pink waist-coat only confirmed her suspicions. Perhaps he was the birthday entertainment, a drag act about to pop to the changing rooms in time for the magic transformation.

Upon their arrival, Josh and his companion stood smiling excitedly before Danni.

"Danni." Josh pulled Danni's hand into his own. "This is my dad. Dad, this is Danni, my beautiful fiancée."

"Your … dad?" Danni blurted, nearly choking on her Pinot Grigio. *Dad?* Could she alone see the obvious irony? Josh was standing proudly next to his father, like a young Ricky Martin embracing Liberace. Was she really the only one who could see behind the candelabra?

"Danni, darling! So wonderful to meet you at last," he bellowed in a rather theatrical voice.

"Ahh! Yes, you too, Mr …"

"Just call me Roy, dear, short for Royston," he said leaning in to kiss her flushed cheek. "What a beauty. I've been looking forward to this moment ever since Josh told me about you. I'm so glad he's met someone at last. After his mum died, I thought he'd never get over it – they were so close you see."

Danni nodded robotically, still dumbstruck. "Yes, I can imagine. She sounds like she was quite a remarkable woman," she said genuinely.

"Yes, she was, she was. It will be good to have another woman in the family. You've met Josh's cousin Helen I take it? You two minxes will get on like a house on fire. Josh tells me you are quite the life and soul. I love a woman with spirit. Now," he whispered taking Danni's hands and holding them in his soft, manicured own. "I don't want you two being strangers, you are always welcome here – especially when the grandchildren are born! One big happy family we are," he said, winking at Josh.

Danni gasped. "*Grand* …"

Josh let out an awkward laugh, so loud that it attracted the attention of a nearby group who nodded and raised their glasses.

"Give us a break Dad. We aren't even married yet," Josh retorted.

Roy shifted his weight to one side, and placed his left hand firmly on his hip. "Don't be so timid Josh; your mother had you when we were barely twenty. Our seed is unstoppable."

Danni felt quite nauseous with the mention of "seed" and "grandchildren". She could only hope for a switch to a more palatable conversation.

"So Dad, Danni's writing a fantastic book at the moment."

"Really?" he said eyeing her with renewed interest. "Let Brooke have a look. We're after some talented female authors. Brooke has a good eye, best in the business. If it's any good we'll see what we can do."

Brooke appeared as if from nowhere and took her place next to a rather merry Roy.

"Ah Brooke. I was just saying how you have an excellent eye for talent. Danni may just be the girl you're looking for!"

Is Brooke blushing?

"Right," Roy declared decisively. "I'll leave you young ones to chat. Wonderful to meet you, Danni," he gushed, gyrating his way onto the now busy dance floor.

Danni looked after him. A good dancer too? The evidence sure was stacking up, she concluded.

"Josh, can I have a word?" she asked, grabbing him by his arm and leading him a few feet away from Brooke and Ethan.

"Josh, about your dad ..."

Josh grabbed her hands. "I know, I know. You're worried if he liked you. Well he did. He loved you, I could tell."

Josh was looking at her with the eyes of a puppy, all soft and gooey. Could she really tell him he had the campiest father in the western world? That his own dad was probably not averse to the odd portion of toad in the hole? Of course not. That's not what friends do to one another.

"That's good. I really like him too."

"Enough about my dad, what do you think about Brooke?" Josh's face broke into a big grin. "She's hot isn't she?"

"Sizzling more like!" Danni quipped. "Did you know she's gay?"

"Yeah I did. I couldn't risk telling her about myself though – in case she told Dad."

"Your dad seems to think highly of her, so maybe he's not quite the homophobe you think."

Josh's features darkened. "Don't be fooled by

appearances."

Danni swiftly changed the subject, the last thing she wanted to do was spoil Josh's night. "So, about the Brooke thing. You can see my predicament. I can't exactly make a move on her without you looking like a complete idiot. Oh Josh, what am I going to do? I really like …"

"Oh, hi there. Am I interrupting?"

Danni swallowed her words and spun around to face the direction of the questioner.

"Brooke. Not at all."

"I just wanted to say goodbye."

Danni instinctively reached out her hand to touch Brooke's shoulder and quickly snatched it back. "Oh no. You're not going already, are you?"

Brooke responded with a faint smile. "'Fraid so. I've got a busy day tomorrow."

"But it's Sunday."

She swept her hair back away from her face. "I know, but I have things planned. It was really nice meeting you," she said outstretching her hand.

Danni inwardly groaned. She didn't want a handshake she wanted something more meaningful, like a hug or, dare she wish for it, a promise of a second meeting. "Wait a second," Danni said boldly, falling into step beside her as they walked toward the entrance. "So." She tried to keep her voice casual, a desperate attempt to hide the excitement she felt at being so close to her again. "I'd, um, love to talk more about the publishing world, if you have time of course.

I know how busy you must be." She looked at her expectantly.

Brooke stopped in the doorway and turned to Danni.

"Of course I have time. I'd be more than happy to. I'd like to hear more about your book as well."

"Let me give you my number."

Brooke slipped her hand into her pocket, withdrew her phone and tapped in the numbers as Danni called them out.

"Great. I'll speak to you soon then," Brooke said as she walked out of the house and down the stairs into a waiting taxi.

A warm fuzziness spread through Danni's body as she watched the car disappear down the driveway and into the night. She stood grinning to herself, possessed by an incredible inner joy that was desperate to burst out. *I'm going to see her again! I'm really going to see her again! Could this be the greatest day of my life? God yes!*

Chapter Ten

The bathroom air was pregnant with the sweet scent of honeysuckle as the two women luxuriated, top to tail, in the free-standing bath. Candlelight illuminated the small room, golden flames flickering against the white tiled walls.

"This is what I miss most when you're not here." Alison grinned, rubbing the ball of her foot over Megan's left breast in a circular movement.

Megan reached for her glass of red wine on the wicker chair next to the bath. "Hmm, I know. This is paradise."

"Isn't it? Oh when are you going to get a job on the ground? Kelly misses you. *I miss you.*"

Megan tilted her head forward a little and took a sip of her blood-red drink. The warmth of the Pinot Noir trickling down her throat made the moment all the more delicious and decadent.

"You know I love my job, Ali. I'd go insane cooped up behind a desk all day. It's just not me."

"Then why don't you look for another job outside the industry – something nearer to home?"

Megan returned the glass to the seat. "Oh come on, babe, what – retrain? Start from the beginning? Realistically what would I do?"

Alison shrugged defiantly, the bubbles sloshing over the edge of the bath lip. "I dunno, anything. Don't you want to be here all the time, with us?"

Megan took hold of Alison's delicate foot and began to massage the heel. "Would you want me to be miserable in a job I hated? 'Moody Megan' wouldn't be good for any of us, now would she?" She smiled, trying to lighten the mood.

"I thought Kelly and I would be enough for you to be happy."

Megan brought Alison's foot to her face and kissed each of her toes individually. "You are," she answered in what she hoped was a reassuring tone.

"But what? You think family life is too mundane for you, not exciting enough, is that it?"

Megan raised her eyes up towards the ceiling, as if seeking some divine intervention. "I didn't say that, did I?

"Then prove it!" Alison snapped, in a voice that heralded the beginnings of an argument.

The last thing Megan needed was another argument. Why did things have to get so damn emotional all the time?

She sat up, the soapy suds sliding down her firm breasts and pulled Alison up to meet her halfway, cupping her lover's glowing face between her hands and drawing her close. Her voice deepened as she leaned forward to whisper in her ear. "When I'm away, do you know what I think of when I'm touching myself," she asked, as she slowly traced her finger around the outline of Alison's breasts.

Alison tugged on her bottom lip with her teeth, before a smile slowly crept onto her face. "No tell me," she breathed more than said.

"I think of you … watching me." Megan looked at her through half-open eyes as she slid her hand slowly down her moist body. Her skin glistened under the seductive glow of the candle light, her hand coming to a halt between her own legs. She loved to watch Alison's face when she was aroused.

"Do you like me touching myself?" Megan moaned huskily as she sank back in the tub to rest her head on the edge, her finger rubbing against her clit.

"Yes," Alison answered with a gasp.

Megan bit her bottom lip, feeling the pressure mounting within her, building and deepening, until she was nearly ready to erupt.

As if sensing the impending final moment, Alison slid her fingers deep into her, increasing the speed as Megan's hips pushed upwards towards her, hitting her sweet spot with every thrust. The sexy, encouraging groans from Alison pushed her faster and closer to the brink of pleasure, as waves of water lapped against their skin like the surf on a beach. Megan gripped Alison's wrist as her fingers buried themselves inside her. She begged her to press harder as her breasts rose and fell rapidly. She was so close. Megan cried out as she felt the explosion between her legs, her body going limp as she basked in the final seconds of ecstasy.

Megan inhaled sharply through her nose, then released a long deep breath as she raised her hand and twined it with Alison's resting on the edge of the tub. Pressing their palms together, Megan pulled both hands back to kiss Alison's fingers. "Hmmm, that was so good."

Alison smiled as she untangled herself from Megan's legs and moved to lay over her, delivering a trail of kisses along her blood-flushed neck. "Just imagine Megan, it could be like this every day."

Megan let out a sigh as she began an internal debate. *But what about Brooke?* Her thoughts drifted from the pleasure of the moment to the cold reality of her other lover, miles away. What was the solution? Brooke drove her to distraction but like Alison, she had something that Megan wanted. Something that would be hard to relinquish. She loved to be needed and nobody needed her as much as these two women – she had made sure of that.

She ran her hand over Alison's short hair, stroking the planes of her back. She felt so good. She loved this woman's body, every glorious inch of it. And each time she devoured her, she wanted her more and more. Feeling the shudder of Alison's shoulders, Megan could sense the unfulfilled lust still burning within. She moved her mouth towards Alison's, feeling a warm throb between her legs as her tongue found its way into her lover's hot mouth. She was divine. She was beautiful. She was all hers … all night.

Chapter Eleven

"The mobile phone you have called may be switched off. Please try again later."

Brooke slammed her mobile on the dresser. A knot tightened in the pit of her stomach. The feeling that something was amiss had led her to leave a highly enjoyable party earlier than she would have liked.

Since arriving home she had called Megan several times without success. She felt a stab of annoyance towards her for being so inconsiderate. Didn't she realise how worried she would be not hearing from her? She should have arrived hours ago. Wasn't it just courtesy to let your partner know you had got there safely?

Why should it surprise me she didn't?

It was morning in Sydney, surely Megan would be up and about by now. She claimed she never suffered from jetlag and was always the first one up and ready for the day's adventures. Strange then that she hadn't heard a word. She sometimes wondered if Megan behaved this way just to torment her.

Her frustrations towards her own relationship made her mind jump to the subject of Danni and Josh. *Now they seem like a couple that really work.* Brooke thought of how nice it must be to be with someone more caring, someone more thoughtful. Danni and Josh seemed to have that, a real respect and understanding. But of course, nothing is ever as it seems, she consoled herself. Who knows what really goes on behind closed doors?

To be honest, she was feeling a little confused by her feelings towards Danni. There was something about her that she couldn't quite put her finger on. She just couldn't get her out of her mind. Was it normal to feel attracted to somebody when you were supposed to be happily in love already? Maybe that was it – maybe she didn't really love Megan anymore. Perhaps she was just trying to cling on and make it work.

Brooke continued the debate in her mind as she walked to the kitchen to grab a glass of water. Despite her annoyance with Megan, a smile played on her lips as she thought about the party and more importantly, Danni. She wondered if it was such a good idea taking her number. Surely that was asking for trouble.

Hey, stop getting ahead of yourself! Danni's engaged - to a man! But then, what about that spark she had felt between them – surely she couldn't have imagined the way Danni looked at her. Brooke was always the last person to realise anyone was attracted to her, it was a long-standing joke amongst her friends.

Dismissing thoughts of Danni, she filled a glass under the tap then walked to her bedroom and sat on the edge of the bed. She picked up her phone from the side and pressed redial, "The mobile phone you have called may be switched o—"

She cut off the message abruptly as paranoia rose within her. A vision of Megan in the arms of another woman leapt into her mind. The ugly image of Megan giving all her love and attention to someone else.

Laying back against the cushions, her torturous thoughts were interrupted by the ringing of her mobile. It was Megan. She hesitated before answering it – she didn't want her to hear any annoyance in her voice. She pressed accept and put on her best upbeat voice.

"Hi, sweetheart."

"Hello," Megan's voice was barely a whisper, she sounded strange.

"Are you okay, Megs?" Her heart rate started to increase. She pressed her ear closer to the phone trying to hear some background noise. There was none.

"I'm fine, I'm just tired."

"You should have a nap."

"I will. How did your party go?"

"Oh that." Her thoughts immediately went to Danni and the guilt she felt at the attraction. "It was okay. I wish I was there with you. Why do you have to stay there so long?"

"We discussed this Brooke, It's only for a two weeks. There was no point me travelling all this way without staying on to see the sights. Oh, uh, sorry I have to go. Call you later."

There was silence, a strange ruffle, and then the phone went dead. Brooke immediately called back but it went straight to voicemail.

Confused, she rolled off the bed and wandered into the living room. She couldn't sleep with her mind racing with so many crazy thoughts. Slumping down into the brown leather sofa, in the clutter-free, spacious room, the sight of Megan's laptop under the white lacquered coffee table caught her eye. She couldn't believe that she had actually forgotten to take it with her. Normally that was the first thing she packed. Was this an omen? What if she looked at it? What if she actually turned it on and checked her email? In an effort to dismiss the impulse, she grabbed the TV remote, trying to stay focused as the plasma screen jumped to life.

Seconds later, her attention was drawn back to the silver lid of the laptop. An inner conflict began inside her. Wouldn't it be better to know the truth? That way at least she'd know what she was up against. *No, Brooke,* another voice contradicted. What did that say about their relationship if she had to stoop to such levels? She was not a spy, that was not her way.

One thing was for sure, the fact she was even tempted to look spoke volumes. It told her she didn't trust Megan. Something in her gut was setting off alarm bells but the question was, did she have the courage to do anything about it?

Chapter Twelve

It was exactly two seconds after Danni opened her eyes that the horrific flashbacks began. What the hell had she been thinking? Her drunken alter ego "Danni Diablo" had taken possession of her earthly body after her fifth glass of wine, or thereabouts. Who was counting? Frankly, not her. What she yearned for more than anything was a deep dark hole to crawl into, or better still, a time machine. The latter not yet available on Amazon, she would have to settle for the solace of her fourteen tog duvet.

She heard Josh's footsteps outside the door and in anticipation of his arrival, peeped from beneath her blanket of shame through one blood-shot eye. She cringed as she watched the handle turn and the blurry image of Josh grew clearer in the den of doom.

She was too embarrassed to even look at him. "Josh, I'm so sorry about last night," she said. "I don't blame you if you want to call off our fake wedding and end our pretend relationship."

Josh's face cracked into a warm grin as he walked over to the window and drew the curtains open.

"What are you talking about?" He laughed. "I had a great time last night, and from what I remember, so did you! Not that you look quite as enthusiastic now, Miss '*Sambucas for everyone!*' So, guess who has the evidence?"

She looked up at him timidly. *Evidence?* She prayed

she hadn't been snapped doing her famous dance-floor cartwheel manoeuvre, not in that skirt!

Josh flopped on the bed beside her and thrust his phone into her pallid face. *Oh Lord, here we go.* She winced. Daring to open just the one eye, she reluctantly looked down at the screen to behold the full horror of the picture. *Sweet baby Jesus in a manger! Was that really her?* Exhibit A: A shoe-less Danni, legs akimbo, performing the Macarena with six unnaturally supple O.A.Ps! *How is it even possible for a human to get their leg up that high?* She pushed the phone away. "Oh my God. What must your dad and cousin think of me?"

"They *loved* you! They think you're great. Last night was a total success."

"Are you serious?" she mumbled, her face now thrust into the pillow.

"Yep."

"That's unbelievable. Speaking of your dad, he's pretty, well, very, uh. " She rifled through her fuzzy brain for a polite description as she looked up at him. "*Flamboyant*, isn't he?"

"Do you think? He's just 'Dad' to me. I guess he is pretty flamboyant."

Hello? Josh? Wake up and smell the camp coffee! Was she missing something or was Josh simply in denial?

"Josh, most dads don't go around in shocking pink waistcoats with hair like a member of One Direction!"

"He just likes vibrant colours, that's all – he says

it cheers him up. Anyway enough about my dad. Let's talk about you and a certain Brooke," he teased, nudging her playfully in the ribs.

"Brooke!" A sense of excitement rose within her.

"Yes, Brooke. You two looked such a cute couple." He grinned, raising a single eyebrow.

"Yeah right," she scoffed. "Fat chance of that ever happening, and it's all your fault, Mr 'Please pretend to be my fiancée.'"

"Come on. I didn't think she'd be your type."

"And what is *my type* exactly?"

"Well after that last girl you were seeing, I'm not really sure." He laughed, ducking as she tossed a pillow square at him.

"Very funny, Josh!"

He straightened up. "So, are you going to call her?"

"I gave her my number. I'd really like to get to know her, even if it's only as a friend."

Josh looked at her incredulously. "Yeah right, and you expect me to believe that? I know you Danni. You wouldn't be able to resist her."

"Could any sane woman? Anyway, there's no point of going into the ins and outs of what might be. In Brooke's eyes, I'm some straight woman and not just any straight woman but the fiancée of her boss' son. I don't think I will be getting myself out of that one too easily."

"I suppose not. But on the positive side, just think of how you helped me out. I'm really grateful."

"I know. I'm just sorry you can't be yourself. Oh anyway, my head hurts too much for such a heavy conversation." All she wanted right now was a little *Danni* time to replay the evening with Brooke in her head. She wanted to relive every delicious minute of it.

"Are you going to write today?"

She closed her eyes. "Yeah later." The thought of writing the book was actually more appealing to her now that Brooke was on the scene. She imagined if Roy did publish her book she'd be able to have a lot more encounters with Brooke, which could only be a good thing. She rubbed her hand over her face and yawned. "It's coming together a lot better than I thought. I'm thinking if I carry on like this, I should have a full synopsis and first chapter finished within a week."

"Don't forget to mention it if, sorry, I mean *when* she calls you. She seemed pretty interested and she might even look at your book too!"

"JOSH!" Danni's eyes opened as she burst into laughter and launched herself at her tormentor, wrestling him onto the pillow.

"You fancy Brooke … you fancy Brooke!" He chanted in a childlike voice.

A new book *and* a new love interest. Things really were looking up.

Chapter Thirteen

Despite it being the middle of October, the morning sun descended through a break in the clouds, its rays caressing Megan's neck and shoulders as they filtered into the bedroom where she stretched out underneath the cotton sheet. The smile that illuminated her face had been there since she had awoken minutes earlier. Thank God for schools. The last thing she wanted today was to have to plan all her activities around a five year old. She didn't know how Alison did it; or any mother, for that matter. She would have been carted off to a mental institution if she had to watch one more brain-numbing children's TV programme, while all the time pretending to be engaged with Kelly. *What a drag.* Now if every night was like last night, she could see herself hanging around just a little while longer than she intended. She slipped out of the bed naked and walked to the bathroom, eyeing her toned body in the mirror as she entered. Women just loved her body, not that she blamed them of course. Turning to the left then to the right as she admired her firm breasts, a grin slowly formed on her face as she relived Alison's tongue caressing them. She couldn't wait until tonight. Maybe she'd get Alison to take Kelly to her mum's for the night. *As if that would ever happen!*

Irritation swept through her as she leaned over and pushed the plug into the bath. What was the likelihood of separating Alison from her precious Kelly for one night? The way Alison carried on, you'd think she loved Kelly more than she loved her. Bloody kids. The whole nation seemed to be fascinated with them. Why, she didn't know. They were just needy little parasites who turned into entitled nasty adult ones. Well that wasn't going to be a problem for her. She had no intention of being around the kid in one year's time, let alone thirteen. She wasn't going to waste the best years of her life looking after somebody else's child. She totally accepted that this predicament was her own fault. When her friends had started to drop off the radar as a result of finding partners and consequently having children, Megan had felt alienated. As there was no way on earth she was going to have a parasite living inside *her* body and ruining her figure, the idea of a readymade family had appealed to her, hence Alison and the brat's arrival into her life. But the reality was just too much for her.

She slid into the bath and dunked her head under the warm water, closing her eyes. The water soothed her racing mind. She sighed, letting calmer, more pleasant thoughts flow through her. Alison's body for one. She slowly opened her eyes and let out a scream when she saw a figure looming above her.

She jerked up into a sitting position and ran her hand over her hair. "Are you trying to give me a heart attack?"

Alison laughed. "I was calling and calling for at least a minute. What were you so deep in thought about?"

Megan's mouth softened into a smile. "Oh, just about you … and Kelly and how happy I am."

"Likewise," Alison said unbuttoning her dress and letting it drop to the floor. "Anything else?"

"Hmm, let's see," Megan said reaching out for Alison's hand and tugging on it. "Last night …"

Alison stepped into the bath. "I haven't stopped thing about anything else. How about a repeat?"

"Definitely. As long as I'm all you think about, you and me are going to do just fine," Megan said as she pulled her into her arms.

Chapter Fourteen

Josh kicked the empty beer can lying in the middle of the pathway as he made his way through the alleyway that divided the shops on either side. The usual hustle and bustle of busy shoppers had died down making the dimly lit area seem creepier than usual. Why his dad chose to play snooker in such a rundown area he could never fathom. Each Monday at eight o'clock his dad could be found racking up the balls and getting ready to whip any worthy opponent. It wasn't the most private place he could think of to talk to him, but he hadn't wanted to go to his house. What he needed to tell him was best said on neutral ground.

He stopped when he reached the neon-lit entrance and took the stairs two at a time to reach the landing. Glass doors led the way to a dank, large space with fading paintwork and a stained carpet. A bar scaled one side of the wall and at least six full sized snooker tables occupied the remaining space; a brass rail and green light shades hung low above each of them.

Josh's view was obstructed by groups of young men surrounding the first few tables. On tiptoes, he peered around the room until he caught sight of his dad bent over the far table ready to take his shot. Perfect. At least he was alone. Josh took a deep breath as he made his way over to him, stopping a few feet away until Roy had successfully potted a red.

"Hey, Dad."

Roy looked up at him, squinting his eyes. "Josh?"

Josh smiled nervously. "The one and only."

Roy moved around the table and briefly embraced him. "It's good to see you, son. Can I get you a beer?"

Josh shrugged off his jacket. "Sure, why not?"

Roy called over to the barman. "Bert! Can I get a couple of beers and my usual over here?"

"No problem," Bert replied.

Josh's heart sank when he noticed a jacket on a stool next to Roy's. He wasn't alone after all. "Who are you playing with?"

"Ethan." Roy laughed. "As you can imagine, the poor boy doesn't know what's hit him."

Josh slipped onto a stool as Bert brought over the drinks and set them on the circular table before heading back to the bar.

"Thanks, Bert," Josh called out after him.

Roy sipped his pina colada, complete with blue cocktail umbrella, through a straw before casting his gaze on Josh.

Josh raised his eyebrows. "You've got Bert making cocktails as well now?"

"He learnt to make them especially for me. So what brings you down here?"

Josh sucked in the stale air and blew it out slowly. "I need to talk to you."

"About?" Roy asked, walking over to stand a few inches away from him.

"Me and—"

Ethan's voice rang out from behind him. "Hey! Good to see you, Josh. Roy never said you were playing tonight."

Josh shot a glance at Ethan. *Maybe this is a sign to keep my mouth shut.* "I'm not. I was at a loose end so I thought I'd pop by to see how my dad was getting on." As much as he loved playing pool, snooker confused the hell out of him – what with all those different coloured balls. It made absolutely no sense.

Ethan picked up his drink and took a swig, looking at Roy in admiration. "Winning as usual. Maybe you can give me some tips on how to beat your dad. It's not right him white washing me all the time."

Josh let out a weak laugh. "No luck here I'm afraid. I'm yet to see anybody beat him."

Roy looked at him, worry in his eyes. "Ethan, would you mind getting some crisps from the bar?"

Ethan looked from father to son. "No, of course not."

"Thanks. Now Josh, you were saying?" Roy said as soon as Ethan was out of earshot.

Josh slipped off the seat, feeling defeated. He really thought he would be able to tell his dad the truth. But just like everything when it came to him, he hadn't wanted to disappoint him. Josh shrugged. "It's nothing. Don't worry."

Roy clamped his hand on Josh's shoulder. "Are you having problems with Danni, son?"

Why couldn't he just say it? Why couldn't he just

open his mouth and tell him and have done with it – exorcise the demon once and for all? It wasn't fair to have entangled Danni in his web of lies. He felt terrible that she'd met a woman she had finally connected with and could do nothing about it – all because of him. Some friend he was. He opened his mouth but nothing came out.

"Look, Josh," Roy began. "Relationships don't always run smoothly for anyone, you have to take the good with the bad. It's normal to be feeling a little apprehensive. Marriage is a big step."

"Dad, it's nothing to do with that."

"Then what is it? Do you need money?"

Josh shook his head as he pulled on his jacket. "It's nothing, really. I'm sure it will be all right."

"Josh, you know you can tell me anything. I won't judge you."

Josh's eyes begin to tear up. *If only that were true.* "I'd best be getting back. Danni will be wondering where I am. Tell Ethan I said goodbye."

"I will. Listen I've got an idea. Why don't you bring Danni over for dinner tomorrow? That way I can get to know her a bit better."

"I dunno …" Josh mused.

"Josh, if she's going to be my daughter-in-law, don't you think it makes sense I should at least spend some time with her?"

"I suppose."

"Good. That's settled. I'll see you both tomorrow."

"Ok," Josh said reluctantly.

As he walked towards the entrance he sensed his father's eyes boring into his back. He was going to have to find another way to tell him. There was no way he could let Danni carry his burden at the cost of her own happiness. And now he had just made matters worse by agreeing to take her round for dinner.

Chapter Fifteen

Danni reread the instructions in the recipe book. What the hell were mungo beans? She shook her head in disgust as she read the remaining ingredients for the soup Josh had suggested they try. Josh and his bloody eating fads. Just because he wanted to purify his body didn't mean she had to follow suit. She opened the fridge and brought out the homemade pizza she had prepared earlier, covered with lashings of cheese and every leftover vegetable she could find.

Hearing the front door slam, she wiped her hands down the front of her apron, walked to the kitchen doorway and peeked around the corner. Josh's face was partially hidden by the large bunch of flowers he held in his hands.

"Who are the flowers for?"

Josh was by her side in a few strides. "Who else but you?" he said handing the dozen red roses to her.

Danni looked at him suspiciously. Josh was not a flowers sort of guy. "Okay. What do you want now?"

"Don't be silly. Nothing." He pulled his face as he sniffed the air. "What's that rancid smell?"

"That soup you said would give me glowing skin."

"Urgh. Do you fancy a kebab instead?"

Danni shook her head. "Right. Come on out with it. What do you want? You only try to buy me off with a kebab when you want me to do something."

"You're so suspicious, Danni," he said looking at her in disbelief.

Danni wasn't falling for his schoolboy charm. The last time she did, look at the mess she had got herself into. "No, Josh. I just know you. Come on, spit it out."

He rubbed his hand over his chin. "Well, if you insist."

Danni took a step back and looked at him though squinted eyes. "Ha! I knew it. You want me to pretend I'm pregnant, don't you?"

"Oh God, no!" He scrunched his face in disgust. "My dad's invited us round for dinner."

He said the words so quickly Danni thought she'd misheard him. When he wouldn't meet her eyes, she knew she hadn't.

She slapped her hand against her leg. "Oh, come on Josh. You promised it would be a one off. I don't do parents and I definitely don't do dinners, I get all flustered and spray food everywhere."

His lips held a hesitant smile. "Come on, it'll only be the three of us. It's no biggie."

She turned and walked to the living room. "Yeah, like it was only going to be the party. I couldn't care less if Jesus himself was cooking the entre. The answer's no."

"Please. Pretty please. You really enjoyed the party."

Danni shook her head. "No, no, no, no, no!"

"Do you remember those jeans you liked in Top Shop?"

"Yes. What about them?"

He lifted the bag he held in his hand up in the air. "Well, I thought I'd get them for you, since you've been such a good sport."

"That's bribery, Josh," she said, reaching out to grab the bag.

Josh pulled his hand away. "Yeah. But just imagine how hot you'd look in them." He laughed.

She pulled her face. "I hate you."

Josh gave a short shake of his head. "No you don't. You love me. Come on, just say yes."

"No."

"Yes," he said dangling the bag in front of her.

"No!"

"Yes!"

She looked longingly at the bag. "All right but I'm not bloody happy about this."

"Believe me, neither am I."

She playfully punched his shoulder as he handed her the bag. "And I am not wearing a skirt!"

Chapter Sixteen

Danni and Josh sat at a long opal table set with china plates and crystal glasses. Candles in silver holders topped off the setting, giving it an air of elegance. Sipping a glass of champagne, she glanced around the well-designed room. Two large sparkling chandeliers hung from the ceiling, throwing patches of light onto the pastel-coloured walls. Dark wooden furniture was neatly arranged at the opposite end of the room. A colourful bouquet of flowers sat above the marble fire place where a fire crackled and hissed, barely audible to the human ear.

"I hope you like steak tartare," Roy said to Danni with a smile.

She bit down on her lip. "Um, yeah love it." She looked to Josh through narrowed eyes. He looked away stifling a laugh.

Josh nodded towards the empty chair next to his dad. "Is someone else joining us tonight?"

"Yes." The doorbell sounded. "Ahh. Here she is now," Roy said rising and heading for the door.

Danni swung her head around to Josh. "Josh, are you crazy? I am not eating raw meat, do I look like a Bengali tiger? You'd better make sure–" she stopped as Roy appeared in the doorway with Brooke. A small sound escaped her lips as she gulped in as much air as her lungs would hold. Her heart was racing and so was her head. *What was Brooke doing here? Had Josh known she was coming?* She turned to look at him, asking him with her eyes whether he knew about this surprise guest. Josh frantically shook his head in denial. She slid her hand under the table and over Josh's leg to pinch the inside of his firm thigh.

"Ouch!" he yelped, jerking back in his seat.

Danni rolled her eyes. "You knew about this didn't you?" she whispered.

"I swear I didn't. Don't you think I would have told you?" he hissed back.

"I'm going to kill … Brooke!" Danni said changing her tone of voice in an instant. "It's nice to see you again."

"You too," Brooke replied, pecking Josh on the cheek and then Danni.

Roy gestured for Brooke to sit. "You all chat amongst yourselves. I'll go and sort out the food."

"Hmm, yummy," Brooke said sitting next to Roy's vacant chair.

Danni frowned. "You like steak tartare?" She felt so flushed with nerves that she thought she might spontaneously combust over the dinner service. It was the Brooke effect – she looked every bit as captivating as the first time she had met her.

A smile lit up Brooke's face. "Love it. I take it you're not too fond of it?"

Danni had no idea why she had to think for a brief moment before responding, but she quickly pulled her senses back into check and nodded. "Me? You're joking. I love it – just love it."

Josh looked at her puzzled. "You do?"

Danni moved her foot to the side and pressed steadily onto Josh's trainer. "You know I do. We eat out at Le Sacre Coeur in Islington all the time."

Roy brought in four plates as expertly as a silver service waiter. "Here you are."

"I think I'll pass," Josh said as Roy put the plate in front of him.

"Sorry?" Danni blurted out as she turned to Josh, her eyes widened in sheer horror. Was he going to send her down this slippery path of sinew all by herself?

Josh patted his stomach. "Sweetheart, I told you before we came out I was feeling a bit dodgy." He smiled at her sweetly. "At least that means there's more for you, you loving it and all."

"You don't want anything, Josh?" Roy asked.

"I'll just stick to the vegetables, thanks," he said using a fork to push the steak tartare to one side of his plate.

Danni gulped. She looked over to Brooke who had already forked some of the raw meat into her mouth. Danni wanted to retch. Tentatively, her hands picked up the knife and fork, her stomach already considering evacuation before she had even tasted it.

Josh smirked and waved some of the meat at the end of his fork in front of her face. "Here have mine."

She looked at him and hoped he could read her eyes – she was going to strangle him with her bare hands when they got back home.

"I think I'll just stick to my own first, thanks," she said through gritted teeth.

His face broke into a grin.

Danni held her breath, counted to three and took a ball of the minced beef into her mouth. All her thoughts instantly turned to the reports of Mad Cow disease. *I'm going to die.*

As she chewed and the flavour hit her taste buds, she decided it really wasn't that bad. But it wasn't good enough that she could eat the whole lot.

After a few more mouthfuls she pushed her plate away and said, "That was really lovely Roy but I couldn't possibly eat any more."

"Trying to keep slim for that wedding dress, Danni?" He laughed. "I'm glad you enjoyed it. It's one of my favourite dishes."

She watched as Roy and Brooke finished their meals. Roy stood and headed back into the kitchen to prepare the dessert. When Josh followed him, she felt like she had been set adrift in a sea of awkwardness. Being there with Brooke felt so intense, giving rise to feelings that were completely new to her. There had never been an occasion where she had felt so out of her depth.

Danni took a sip of her drink for Dutch courage. What did you talk to an editor about? *Books you idiot!* "So, who's your favourite author?" she asked calmly despite feeling like a nervous wreck.

Brooke didn't skip a beat. "That would have to be Wayne Dyer. How about yours?"

"Hmm … let's see," Danni said, racking her brain. Who was that small guy who barely spoke above a whisper? Ek somebody. The name of one of Josh's favourite authors was on the tip of her tongue. "Ekhar–"

"Eckhart Tolle?" Brooke filled in for her.

Relief flooded her. "Yes, that's him," she said triumphantly.

Brooke gave her an approving look. "I've been to one of his talks. It was very insightful."

Danni leaned back in her seat. "I can imagine."

Seeing Brooke's empty glass, Danni scooped up the bottle and refilled it.

"I must say I was impressed by your effort to look as if you liked steak tartare."

Danni's eyes widened. "Oh my God, was it that obvious?"

Brooke laughed. "No, it wasn't so much your body language. Your eyes gave you away."

"Oh no, I really thought I'd pulled it off." She prayed Brooke couldn't see her blushing as she felt her cheeks burning with the ferocity of Pompeii.

Brooke lowered her voice and said in a slight whisper. "Don't worry, your secret is safe with me."

Danni muffled a laugh with her hand. Now she had yet another secret. How had she come from being a straightforward honest sort of person to this cloak-and-dagger pretender. If she had her way she would just blow the lid off everything by telling Josh's dad exactly what she thought of his outdated views and after that, ask Brooke out. The fantasy pleased her to no end.

Danni tapped her slender fingers on the table, blurting out the first thing that entered her mind. "So, do you have dinner at your boss' often?"

Brooke nodded. "Oh yes. Roy and I have been friends for years. He mentioned you were coming tonight and thought it would be nice for us to meet again to discuss your book."

"Oh," she started slowly. "So you knew we'd be here?"

"Yes."

It was a pity Josh's dad hadn't given them the heads up as well. Had she known beforehand that Brooke was going to be there she would have at least put some make up on and worn her hair down, not to mention putting on a more revealing top. Instead, she sat there in a white cotton shirt buttoned up to her neck like the most conservative member of the Amish. She dreaded to think what Brooke made of her fashion sense.

There was a brief awkward moment as the women looked at each other, neither breaking eye contact. Danni didn't know why Brooke didn't look away but her own motivation was simple: she couldn't. Brooke held her gaze like a magnet.

"Hmm," was all she could think to say to end the silence. Why on earth was this woman causing her to clam up like this? She could normally talk the hind legs off a donkey, cow or any other farmyard animal.

"So, tell me some more about the book," Brooke asked, finally looking away and focusing on her drink.

Danni hesitated. Twirling the ends of her hair with her finger, she said. "The book, well um, it's about … let me see …" Her brain was failing her, she just couldn't get the words out. She was well and truly tongue-tied. "It's about–"

"Expectations," Josh exclaimed as he entered the room and picked up his drink from the table.

Brooke looked up at Josh then back to Danni. "Expectations?"

"Yes," Danni said finally finding her voice. Suddenly she felt her confidence rising a little. Having Josh around sometimes really did have its advantages. He made her feel protected when she was at her most vulnerable and sitting opposite Brooke, she felt as exposed as she had ever been. "In a nutshell, I'm writing about expectations and the harm they do to relationships."

"Really? And what harm do you think they do?"

"Where do I start?" Danni grinned, gulping the fizzy liquid.

"At the beginning, darling," Josh said swigging his beer before dashing out of the room again.

Danni stared after him. She hadn't spent three years at university studying creative writing to not be able to talk about storylines and ideas at the drop of a hat. She had to get her act together. "I truly believe," she started, a slight tremble in her voice as if she were giving a presentation for the first time in her life, "that you can't build a solid foundation between two people whose relationship is based on unrealistic expectations."

"But everyone has certain standards they expect from a partner? What might be considered unrealistic to one person might not to another."

Danni cleared her throat before pushing her glass to the side and leaning forward on the table with her elbows. "In which case they aren't compatible. What I'm trying to say is that I don't like the idea of obligations or expectations in relationships. If somebody wants to do something, they should do it because they want to, not because it's expected of them."

Brooke cocked her head. "For example?"

"Take sex." Danni shifted to the edge of her seat and joined the tip of her fingers in a steeple position. "Do you think it's right that some people believe it's their God-given right to expect sex just because they're married?"

Brooke shook her head. "Most definitely not. I agree that it defeats the object of what should be a very loving and natural thing to do."

Danni slapped the table with her hand. "Exactly. I would hate for my partner to do something she," Danni quickly caught her slip-up, "or he didn't want to do. I know the premise of it sounds naive and unrealistic but I think relationships would have a better chance of success if people just dropped their goddam expectations."

Brooke smiled as she looked up at Danni from under her lashes. "You're quite passionate about your book, aren't you?"

Until that very moment Danni hadn't even realised it, but yes, yes she was. It wasn't that she didn't believe in what she was writing, she just didn't feel qualified. But sitting there as Brooke listened, Danni realised she had just as many qualifications to write this book as the next person.

"Yes, I suppose I am."

Brooke clasped her hands together. "Good. I like to see that kind of passion in a writer."

"Passion?" Roy asked as he followed Josh into the room carrying a strawberry cheesecake on a tray.

"I was just saying that Danni is very passionate about her work," Brooke said.

"Ahh, that she is," Josh said bending down to kiss her. With a slight shift of her head, Danni managed to avoid kissing him on the lips.

"Young love," Roy said as he put the tray in front of the women.

Danni clenched her teeth together. *Shit. I hope Roy didn't just see that.* Some fiancée she looked – one that couldn't bear to kiss her husband-to-be on the lips.

The next few hours were filled with laughter as Roy recounted funny anecdotes about Josh as a boy. Seeing how Roy watched Josh with pride, she still found it hard to believe he would even care if Josh was gay. He seemed such a warm and loving man, but then they say Hitler was kind to animals. Looks could be deceiving.

Beside him, Brooke seemed delicious enough to

eat. Her face had a permanent smile on it. Not for the first time that evening, Danni wished both men would disappear and leave them alone in their own little cocoon of lady-love. Danni was in heaven, staring at Brooke so intensely that she didn't realise Josh was talking to her.

"Danni, we're going now."

Her hopes of being in Brooke's company for any longer were brought to an unwelcome end. How had the time managed to pass so quickly? Rising from the table, she followed Josh to the door where they said their farewells to his dad, thanking him for a wonderful evening.

Josh turned to Brooke, bending to kiss her cheek. "It was good to see you again. Really great."

"You too."

"I'll wait in the cab," he said to Danni.

"Sooo," Danni said swinging her arms to her back.

Brooke cocked her head. "So."

"I, um, really enjoyed our talk this evening." Danni brought her arms forward and crossed them over her chest.

"Me too."

If this were the movies, it would be at this point Danni would step forward, take Brooke in her arms and kiss her beneath a canopy of glistening stars. But, alas, this was not the movies. It was real life and they were standing on the doorstep of her pretend fiancée's dad's house.

"Well you've still got my number, make sure you call me."

"I will," Brooke said.

Reluctantly, Danni stepped past her and headed down the stairs to the cab where Josh was in deep conversation with the driver. As she closed the door she took one last look at Brooke. There had to be a way around all this. *There just had to be.*

Chapter Seventeen

Brooke smoothed her palms over her pristinely tailored shirt, knocked on the heavy wooden door and entered. Roy Reynolds was lounging on his dark leather chair in a reclined position, legs crossed at the ankles and resting casually on the large mahogany desk. Upon seeing Brooke he lowered them to the ground.

"Ahh, Brooke. Take a seat," he said gesturing to the wooden chair opposite him.

Brooke slid elegantly upon the seat and waited. She loved Roy's office. It was exactly how a publisher's office should be. Shelf upon shelf of books – many first editions, expensive art work adorning the walls and antique furniture scattered throughout. The room had a wonderfully rich smell of leather, which made her feel immediately at ease, yet aware that this was a room that commanded authority.

"Sorry to have disturbed you, Brooke, I just wanted to let you know the release date for Rodger Holt's book has been finalised. I'm going to throw him a small bash here to coincide with it."

Brooke nodded approvingly. She had been the editor on his book and was pleased for him. "That's good to hear. It'll be nice to see him again."

"I'm relieved if I'm honest. His agent was getting a bit arsey with me. She thinks he's been out of the spotlight for too long and that his readers have forgotten about him."

"That's hardly likely, he was on the Sunday Times bestsellers list for six months."

Roy raised his hands in surrender. "I know but that's what agents are like. The quicker the author gets a book out the quicker they get paid."

"Yes, I suppose so." She rose to stand but he waved her back down again.

"Just one more thing. I hope you don't mind me asking, but I just wanted to hear your opinion on something."

She sat back down, crossed her legs and rested her hands on her knee. "Of course, anything. I'd be happy to help."

"It's about Danni."

The very sound of her name made Brooke's stomach somersault and her heart pump a little faster. She only hoped that her cheeks hadn't flushed, betraying her true emotions.

Brooke paused and pretended to think. "Oh, yes Danni. What about her?"

He leaned forward, resting his elbows on the desk. "What do you think of her?"

What did she think? Where should she start? Smart, funny, warm, beautiful … incredible even.

"I think she's lovely. And Josh certainly seems to be fond of her."

"Yes, yes, he does. Is there anything else?"

Brooke was confused. What more did he want her to say about a woman she barely knew?

"Well no, not really. I don't feel particularly

qualified to comment Roy. Why? I'm sensing a certain 'malaise' from you? What did she do exactly?"

He leaned back in his seat smiling. "Nothing at all. In fact I like her very much. Very much. But I can't put my finger on it." He paused and smoothed his thinning hair. "There's just something a little, shall we say, awkward between her and Josh."

She glanced down at the gold Mont Blanc pen on his desk before looking back up at him. "Awkward? I thought they seemed like a great couple."

"Yes, they are … yet … I can't explain it." He frowned. "Their affection for each other just seems a bit … stilted. It's been playing on my mind."

Brooke cocked her head. "Really? I didn't get that impression at all. I thought they looked a very loving couple. Maybe Danni just feels nervous around you. What did you want them to do Roy? Make out on the cheesecake?"

The pair laughed for a few seconds.

Roy looked thoughtful. "Yes, you could be right. What does an old man like me know? I'm sorry to have taken up so much of your time."

Brooke stood up. "Not at all. It's natural to be concerned for your son's happiness. For what it's worth, I think he has a good woman there."

As she reached the door and turned the handle, Roy quickly rose to his feet and cleared his throat. "Actually, there is one more thing I'd like you to do, if you don't mind."

Brooke turned to face him. "Just name it."

"I was thinking, maybe you should be the one to look over Danni's submission when she sends it in. As you said, she seems pretty passionate about it. I know you have piles of manuscripts to get through, but I did promise Josh. He's an astute boy. If he thinks she has something, I believe him."

"Well, perhaps Ethan would be better placed to help. I've got so many new titles on at the minute … and," Brooke stammered.

"Ethan! No, no. You are much more suitable. Besides, you two ladies looked like you had lots in common."

"Yes, okay. If you want me to take a look at her ideas, of course I will. You're the boss after all."

"Fantastic, thanks so much."

Brooke remained where she stood. "Anything else?"

Roy's expression was neutral for a moment, then the edges of his mouth began to turn upwards as he sat back down. "Yes. I've got a surprise for you."

"Really?"

"Yes. I've got two tickets for Michael Fitzgerald's book reading next Thursday. Why don't you take Danni along and see what she thinks of it. She's writing about relationships, it might be of interest to her."

Brooke gasped, a sense of panic rushing through her. A night out, her and Danni, alone?

"Really. I thought Fitzgerald's reading was all sold out?"

"It is, but I managed to secure a couple of tickets, pulled in a favour." Roy winked.

She couldn't turn down such an opportunity. "I wish I had friends like that. I suppose there's no harm in giving Danni a call. I said I would anyway."

He clasped his hands together. "Good, good."

Brooke opened the door and was halfway through her exit, when Roy said, "I'm sure you'll enjoy yourselves." Brooke turned back and he nodded with a warm grin. "By the way, are you and Ethan still up for drinks tonight?"

"Yes sure. We'll pop by at five."

Brooke smiled and made a hasty half-run back to her office.

She didn't know whether she was excited or terrified at the thought of next Thursday. The chance to see Michael Fitzgerald was an unimaginable treat, but although the idea of spending time with Danni excited her, it also filled her with fear.

Fishing out her mobile from her bag, she scrolled down until she reached Danni's number. Without hesitation, she pressed the screen and after two rings, Danni's bright voice sung into her ear. There was no going back now.

"Hello."

"Oh, hi, Danni. It's Brooke." A pause. Then. "I hope it's okay to call?"

"Oh Brooke. Um, yes, of course. It's good to hear from you."

"The reason I'm calling is, I was wondering if

you're doing anything next Thursday?"

Another pause.

"Next Thursday?"

"Yes."

"Doing anything? Um, let me think. No, why?" Danni answered.

"Well, I thought it might be good for you to attend a book reading. I have tickets to see Michael Fitzgerald and wondered if you'd like to go?"

"Michael Fitzgerald?"

"Yes. Are you interested?"

"Um, sure. It sounds amazing. Wow. Thanks so much for thinking of me."

"Brilliant. I'll text you the details as soon as I have them. I'd better run, I have stacks to do. Take care."

Hanging up, Brooke clutched the phone to her chest, took a deep breath and exhaled loudly as if to release the tension. There was no reason for her to feel guilty about the call, but still she did. Should she tell Megan about the arrangement? She would be back from Australia the day after the reading. It wasn't as if she was planning anything inappropriate though. And even if she was, would Megan care?

Chapter Eighteen

Hearing the unexpected sound of Brooke's voice was still playing havoc with her pulse as Danni laid her mobile on the coffee table. The living room seemed to be getting smaller as the sound of her heart thumped between her ears. It had taken a few seconds for her brain to decipher who she was talking to. After all, she hadn't thought Brooke would *actually* call her. She had just thought Brooke was being polite when she said she would. But she *had* called, she had actually called!

Danni stared down at her twitter page. Suddenly the tweets about Kim Kardashian's new handbag seemed even less interesting, if that was possible. Now all she could think about was *who the hell was Michael Fitzgerald?* This man responsible for bringing them together again.

Seated on the sofa, she trawled through her internal Michael database. Michael *Douglas* – dirty one from Basic Instinct, Michael *Jackson* – glitter glove with a passion for monkeys. Yes, she could picture them, but Michael Fitzgerald? Danni had a brief recollection of the name, a small inkling that Mr Fitzgerald was one of Josh's favourite gurus. The man who had promised a *Life Transformation,* but she couldn't be sure. She could only hope that Brooke had believed her excitement, which was more about spending an evening with her than a Michael she couldn't really place.

This was one of the millions of reasons why she thought she was unqualified to write a self-help book. It wasn't as if she had any great knowledge of the genre. Once again, she felt like a big fraud – writing about things she didn't really know about and pretending to be engaged to her gay best friend. Cut her in half and she would have "fake" written through her middle. God, she hated feeling like this. It just wasn't her. The only things that were genuine right now were her need for a vodka cranberry and her feelings for a woman she hardly knew.

"Oh shit, what am I going to wear?" she said to herself, springing to her feet. What would she wear this time? She had to impress. Would she have to purchase another skirt, and God forbid, more nightmare heels? Hell no! The very thought of it gave her the heebie-jeebies. The wearing of skirts and heels (so high that one might clean the windows of the International Space Station with just one small stretch) were now prohibited items. She would not wear them again – not for Josh's dad, not for anyone. She sniggered at the thought of herself wobbling around at the party. How had she managed it? She now had the scars that would forever remind her of that night – six bandaged toes, and a blister the size of Lake Tahoe on each heel. Danni glanced upwards to the ceiling, shaking her head. What did clothes matter? She was going to see Brooke again, and this time, she would be herself.

There was something about the brunette that Danni had taken to, something that stirred her, and that rarely happened to Danni. Up until now, her love life had been nothing more than a few fleeting romances. Not that she was short of offers. It was simply that no-one had ever managed to tick the right boxes for her. Until now … until Brooke. A woman who worked for her fake fiancé's father and was proudly gay – one out of two wasn't bad.

She pondered the implications of the invitation. She was sure Josh would be okay with her seeing Brooke again and that he would trust her not to blow his cover. Still, she felt it was best to tell him, partly out of respect, but more because she was so damn excited. Hell, she wanted to tell the whole world! *What kind of saddo had she become?*

She could contain her excitement no longer. When Josh answered his mobile, she heard the clanging of metal and the holler of male voices in the background. She would never understand why he had chosen to work in such a harsh industry, and more bizarrely, how his hands were still so ridiculously soft!

"Hey, D. What's up?" he said shouting above the noise.

"Well, guess who has a date with Brooke next week?" She laughed with a distinct air of pride.

Her laughter increased when she heard the absolute disbelief in his voice.

"Noooo! Are you serious? You actually called her?"

"No, she called me. Can you believe it?"

"She did? Wow. What did she say?"

"Nothing much. She only invited me to Michael Fitzgenital's reading next week."

"*Michael Fitzgerald!*" he corrected her. "You're kidding. The guy's a legend, D."

"Fitzgerald – can't say it means much to me." She giggled. "I'm going to have to look him up online so I don't look like a complete vacuous twat!"

"Hmm, bit late for that, D!" he teased. "Hey, you aren't going to let the cat out the bag about your rampant lesbianism are you? She might go back and tell my dad."

"Why on earth would she do that?"

"They are good friends, D."

"Fear not. I promise to be on my best behaviour."

"Oh Lord, I've heard that one before. Anyway, how's the writing going?"

Danni looked at the computer screen. "Good, I've written the outline and synopsis and made a stab at the first two chapters. Pretty good going, really. I hope it's something they will go for."

"Have faith. Look, I'm going to have to go, my boss is calling me. Sorry. We'll speak about it later."

Alone once again, Danni sat in the lounge, staring down at her laptop. All she could think about was Brooke – Brooke and the impending evening. *Expectations, expectations, expectations.*

Chapter Nineteen

Megan stood by the old French doors that overlooked the small tidy garden, watching intently as Alison and Kelly planted pansies in the flowerbed. The sky was grey and moody, mirroring her own feelings. She was going back to London and most probably back to Brooke wanting to know every detail of her "holiday". Sometimes she grilled Megan like an inquisitive child – where she had been, who she had been with, the name of the hotel she had stayed at – if Megan wasn't so good at covering her tracks, she'd think Brooke was suspicious of her.

Glancing up, she was startled by the sight of Alison staring at her from the garden, a puzzled look upon her face. "Are you ok?" she mouthed.

Megan smiled and nodded, before turning away and heading for the bedroom. She'd better get packing if she was going to get there by nine. She heard Alison's light footsteps behind her as she zipped her case closed.

"I'm gonna miss you so much, Megs."

Megan pulled the case off the bed, turned and rested it on the floor. She saw the sadness in Alison's eyes and for a brief second wished she could just be enough for her.

"Me too." She smiled.

"So, any idea when you'll be flying back?"

"Not exactly. I've got a pretty busy schedule for

quite a while; we have a few cabin crew off sick. I'll be able to tell you exactly when the rosters are drawn up. They can be so slack sometimes."

Alison smiled, wrapping her arms around Megan's waist. "Perhaps we can meet you in London at some point and do some Christmas shopping?"

"Yes, maybe. I'll see what I can do."

"You don't want to?" she asked, pouting like a child.

"Ali, of course I do. Christmas is bloody mayhem though. I don't want to make any promises I can't keep."

"But Kelly—"

"—Oh, just stop it with the emotional blackmail Ali. I said I'll see what I can do now leave it at that," she said abruptly, removing Alison's arms from her.

"I don't get you, Megan. I'm so understanding about your being away all the time. I rarely, if ever, put pressure on you and look how you're behaving. This isn't fair on Kelly and it isn't fair on me. Don't you think we have a right to spend time with you at Christmas? Is that so strange?"

"You're not my wife, Ali. We're lovers. You don't get to dictate how I spend some over-commercialised holiday. God, I hate Christmas," Megan snapped. The phone calls from Brooke coupled with the current tension was just too much.

"Even though it affects mine and my daughter's life?"

Alison let out a sigh and sat down on the bed.

"I'm tired, Ali. Tired of all of the questioning, the demands."

"*Demands?* What do you think relationships are about – you coming and going as you please, uprooting my life as and when you see fit? No, Megan. That's not cutting it with me. I'm not one of those desperate women who will put up with any old shit thrown at her because I'm scared to be alone. You should know by now that isn't me. My daughter comes first and I will not tolerate anything that might hurt her. Simple."

Megan's shoulders sagged as she held out her arms, beckoning Alison to sit beside her. By the look on Alison's face, she realised she'd overstepped the line this time. The only way to win her over was to use Kelly as a carrot. "I know, I know and I'm sorry. I think the thought of leaving you both has got me on edge. I will try and sort something for Christmas, I promise. In fact, why don't I book us some tickets for a children's show? We can stay in a hotel for an extra treat."

Alison's features softened as she looked down to the ground.

"Oh, come on, Alison. I'm sorry. I really am. I will make it up to you." Megan stood and walked over to her, tilting her head up with her hand to kiss her mouth. Feeling Alison press back with her own lips, Megan straightened up. "So, are we good? I don't want to leave with any bad feelings."

Alison raised her eyes and managed a slight smile.

"Yeah we're good. But you need to watch how you talk to me. You can be so hurtful, Megan."

"I know, and I will watch it in future. So I'll see you both as soon as I can, I promise." Megan smiled, tilting her head.

"Yep."

"Good. I'll call you before I go to bed tonight."

"Is that promise?"

"Yes," she said kissing the tip of Alison's nose. "And you know I'm true to my word."

Chapter Twenty

A silver sign above a glass-fronted shop read "Discovering Books". Brooke glanced up at the night sky as she felt the first patter of rain. Despite the threat of a downpour, she was glad she'd arranged to meet Danni outside. By the look of things, trying to find one another in the overcrowded book shop would have been like finding a needle in a haystack. Brooke crossed her arms over her chest. She was trying her hardest to treat the evening as nothing more than a casual meeting but her nerves were getting the better of her. Her stomach flipped and gyrated as if performing a less than graceful lambada to the soundtrack of the passing cars.

Though her mind assured her that there was nothing inherently wrong with meeting Danni, her heart was telling her otherwise, as if privy to some secret confidence. Since being with Megan, Brooke had never so much as looked at another woman. Not a glance. Not even a peep. Brooke was just not the cheating kind, if there was ever such a type. She was clear on where she stood on the matter of infidelity – zero tolerance. So why was it that she couldn't stop thinking about this woman? Why was she occupying her every thought, consuming every waking moment? Perhaps it was because she knew her relationship with Megan was faltering, taking its final sorry breaths.

Breaking free from her inner dialogue, she

caught sight of Danni across the busy street, artfully playing dodgems with the oncoming traffic. A few angry hoots later, Danni had safely negotiated the crossing, and was smiling proudly as if she had won a small victory over the rush-hour traffic. Unravelling her grey snood, she approached a nervous Brooke standing at the entrance.

"I'm not late am I?" She smiled, a pair of cheery dimples breaking forth from each cheek.

Brooke glanced down and pretended to consult her watch, being momentarily unable to hold Danni's gaze. "No, not at all, I've only been here five minutes."

"Oh that's good. I left my phone at home and had to go back for it."

Brooke smiled, discreetly eyeing her new friend from top to toe. She looked even better than she had at dinner – effortlessly stylish. Black jeans, ankle boots, and a black leather biker jacket. The understated chic look suited her.

"Do you want to get a quick drink before we head up to the reading?" Brooke asked.

"Oh, that sounds perfect."

"Good. After you." Brooke gestured as she held open the bookshop's heavy glass doors for her.

The lower floor was buzzing with people chatting in groups near the shelves. A large picture of Michael Fitzgerald, white-toothed and clean-shaven, sat on a stack of hard-back books, giving information about the time of his reading.

Brooke nodded towards the picture. "Have you

read any of his work?"

"A little. If I'm honest, I found his views on monogamy a little strange," Danni responded with a frown.

"I suppose so. He is seen as quite controversial. In the book he's reading from tonight, he talks about why he believes monogamy is unrealistic."

"Does he now? Hmm, I'm not convinced." Danni grinned. "Anyway, I'm an open-minded kind of girl; I'll wait 'til I hear what he has to say."

"Glad to hear it," Brooke answered, weaving her way through the crowds to the small make-shift bar at the back.

"So, what do you fancy?" Brooke asked, taking her purse from her leather satchel. She hoped it didn't come across as a leading question.

"Uhh, vodka cranberry please," she answered. "Just a single please, I don't want you getting me drunk now." Danni smiled.

Brooke raised her eyebrows. "I'll try not to. You find us somewhere to sit and I'll bring them over." Eyeing an empty table, she pointed it out to Danni. "Look there's one over there."

A few minutes later, Brooke laid the drinks down on the table. "There you go, one vodka cranberry.

"Thanks," Danni said as she put the glass to her lips and took a sip.

"So, I have to say, if it wasn't for your hair I would have hardly recognised you from the party or from dinner at Roy's. You look really different,"

Brooke said as she sat down.

Danni glanced around and toyed with her drink. "Ah well yes, I can explain," she said, pausing to take another sip of her drink. "The skirt and high heels were Josh's idea. It's not really my thing. He thought it might impress his dad. You know what men are like."

Brooke laughed, amused by Danni's explanation. No wonder Roy thought she was on edge. "Well it seems to have done the trick. Roy really likes you."

"He does? Oh good. I like him too. He seems quite a character."

"Yep, he can be pretty flamboyant. He's firm but fair, and that's what I like in a boss. So, about you and Josh. You said you hadn't set a date yet, but are you planning on getting married anytime soon?"

Danni scanned the room before settling her gaze back on Brooke. "No, not as yet. It could be years before we tie the knot. We aren't in any rush. How about you? Are you married, in a relationship, none of the above?"

Brooke smiled faintly, in a way that meant "it's complicated". For some reason she didn't want to tell Danni she had a partner, but her innate honesty compelled her to.

"Yes, I am in a relationship."

Danni raised her eyebrows. "Long term?"

Brooke nodded. "If you call eight months long term, yes."

Danni looked at her quizzically and cocked her head. "I'm sensing you don't really want to talk about this, am I right?"

Brooke shrugged and smiled faintly. "You could say that. It's just that we're having a few issues at the moment."

"Oh, sorry to hear that. I hope it's nothing serious."

"Not really. At least I hope not," she said with resignation. "So, enough about my problems. How long have you and Josh been dating?"

Danni shifted in her seat. "Um, let's think now, um, a year I think. Yeah, a year."

"And you just knew he was the one?"

Danni held her gaze. "You know I never used to believe in 'the one', but lately I'm beginning to think there is some truth in finding your soul mate. Even though you might not be able to be together, the connection is still there. Even if fate is against you."

Brooke sat transfixed. That's exactly how she had felt when she first laid eyes on Danni. As much as she believed she loved Megan, she had never felt that omnipotent connection. She was hugely attracted to her, of course, but nothing more. "It sounds sad – to have a soul mate you can't be with, I mean."

Danni looked at her with a heavy, thoughtful expression. "Heartbreaking even," she added softly, smiling.

Brooke felt as if Danni could see into her soul, read her thoughts even. "Anyway," she said, breaking the spell, "Tell me about your book. How is it coming along?"

Danni leaned back in her chair. "Good thanks. I'm actually surprised at how much I'm enjoying writing it."

"I've always wanted to be a writer," Brooke said, playing with her hair.

"Really? Why aren't you then?"

Brooke thought about it for a few seconds before answering. "If I'm honest, I really don't know. I've just never had the headspace to do it. Perhaps that's just an excuse. Maybe, I'm just not cut out to be one. I really love working with new writers, helping them develop their style. But maybe one day," she said pensively. "So, how long have you been writing for?"

"For as long as I can remember. Even when I was a kid, I had a fascination with words. I used to read the dictionary – how weird is that? No, I just love the power of words, how they can make you feel. I love how they can inspire people, empower them. Change lives even. Sounds really corny I know." Danni blushed slightly

"No, it doesn't." Brooke smiled reassuringly.

'Ladies and gentlemen, the Michael Fitzgerald reading will commence in five minutes. Kindly take your seats.' The bookstore announcement shattered the moment. For once, Brooke didn't want to go upstairs and enter into someone else's world. She wanted to stay there, in her own with Danni.

Neither of the women moved, it was as if they had not heard the perfectly clear announcement that boomed through the air. Even the sound of screeching chairs as people stood up and walked from the bar area had little impact. Instead, they continued their conversation about the joys of literature, their favourite authors, books that had changed the way they saw the world. With every word, Brooke felt herself being drawn further to her companion. She was energising, full of wild excitement. She sat wide-eyed and smiling, drinking in every word as though she was afraid Danni might suddenly stop speaking upon realising the reading was about to start.

This new-found rebellious streak was a novelty for Brooke. She was not the type to act in a way that might be deemed unprofessional. Ever. Even as a giggling schoolgirl, she had politely declined her friend's numerous appeals to play truant. But for once in her life, for this one special time, she wanted to do what *she* wanted and it felt good. Bloody good.

Looking around the near empty bar, Brooke knew she had to react. "Everyone has gone! Oh shit – we've missed the reading."

"Oh no. Sorry, it was my fault. Me talking too much as usual," Danni answered.

"No, don't be silly."

"Anyway," Danni grinned, "it would be a shame to rush off." Danni stood up and picked up their glasses. "Same again?"

"Why not." Brook smiled, lowering her head to hide her obvious happiness over the offer. Danni headed to the bar, leaving Brooke to ponder the situation. Was she playing with fire, starting a

friendship with such an attractive straight woman –
especially one she had feelings for? She quelled her
fears, taking solace in the fact that Danni *was* straight,
and therefore no real danger. She dreaded to think
what would happen if that wasn't the case. *Let's not even
go there. Danni is not gay, so there's no problem. Relax.*

She glanced up as Danni placed the Pinot Grigio
in front of her.

"There you go. Bottoms up." She laughed. "What
does that even mean, anyway?"

They laughed and clinked glasses.

Brooke felt the buzz of her mobile vibrating in
her pocket. She was pretty sure who it was but for the
first time in an age she didn't want to speak to her. As
astonishing as it seemed, she just didn't want anything
to ruin her night. It wasn't about being sneaky or
underhanded, she simply wanted to enjoy the best
evening she'd had in ages without Megan ruining it.

She ignored the buzz and attempted to concentrate
on Danni's words – something about Brooke's job – but
all she could do was stare at her lips, plump and red. Her
concentration had gone.

What did Megan want? Brooke had been trying to
get hold of her all day to find out what time she'd
arrive back in London tomorrow and she hadn't
bothered to reply, so why now of all times had she
decided to call? The phone began to vibrate again and
her compulsion to do "the right thing" took hold.
Resigned to the interruption, she smiled apologetically
at Danni.

"I'm so sorry to interrupt, Danni, but I really have to take this."

"No problem. Take your time, I was just warbling on anyway," Danni said grinning.

Brooke let out a sigh before sliding the screen to accept the call.

"Hello?"

"It's me. I called you a minute ago." It was Megan and she wasn't sounding very friendly.

Brooke rose from the table, signalling to Danni that she wouldn't be a minute and headed to the ladies. Once inside, she rolled her eyes and leaned back against the basin as if anticipating the upcoming discord.

"And I've been trying to get you all day but that doesn't seem to matter to you, Megan."

"I was in the air, Brooke. I've arrived back a day early. Anyway, where are you?"

"I'm–" Brooke answered, immediately being cut off.

"–Look I haven't got much time, I'm getting on the train in 10 minutes. Can you pick me up? The queue for cabs is always a nightmare."

"Tonight? What time?"

"In an hour."

"Uh, you are aware that I actually have a life too and I can't just drop everything?"

"Have we got to argue about everything, Brooke? For once, can't you just do as I ask without the fucking drama!"

"There's no drama here. The fact is, you're a grown woman, make your own fucking way."

Before Megan could utter another word, Brooke pressed the end button.

Within seconds the phone was buzzing again. Her resolve fading, Brooke reluctantly answered the call.

Megan's voice held a ragged edge of hysteria. "I hope to hell you didn't just hang up on me?"

Brooke inhaled. "No, I think the reception's bad."

"Where did you say you were?"

Brooke closed her eyes. "I didn't. But I'm at a, a book reading."

"Oh, with who?"

"What?"

"I said who are you with?"

She said the first name that popped into her head. She didn't know why but she didn't want to say Danni's name in case Megan's super senses picked something up in her voice. "Ethan."

"Oh really? Put him on the phone."

The hand she held the phone in began to tremble. "What, why?"

Megan gave a brittle laugh. "Brooke, I know when you're telling porkies. You're a terrible liar."

"I'm not lying, I'm with Ethan and I'm in the toilets and even if I wasn't, I wouldn't put him on the phone, I wouldn't embarrass myself."

"Whatever. Do what you like. Look, just be at the

station in an hour."

The line went dead. Brooke slipped the phone back into her pocket and cupped her head in her hands. How much longer was she going to be able to put up with this? She could feel her self-worth being chipped away with every interaction with Megan.

She dropped her hands to her side as she heard the door squeak open. Danni appeared in the threshold.

"Is everything okay?"

"Yes, everything's fine."

Danni looked doubtful before walking to stand in front of her. "Was that your girlfriend on the phone? I could hear you from outside."

Brooke nodded. She didn't trust herself to speak; she was so annoyed and hurt.

"Do you want to talk about it? I might not be great at giving advice but I'm good at listening – have you seen the size of my ears?" Danni joked, tugging at her lobes.

Brooke smiled, grateful for the injection of humour. *Where would I begin?* She knew what the solution was, but nobody could give her the courage to do what she knew she must. She was going to have to do that by herself. But when and how she didn't know.

"No, it's okay, really. I didn't invite you out to bore you to tears with my relationship problems. I'm fine, honestly," Brooke said, embarrassed by the attention.

"If you're sure."

Brooke nodded.

"Come on then, your wine is getting warm."

Brooke followed Danni back to the table. "Look, I'm really sorry to do this, Danni, but I need to shoot off. I've got to pick my partner up from the station."

"Don't worry. My liver will be relieved." She laughed. "It was nice to see you again Brooke. It's good to talk about the book and writing. Really inspiring."

"Yes, I've enjoyed myself too. Shame about the reading."

Danni grinned. "Well, perhaps we can meet up again to talk about the book, and about publishing? I'd love to know more."

Brooke adjusted the straps of her bag over her shoulder, prolonging the agony.

"I'd like that. I'll call you soon."

"Great," Danni answered.

The two women stood up and faced one another. There was an uneasy pause – should they embrace? Shake hands? Embarrassed by the awkwardness, Brooke extended her hand to Danni. "I'll see you soon."

Danni's hand reached out, her delicate fingers wrapping around Brooke's own. Brooke's eyes widened involuntarily as if waking from a dull slumber. She felt alive, re-energised. Unable to hide the pleasure of the touch, she looked down. Her system was barely able to withstand such intensity, let alone the added power of Danni's gaze.

"Bye then." Danni smiled.

"Yes, bye, Danni. Goodbye."

Chapter Twenty-One

Come on Danni, save yourself the heartache – she's not available!

Leaving the bookstore, Danni crossed the road and began her brief walk to the bus stop nearby. Her mind was pre-occupied by the events of the night, and more precisely, its rather abrupt end. *Poor Brooke.* How could she put up with a partner that demanding? She didn't want to be judgemental, but from what she had heard that evening, Brooke certainly didn't have it easy. It seemed to Danni that Brooke was being manipulated; having to change her plans last minute upon her partner's whim. Worse still, it had meant the end of a perfect night.

Within minutes, she had boarded the bus – one of Boris' iconic new London route finders, and was settled into her window seat on the upper deck. The sound of the humming engine made her feel relaxed, allowing her mind to drift quickly back to her new favourite subject – Brooke.

For her, it had been an incredible evening. From the very moment Brooke had greeted her outside the bookstore, Danni had felt such a connection to her, a oneness even. She laughed to herself, realising how wet she sounded. Yuk! She grinned. *What have I become? I'm even making myself feel nauseous.*

Danni was not one for overly romantic sentiment; she had always poked fun at her friends for getting all soppy. However, since meeting Brooke, she found it impossible to think in any other terms.

Brooke was fascinating. Amazing. Beautiful. Bright. Charming. Insightful. Eloquent. Witty. Brooke was Perfect.

Her face lit up. She had become one of those mad people occasionally spotted on night buses, who just sit there smiling to themselves. There was no denying it; she had become a hopeless romantic. *My name is Danni and I'm a big soppy drip!*

As her journey progressed, questions began to pop into her mind. She had not meant to eavesdrop on Brooke's call, but she had the distinct recollection of Brooke telling her partner that she was out with her work colleague Ethan? Her pulse quickened. Why would Brooke feel the need to lie, unless of course she had feelings for her?

Could she? It wasn't inconceivable, was it?

The possibility filled her with an all too joyful happiness – a sense of elation which was quickly disturbed by the beeping of her phone.

A message.

It was most probably Josh being nosy. She smiled as she glanced down at the slightly scuffed screen, expecting to read some wildly inappropriate comment from him.

Brooke!

She opened the message excitedly.

"Danni. So sorry I had to run off abruptly. It was great to catch up with you. Once again, sorry. Brooke x"

Danni read the message again, desperately trying to uncover any innuendos that might be contained within the twenty-five word text. She hadn't done that in years, not since her very first date with a girl.

She quickly started to text back,

"Hi Brooke. No problem."

Delete.

"Hey Brooke – that's fine."

Delete.

As if seized by some new-found courage, she tapped the screen and produced a message so bold that it made her feel quite unwell.

"Hey Brooke, absolutely no problem. I had a fun night too. Would be lovely to meet again to continue our chat. How are you fixed this weekend? Danni x"

Oh God! It was done. She had put her wish out into the universe, now all she could do was wait.

***

Danni felt like the lion in *The Wizard of Oz*. Her newly acquired courage had put her in an upbeat and inspired mood. Arriving home, she grabbed a beer from the fridge, collected her laptop and went straight to her bedroom to continue work on her book.

She was buzzed.

It was as though Brooke was her muse. One single evening had seemed to give her that final push she needed.

Her fingers skipped and danced over the keys

with renewed vigour. Every word being conjured easier and quicker than the last. Letters became words, words became sentences, sentences became paragraphs. Paragraphs became chapters.

After five hours, she pushed her chair back from the desk, rubbed her eyes and let out a satisfied sigh. The synopsis and first four chapters were complete. It was more than enough to show any potential publisher, and moreover, Brooke.

Doubt flooded her as she closed the lid of her laptop. Did she really want Brooke to read her latest literary creation? Could she cope with a rejection from this woman, the object of her affections? The thought made her stomach turn. It didn't matter if she sent her work off to some faceless publisher whom she didn't know, but to have Brooke tell her that she sucked would be a bitter pill indeed.

Danni undressed, slipped into bed and snuggled under her quilt. It was late. She was tired. It had been quite a day. Glancing down at her phone, there was still no word from Brooke. Danni felt philosophical about the situation. She had been bold, perhaps foolish – she had asked Brooke out. If she didn't reply, then at least she would know. It occurred to her that it was just the same with her book. If it turned out to be dire, at least she could accept it and move on, after all, the truth sets you free.

Rolling onto her side, she made the second brave decision of the day. Tomorrow, she'd go through her manuscript again then send it to Roy. If he didn't bite, she would reconsider her future.

This bravery lark felt good. *Scary* but good. Like her nan always told her:

"Faint heart never won fair lady … nor a fabulously lucrative book deal!"

Chapter Twenty-Two

Brooke sat staring at the TV, trying her hardest to block out Megan's voice by turning the sound up.

Megan threw her hands up in the air like a spoilt child and blocked her view. "So you're giving me the silent treatment now?"

Brooke threw the TV control down beside her. "No, Megan, I'm not. I just don't have anything to say to you right now," Brooke answered calmly, holding her ground.

Megan snorted. "That's a first. Normally you never stop nagging."

"*Nagging?*" Brooke looked up, meeting Megan's eyes with a narrow stare. "Is that what you call it when somebody attempts to get a bit of respect?"

"Look, I'm sorry to have dragged you away from your fun night out, Brooke. God. I can't believe I've been away for two weeks and I come back to this bullshit again. Jeeesus," Megan hissed.

Brooke felt her jaw tighten. "Megan, I …"

The words were right on the tip of her tongue, ready to throw themselves off, if only she had the courage to let them. She was confused. She felt numb towards Megan. Exhausted. Spent. Done. But were these feelings real, or merely the effect of Danni's unexpected entry into her life? In any case, she couldn't make life-changing decisions based on an attraction she might have towards a straight woman, however real it might feel. If she was to let Megan go, it had to be for herself, for her own sanity.

"What?" Megan snapped. "What are you trying to say, Brooke?"

Brooke frowned and looked down at the ground. "I, we can't carry on like this."

Megan dropped down into the leather armchair in the corner of the room. "Like what? Carry on like what?"

Brooke was silent. She collected herself for a moment before she found the courage to look into Megan's eyes. "I mean it, Megan. I just can't do this anymore."

Megan looked at her in disbelief. "So you want us to break up? You don't really mean that."

Brooke's voice dropped. "I'm not sure. I don't know what I want, Megan. But I'm not happy and if you're honest, neither are you."

Megan quickly rose from her seat to close the distance between them. Kneeling down at Brooke's side, Megan's eyes softened, her gaze submissive, her voice full of a new-found tenderness.

"Look, I know things have been a bit difficult recently, really hard. But Brooke, I know if we both try, we can get back what we once had."

"Do you honestly think that's possible, Megan?" Brooke asked.

"Yes, I do. I really do. I know I can be selfish sometimes but I do love you. We can't just throw in the towel. We owe it to each other to have another try.

What do you think? Brooke?"

Brooke sat staring into space. Just five minutes ago, she had been ready to end it. Now, looking into Megan's eyes, she could see the woman she once knew, the woman she fell in love with. She hated herself for being so weak, but she knew she had to try just once more, just to know she had truly given it her all, should the worst come later.

"I need things to change. I don't just mean you saying it to shut me up, I need promises, Megan."

Megan smiled softly. "Just name them," she said leaning in, showering Brooke with tiny butterfly kisses on the side of her closed mouth.

Brooke closed her eyes, trying to silence the inner conflict. She was angry, hurt and yet perversely, part of her still enjoyed the sensation of Megan's lips against her own.

"No more cancelling our dates to go out with other people," Brooke said, laying out her demands. "When you say you're going to be here at a certain time, you have to be."

"Uh huh," Megan's hand slid up Brooke's top and made contact with her bare breast, gently teasing her nipple between her finger and thumb. Brooke was simultaneously repelled and aroused. Part of her hated Megan touching her. Part of her loved it. She wanted to push her off, reject her just as she had felt rejected, but there was such a yearning for intimacy that she couldn't resist.

Brooke swallowed hard. "And when you're

overseas, no more being unreachable days on end," she said between breaths.

"I promise," Megan said pushing Brooke down on the sofa and lying on top of her. "Anything else?" she asked in a low husky voice.

Brooke felt powerless to resist.

"Well there is something," she whispered as Megan hungrily covered Brooke's mouth with her own.

***

Disentangling herself from Megan's legs, Brooke stood up from the wide-striped sofa. She stretched, pushing her hair behind her ears as she stepped over the cushions that had been tossed from the sofa half an hour before. The intimate encounter had broken down the barrier that had stood between them for so long, and yet Brooke still felt an ominous shadow hanging over them.

She stood in the lounge, just staring at Megan as she lay on the sofa, delightfully drowsy from pleasure. She loved the contours of Megan's back, the firmness of her shoulders.

"What do you think about having date nights? We never seem to go out anymore," Brooke asked, breaking the silence.

"What did you have in mind?" Megan said sleepily.

"Oh I don't know. We could go to a gay bar or something on Saturday. Like we used to."

"Sure why not. Whatever you want."

"Megan, I really hope we can make it work, I really do."

When Megan didn't reply, Brooke leant over her and brushed back the hair from her face. She was sound asleep. Why couldn't love just be simple – why did it have to be so much work?

She made her way to the bathroom and as she passed through the hallway, she glanced at her phone charging on the side table. She flicked it on and within seconds, it bleeped indicating she had a message. It was from Danni. She slumped against the wall, eagerly reading the text.

The thought of seeing Danni again pleased her, excited her even, however, Brooke was torn. If she was serious about giving things one final go with Megan, she knew in her heart that meant no distractions, no "interests", no outside influences that might derail their relationship. Danni might be straight but she was still a distraction, a beautiful one at that.

Yes, that would be the most prudent course of action, Brooke mused. Her fingers hovered over the keys as if urging her to reconsider her assessment. Perhaps she should sleep on it, decide in the morning. *After all, everything is clearer in the cold light of day.*

Chapter Twenty-Three

Brooke clicked the save button for the final time on the manuscript she was working on. As much as she had enjoyed reading the book, she was grateful she had finished it. It had been a tough one, not the writing itself but the discipline she had to instil in herself to keep her mind focused on the job at hand.

Ethan strolled in past her. She gasped when she realised the familiar sight of his suit was gone, only to be replaced with drainpipe jeans, a blazer, and a scarf around his neck. He smiled at her when he saw her puzzled expression.

He dropped into his seat. "What's up? Cat got your tongue?"

Before she could respond, Roy swooped into the empty seat beside her. He looked over at Ethan for a split second, raising his eyebrow as he did, before turning his back to Brooke.

"How's it going?" Roy asked.

"You'll be pleased to know I'm finished with the Cruz edit."

"Good, good," he said smiling. He cleared his throat. "I take it you had a pleasant evening at the book reading?"

Brooke sat, resting her hands on her lap. "I'm afraid I have a confession to make."

He looked at her quizzically "Oh yes?"

"The Michael Fitzgerald's tickets you gave me

went to waste."

"Really. How so?"

"Well I met up with Danni as planned and we sort of got carried away with, you know, talk about the publishing world, authors, her book. We just totally lost track of time."

He glanced around the office before fixing his eyes back on Brooke. "Well, it's nice to hear you two got along so well." He leaned in towards her, lowering his voice when he spoke. "Looks like you approve of my son's choice then?"

Brooke smiled. "Yes, she's a very interesting young woman. Oh and to put your mind at rest, you were right, she was feeling a bit awkward, but it wasn't anything to do with her feelings about Josh."

Roy nodded for her to continue.

"It seems she felt a little uncomfortable in her outfit."

Roy looked puzzled. "Her outfit?"

"Yes. Apparently Josh wanted her to pull out all the stops to impress you. Anyway, she said she was feeling uncomfortable in herself. So that's what you most probably picked up on."

A wave of relief swept across Roy's face, as he jumped to his feet. "Josh is a strange boy. Why would he make the poor girl do something like that?"

Brooke shrugged. "Probably so you'd like her. It's kind of sweet that he wanted her to make such a good impression on you – although not so much fun for her – especially in those heels at your party."

He smiled as looked down at her. "Yes, I guess so."

Brooke rose to meet him, pushing in the chair. "So, is that all, Roy? I've got to be at a meeting in Soho."

"Okay, don't let me keep you." He gave her shoulder a gentle pat and waltzed off towards his office.

Brooke turned to Ethan. "What's with the outfit?" she asked gesturing to his new style of clothing. "It suits you."

"Thanks. Helen thought I looked a bit stuffy in suits. Said I was a clone."

"Well you definitely stand out now and I mean for the better."

"Thanks. Do you think Roy looked a bit, you know?" he asked pulling his face.

"I'm sure he was as equally impressed as I was. Sorry, I've got to run," she said gathering her bag from the floor. "Speak later."

As she bustled her way to the lifts she was glad the conversation with Roy about Danni was over. Now if only she could get over the woman herself. Maybe her night out on Saturday with Megan was just the thing she needed.

Chapter Twenty-Four

At one time, *Revolutions* was a seedy backstreet bar in the heart of Soho. However, with the revamp of the area it had been magically transformed into a bonafide stylista venue that attracted a mixed crowd on a Saturday night. Without doubt though, it would still smell of poppers and stale B.O. As Danni's nan always said, you can't polish a turd.

It was eight p.m. With its mirrored walls and vibrant red booths, *Revolutions* was slowly coming to life with a steady stream of hopeful revellers. Danni sat perched on a stool at the bar, eyeing Josh in his white vest and black skinny jeans. Fair dues, he did look pretty hot. He was a man on a mission. A man with a twinkle in his eye and an itch just waiting to be scratched – but not in a Y-front infestation kind of way.

She sat there for a while watching the master of seduction in action. So this was his idea of celebrating the completion of her book proposal? Taking her to a bar for Lesson 101 in *How to Pull a Steroid-pumped Barman*. She knocked back a sambuca shot as the two men devoured one another with their eyes like two hungry wolves. *Get a room.*

Just twenty-four hours earlier, Danni had emailed her book proposal to all the publishing houses who marketed books in the so-called "self-help" genre. There was no point in putting all her unfertilised eggs in one basket. If Roy's publishing firm turned her down, there was still hope that the others might be interested. A tiny hope, but a hope nonetheless. Whatever happened, there was some solace in the knowledge that it was out of her hands now and in the lap of the literary gods. All she could do was wait. And have another drink.

The barman was torn away from the serious business of flirting, leaving Josh free to swivel around in his seat to talk to Danni.

"Oh, so you've remembered I'm still here then?" she asked in a subdued voice.

Josh answered in a slurred drawl. "Of course, how could I forget? Little Miss Sulky-Pants. I thought you'd have been happy – what with getting the book off."

Happy? Right what was the definition of happy again – oh yeah, "feeling or showing pleasure or contentment". Hmmm, that didn't quite fit Danni at the moment. Of course she was relieved to have sent off those chapters. She was relieved to have completed what was a tricky, challenging piece of work. But to say she was happy would be an overstatement. Put it this way, if she'd have been auditioning for one of the seven dwarves, it certainly wouldn't be for Happy. In truth, she was feeling pretty darn gloomy and no amount of shots, cocktails, or dry roasted nuts could save her this time. The fact was she had it bad. Real bad.

Was it even possible to feel like you'd lost something precious when it had never belonged to you? That was how she saw things with Brooke. The reply to her text message had never arrived. Maybe it was a good thing – it was all too complicated anyway.

Danni took a long sip of her Mojito. "Just ignore me Josh, I'm just a bitter, washed up has-been that never-was."

Josh looked past her, his eyes suddenly widening.

Danni, oblivious to his astonished look, ignored the signal and leaned in tightly against his shoulder. "I said don't worry, go back to lover boy. There's no point in us both missing out on the true love," she slurred.

Josh looked frantic as he twitched and winked in a desperate attempt to warn her of an imminent arrival. "Yes, D. Very good. Oh, look who it is," Josh said enthusiastically, gesturing to the appearance of someone over Danni's shoulder.

"Hi, Josh. Hi there, Danni," A female voice answered.

Danni froze. That voice, that beautiful dulcet tone. It couldn't be. It couldn't be – *Brooke?*

Danni felt her throat constricting as if she had suddenly been set upon by an over-amorous python.

"Bro … Brooke!"

Danni rose to her less than steady feet and turned to Brooke who had leant in for a welcoming hug. Despite being slightly numb from the sambucca shot, she could still feel the delicious heat from Brooke's body as she held her close. Time seemed to stand still. Danni closed her eyes, wrapping her arms around her friend's shoulders, her face nestling in her vanilla-scented hair, soft and warm. *Bliss*. She discreetly inhaled the odour, drinking in the moment. *She smells like heaven*. Upon releasing her, Danni's eyes immediately fell to Brooke's female companion who was eyeing them both with an ardent interest.

She gave her a faint smile and sat back down.

"So, who's your friend?" Josh asked Brooke, referring to her mysterious female companion.

Brooke looked towards Megan. "Oh, yes. This is my partner. Megan." She began the formalities. "This is Josh and his fiancée, Danni. Josh is Roy's son."

"I can see the resemblance. Nice to meet you," Megan remarked.

She reached past Danni and shook Josh's hand before giving Danni a slight nod in acknowledgement.

Holy crap. Her partner. *This day just can't get any worse*.

"This is strange, meeting you two in a place like this," Brooke said, her gaze finally settling on Danni's favourite "Girl on Girl" T-shirt. A puzzled look crossed her features.

Danni took a few seconds to realise what Brooke had seen then quickly crossed her arms, desperately trying to cover the purple emblazoned letters on her chest. Blood rushed to her face as she searched for an explanation. "Oh um, Josh's just–"

"Hey lover, come back I'm lonely," the barman called flirtatiously to Josh.

Oh Shit. It just did.

Danni felt nauseous, her knees weak. She looked on in horror as both Brooke and Megan both turned to stare at him. This was one of those "abort mission" moments. Surely they were about to get rumbled.

As if by reflex, Josh placed his hand firmly on Danni's knee.

"Oh that's Eric, my best friend. It's his birthday today so we came to have drinks with him. Looks like he's getting a head start," he said with a strained laugh.

Danni gave her quick-thinking hero a grateful smile. She looked down at her glass and swirled the contents around before taking a quick mouthful. Her heart was still pounding from the unexpected intrusion. For some reason she hadn't thought Megan was going to be so pretty. The tight black panel ribbed top she wore with her black trousers, exposed what seemed to be a great body as well. Despite how hot Megan was, she didn't really think they suited each other. Surely a brunette like Brooke would be far more suited to, well, a blonde. Just saying.

"Oh happy birthday," Brooke said, as Eric glided to the counter to take their order.

He looked at her, slightly bewildered by the greeting. "Huh."

"Don't be so coy, Eric," Josh said smiling at him before turning to Brooke. "He hates people knowing it's his birthday, he doesn't like any fuss. You know how some people are about their age."

"I know the feeling," Brooke said. "Can I have two dry white wines please and whatever you're all having?"

"Oh, thanks very much. Hey, why don't you girls join us?" Josh said indicating to the vacant seats next to Danni.

"Thanks but we're—"

Brooke interrupted Megan before she could even finish the sentence. "Thanks we'd love to," she answered, taking a seat and giving Megan a look which implied she should do the same.

Danni tried to remain calm, despite the shockwave that surged through her body every time Brooke's blue eyes fell upon her.

"Sooo," Danni said, shifting in her seat as she looked at each of the women. She was seriously beginning to feel hot under the collar despite only wearing a T-shirt. "What brings you guys here tonight?"

"Does there need to be a reason?" Megan shot back at her, before taking a big sip of her drink.

Danni smoothed her hands over her hair and narrowed her eyes. "No, not at all. Just wondered. Anyway …"

So her first instinct about this woman had been correct when she had overheard Brooke talking to her on the phone. And as her nan always says, if it walks like a duck, quacks like a duck, then it is a duck. Or, in Megan's case – a bitch. There, she said it. Danni didn't like to throw that word around willy-nilly, but in this case, she felt entirely justified. She'd known a lot of women like Megan in her time, and boy, was she a tricky one. Her heart went out to Brooke. How the hell had she got mixed up with someone like that?

Brooke looked at her apologetically. "Uhh, actually, we haven't been out in a while so we thought we'd have a bit of a blow out."

"A blow job?" Eric laughed, ear-wigging from behind the bar. Clearly he'd had one too many, or else rather limited social graces.

Oh God, did he really say that? Danni cringed. Thankfully, nobody else seemed to hear, or at least pretended not to. She gave him a look as he walked away to serve a thirsty customer.

"Have you been here before?" Brooke asked, clearly attempting to alleviate the tension.

Josh nodded. "Yeah, all the time."

Danni discreetly nudged him. "What Josh means is, we come here regularly to hang out with Eric, his best friend who is gay. Not that that matters, who cares in fact? Not us, we love them, uh, yes." Danni was mortified by her foot-in mouth response. She was a lousy liar and as a result ended up saying the most ridiculously inappropriate things.

Megan brushed her finger across her lip to wipe away a droplet of wine and looked at her with a cool expression on her face. "I'm surprised you both don't get hit on, especially a gorgeous boy like you Josh."

Josh tore his gaze away from Eric, tucking his tongue back inside his mouth. "Nah, can't say I do. It's not really a pick up joint."

Danni tried not to laugh as she caught sight of two men fondling each other in the corner as they sniffed a small bottle of naughtiness.

Danni glanced at Brooke out of the corner of her eye and if she hadn't been under the influence, she could have sworn Brooke was staring at her. She was not the only one.

"Have you lost something?" Megan whispered to Brooke with a scowl, making her pretty features turn rather ugly.

Danni looked away, pretending she hadn't heard. She could sense the tension rising between the two.

Brooke picked at the coaster beneath her drink and answered, "Sorry?"

"Oh, I just thought you were looking at Danni as she had something you wanted."

"What? Don't be silly I—"

The whispering over, Megan jumped to her feet.

"Well this has been fun but all good things come to an end." Megan grinned sarcastically.

"But I haven't finished my drink," Brooke protested.

"Yeah, well you can get another one from the next bar. Sorry guys – we have to go."

Danni willed Brooke to stand her ground and not give in. To her disappointment, Brooke stood up and pushed her glass aside. She smiled at Josh and Danni, her cheeks colouring slightly. "It was great seeing you guys again. I'm sure we'll meet up soon," she said looking directly at Danni.

"I hope so," she replied.

Josh stood and embraced her. How Danni wished

she could do the same again. Instead she just smiled at the two women as they turned and left the bar.

"Whoa. That was, intense," Josh said, looking towards the retreating women.

"Tell me about it."

Eric appeared in front of them. "Right handsome. Can I stop being your birthday boy? I've finished work and am ready to be seduced now," he said slapping his hands down on the bar and smiling seductively at Josh.

Josh looked to Danni and then back to Eric. "No, I'm out with Danni."

"Go," she said briefly hugging him. "I'm fine. I'm going to head off now anyway. And be careful."

"Aren't I always? Thanks babe – if you're sure?"

Danni smiled and nodded as Josh grabbed a handful of condoms from the bowl on the bar, stuffed them in his jeans pocket and walked towards the door with Eric. Moments later they were gone, and she was alone in the bar feeling like the loneliest woman on the planet.

Chapter Twenty-Five

Brooke led the way to the corner table in the Dog and Bone Pub. The air whiffed of stale beer, the patterned carpets threadbare and worn. The place was quiet with only two elderly men hunched over the bar, staring vacantly into their drinks. The pub wasn't exactly what Brooke had in mind for their "date night", but she couldn't take the chance of going to another gay bar, in case Danni and Josh decided to move the party on to another venue. She didn't want to witness another uncomfortable encounter between Danni and Megan. She ground her teeth until her jaw ached, waiting until they were seated before casting her narrowed eyes on Megan, her voice low, but full of fury. "Did you have to be so obvious?"

"I don't know what you're talking about." Megan lowered her eyes to the faded beer mat she held between her hands.

Brooke gave a quick glance around the dowdy space, before sliding forward to the edge of the chair and leaning slightly over the table. "Come on Megan, don't play stupid. You were so rude to Danni I actually felt embarrassed."

Megan raised her eyebrows. "Really, but not that embarrassed that you couldn't keep your eyes off her."

Brooke frowned at her accusation. "What are you talking about? Don't try and make this about my behaviour."

"Oh really? And why not? Have you got something to tell me Brooke? Because if you have I'd rather just hear it up front rather than be made a fool out of."

"Are you joking? I haven't done anything wrong. Danni is straight and engaged to Josh."

"Yeah right. Pull the other one. It's obvious she's got a thing for you."

Brooke slumped back in her chair. "A thing for ... ? Have you gone insane? She's straight Megan — do you want me to spell it out."

"I bet Josh is too."

"Well yes he is."

"I don't know if you actually believe what you're saying or if you're taking me for a fool. Did you see her T-shirt?"

Brooke shook her head in frustration. "You really are paranoid aren't you? So what if she wears a T-shirt saying "Girl-on-Girl"? It doesn't mean a thing. She was in a gay bar after all —maybe it was a present from Josh's friend?"

"Come on, Brooke, you don't believe that."

"Yes I do. What's going to be next? I fancy Ethan?"

"Do you?"

"Do you know what? This evening was a mistake. This whole idea of thinking things could work between us." She shook her head and stood up. "I'm going home Megan."

As fast as a cat pounces on its prey, Megan

gripped Brooke by the wrist, her slender fingers turning white from the pressure.

Panic rose in Brooke's voice. "Megan let go of me. You're hurting me."

Megan looked up at her with dark hooded eyes. "Sit down."

"No, I won't fucking sit down. Let go of me." Brooke yanked her arm free and rubbed her wrist. What had got into Megan? She had never seen her behave like that before.

Megan bowed her head. When she glanced up again moments later, her eyes were wide with apologetic humility. "I'm sorry. Please sit down."

"What for? What else do you want to accuse me of?"

Megan circled the rim of her glass with the tip of her finger. The worry lines on her forehead more prominent as she looked up at Brooke with regret in her eyes. "I'm just tired Brooke. All these long haul flights, spending time apart from you." She threw her hands in the air. "It's all grinding me down."

Brooke thought how much she looked like a vulnerable child at that moment, and immediately her heart softened. It hadn't occurred to her that Megan was under pressure recently and she had been adding to it. Brooke slipped into the seat beside her and put her arm around her waist. Her voice softened. "Honestly, you've got nothing to worry about, I promise," she said leaning her forehead against her back.

Her thoughts returned to Danni. What she had was a silly little crush. Lots of people in relationships felt attracted to other people at some stage in their lives – it didn't mean they were going to jump into bed with them the first opportunity they got. It just showed they were human.

When the time came, she would read Danni's draft. She hoped for the sake of everyone involved that she could honestly tell Roy that the idea was a no-go and she could close the chapter on what was a brief moment of madness.

***

Megan stared into the darkness of the night. Brooke was breathing softly beside her, her leg across her thigh. Things were okay for now. But that didn't make it any easier for her peace of mind. She had been right about Brooke. She had seen the attraction between her and that Danni woman the second they came into contact with one another. The energy in the air was undeniable. She didn't know who any of them thought they were kidding – and if pretty boy Josh was straight she'd eat her hat. What was their game? Why were they pretending to be a couple? She didn't want to rock the boat and have Brooke think any different – as long as she believed in their facade their relationship was safe.

She was going to have to work out a proper timetable between the women. Brooke was being left alone for too long and by doing so, Megan seemed to be losing her grip on her. As for Alison, she didn't pose too much of a problem. That was one thing she should be grateful to Kelly for. Motherhood made sure Alison was tied to the home. There was little chance of her meeting anyone else. Megan had the best of both worlds and if she didn't get a handle on them she was at risk of losing it all.

"Brooke?" she said softly. "Brooke?" Megan lifted Brooke's leg off her, slipped out of bed and felt her way to the door. Before heading to Brooke's office she grabbed a dressing gown from the bathroom door.

Sitting comfortably in Brooke's chair she flipped open her laptop and logged into Skype. She smiled when Alison accepted her call a minute later, her face against a pillow came in to view.

"Hey, baby," Alison said sleepily. "What time is it?"

"I couldn't sleep, I can't stop thinking about you," Megan said as she opened the dressing gown and exposed her nakedness. "Are you tired?"

Alison's eyes widened. "Not anymore!"

Chapter Twenty-Six

"Come in!" Brooke heard Roy call from behind the office door.

She entered to see Roy seated in his usual casual manner – semi-reclined in his leather chair and sporting a pin-striped suit.

He gave her a welcoming smile. "Take a seat."

When Brooke was seated, a smile spread over his face. "You did a great job on the Cruz edit, Brooke. A great job."

"Thank you Roy."

"So, how are you fixed at the moment?"

"Got a few edits in the pipeline but nothing urgent. I'm pretty much ahead of schedule."

"That's good to hear."

Brooke looked at him with curiosity. "Why? Is there something you'd like me to do?"

"Yes." He walked behind his desk, sat down and switched on his computer. "It's here."

"What is it?" she asked.

"The synopsis and first few chapters of Danni's book." His perfectly manicured finger pressed the mouse button. "I've emailed it to you. It would be good if you could let me know what you think of it."

"Oh right. Great. Have you read it?"

He shook his head. "I don't want to be biased. I trust your judgement Brooke."

"Flattery will get you everywhere!" She smiled.

"Not flattery. Anyway have a read and let me know what you think."

"Will do."

She nodded and made her way back to her office. As she sank into her chair, she sighed with a mixture of satisfaction and discomfort: If the book was good and Roy decided to publish Danni's work, she would be over the moon that she had got her big break. But that would also mean Brooke would have no choice but to have contact with her. The thought scared the living daylights out of her.

Chapter Twenty-Seven

As the days passed by, Danni tried her hardest to put all thoughts of Brooke aside. She thought she was doing a good job of keeping her emotions in order, until she'd passed by the bookshop and remembered the evening they had spent there together. It had left her feeling helpless and desperate for a final solution. A part of her had toyed with the idea of emailing Brooke and just telling her the truth, but who would that really benefit? It would just complicate things even further. No, she'd just have to suck it up and move on. *Perhaps one day.* She shook her head. *Just let it go!*

Danni sat on the living room floor. Chocolate muffins, a coffee, and her laptop to keep her company. Just as an email alert popped up on the screen, the door flung open.

"What you up to?" Josh asked entering the room.

Danni clicked on her email. "Nothing much. Laughing at pictures of pets that look like Oprah Winfrey." She looked up at him. "I've got some good news though."

Josh lowered himself onto the floor beside her and put his arm around her giving her a quick squeeze. "What's that? You've won the lottery?"

Danni shook her head.

"Well spit it out – and you say I never get to the point?" he said rolling his eyes.

Danni made a concerted effort to sound positive

– despite the fact that she felt she had been kicked in the guts by a herd of angry cows. "Guess who has got a job interview tomorrow?"

"You have? With who?"

"The council. It's just to tide me over until my latest book gets snapped up and I become a best-selling author."

"Oh right. Doing what? Admin?"

Danni pushed herself onto her feet and walked to the window, looking down at the ant sized figures below. "Not exactly. I did apply for that one – didn't get an interview. It seems they don't think my degree in creative writing makes me suitably qualified to write eviction letters!"

Josh laughed. "What? That's crazy. I think you'd have been great at that."

"Me too. I can just imagine someone receiving one of my eviction letters." She cleared her throat, putting on a posh accent. "Well darling, the bad news is that we're being evicted. On the plus side though, the letter from the council is wonderfully worded and the use of commas – exemplary."

The pair broke into hysterical laughter, Josh eventually steadying himself enough to continue the conversation.

"So what's it for?"

Danni hesitated for a moment as she leant her forehead against the cold glass. "Let's say I'm hoping to be a Highway Environmental Officer."

"A what?" he asked incredulously.

"A Road Sweeper."

"Huh?" Josh said, stupefied.

Danni busied herself tidying up – she didn't want to see the pity in Josh's eyes. "A Road Sweeper, Joshua. Don't look so sad for me. It's outdoors, plenty of fresh air, and I get to come up with ideas as I sweep. Plus, the pay is really good. Oh, and I get a uniform and wait for it …" She spun around. "… my own broom."

He jumped to his feet and walked over to her. "You are joking?"

"No, I really do get my own broom, two if I do overtime. How great is that?"

He held her by her shoulders and stared at her with the most earnest of looks. "D, if it's about the money, I can cover your back. You can't really be serious about being a road sweeper. You've got a degree for God's sake."

Danni swallowed the lump she felt forming in her throat. "I know, I know. Hey it's not that bad. Lots of famous writers did menial jobs before they made it, I'm simply following in that tradition. Besides, it's better that I do this than some comfy office job that I get all settled in and forget my dream. I want to do something that allows my mind to be free. So, until I can come up with a better plan, a road sweeper I shall be – and a bloody good one too."

"Okay, D. But you will get your publishing deal, I just know it."

"Yeah, well, I hope you're right dear fiancé. Hey,

I'm a bit tired. I think I'm gonna go and rest my weary head."

Alone in her room, she flung herself down on the bed and buried her head in her pillow. She wasn't one to feel sorry for herself, but with having so many disappointments of late – Brooke, her writing, bloody council admin jobs – nothing seemed to be going right for her. To make things worse, her pillow seemed to be giving off the distinct odour of kebab.

How could this be happening?

She hadn't had one for weeks. Falafel maybe. But no kebabs.

***

Danni sat patiently on the hard, plastic chair. It was the kind of seat you often found in doctors' waiting rooms, the kind you were afraid to touch in case you inadvertently encountered some dried bogey. The office was small and rather empty, smelling of a strange mixture of disinfectant and fruit gums. How on earth did this grey-faced man in front of her cope with it? She'd only been in the interview for five minutes and already she wanted to gag. Now that would make a good impression.

Mr Pompous Ass, otherwise known as Mr Jenkins, studied her with a stony expression on his face. "So Miss Gardener, what skills do you think you possess that makes you right for this job?"

Sweet Baby J in a manger! Was this wacko somehow related to Pete, her old boss? That was exactly the same question he had asked her at her waitressing interview. They clearly both read the same manual.

Danni attempted to muster an enthusiastic smile as she eyed Mr Jenkins opposite her. His grey suit perfectly matched his grey complexion, giving him a look of somebody suffering from the Black Death in the Middle Ages. Not that she had ever seen such a person. Mr Jenkins had an obnoxious habit of peering down at her from the top of his glasses every time he waited for an answer.

"Well, in what other job do you get the opportunity to sweep people off their feet on a daily basis?"

Danni laughed. Unfortunately, Mr Jenkins didn't. His expression remained cold, then he looked down at her application form again.

Come on, Danni! Think brooms, think rubbish. She cleared her throat and spoke a little louder, injecting a tad more enthusiasm.

"Well Mr Jenkins, in all seriousness, I'm a huge fan of the environmental health policies adopted by this local authority. In fact I've written to my MP to express my gratitude for all the changes that have been implemented."

Bingo! For the first time since she sat down, he was looking at her with real interest.

"Such as?" he asked, leaning forward, his top lip quivering with enthusiasm.

"Oh gosh, there're so many … where do I start? Okay. The new recycling plant that's just opened has had a massive impact on the quality of my life – and that of the local community."

The grey man smiled. Danni even thought she saw some colour rush into his ashen cheeks.

"I'm glad to hear it. I was in fact one of the leaders in that project," he responded proudly.

Double bingo! This was going well, now to close the deal.

"You don't say! I imagine your wife must be very proud to have a husband with such vision and integrity."

His eyes narrowed. "Mrs Jenkins left me, for a woman."

Epic fail!

Danni's jaw dropped. "Never. What a shame, what a terrible shame. Well at least you can be proud of what you've achieved, Mr Jenkins. You are a true forward-thinker. I'm so glad to have a man like you working in my local council."

Well recovered, Danni-girl.

"Why thank you Miss Gardener. It's nice to be appreciated sometimes." He gave Danni a smile.

She grinned back. "You're more than welcome Mr Jenkins. More than welcome."

Maybe she'd get her broom after all!

Chapter Twenty-Eight

"Hello? Earth to Brooke. Earth to Brooke – do you copy?" Ethan tapped a vacant Brooke on the shoulder. She started, letting out a sharp scream that resulted in Ethan leaping back a few steps and Brooke banging her knee on the corner of the desk.

"Ouch!" she cried.

He looked at her apologetically. "Sorry Brooke, I was trying to get your attention."

"It's okay, I was a million miles away," she said rubbing her somewhat flushed knee.

Ethan nodded to her computer. "What's that you're reading?"

"Remember Danni said she was writing a book?"

"Yeah."

"Well." She pushed her back against the seat and looked up at him. "These are the first few chapters. Roy asked me to take a look."

"Really?" Ethan said walking back to his desk and dropping into his seat. "And, is it any good?"

Brooke's expression lightened as she looked at him. "Actually it is."

He looked bemused. "You sound surprised."

She wasn't about to tell Ethan that she wished she had hated it, every wonderful word. Every beautifully crafted sentence. She had been hoping that she could tell Roy the book was average, below average even. Fit for neither toilet paper nor hamster bedding. Truth was, she actually loved it. She was blown away by it – from the engaging, warm style to the witty anecdotes. It was refreshing. Different. It had kept her hooked. No, in truth, she was convinced that Danni had real talent. She was onto a winner.

"Ethan how many manuscripts do you think we read in a month?"

He thought for a second. "I dunno, fifteen, twenty – at least I do anyway. You must read loads more considering you take stuff home."

"Okay for arguments sake let's say fifteen. Out of those fifteen, how many do you reckon we recommend for publishing?"

"Hmmm now that's easy – around one or two at the most."

"How many this month?"

Ethan picked up a pen from his desk and tapped it against his chin. "One. I hope this conversation is leading somewhere."

Brooke smiled. "Let's just say this is Danni's lucky day – she's going to be number two."

"Really? You like it that much or is this decision based on something more personal?"

"No, Ethan. I like it because it's good," she said standing up and stretching. "This could really be what we are looking for."

He spun his chair in a full 360 degree turn. "Really? Or could it be more like a nice bit of nepotism. Imagine that, the boss' future daughter-in-law is to become a published author. Roy will be happy to have talent so close to home. Think of all the little baby authors she can trot out. Ker-ching."

"God, you can be obnoxious sometimes."

"Only sometimes?" he teased.

"There's no nepotism going on here Ethan. Just a refreshing and original idea, written with honesty, warmth and a healthy dose of wit. I would have the same opinion, even if you'd have produced it – not that you ever could." She grinned sarcastically.

"All right. I'm just yanking yer chain Brooke. It's so much fun to see you all hot and bothered."

Brooke rolled her eyes and turned to walk away.

"Where you going?"

Brooke smiled sweetly. "To see the boss about a book. Oh and recommend that you be fired."

Within minutes she sat across from Roy who was looking at her apprehensively. She couldn't believe it – he actually looked nervous.

Clasping her hands together in front of her she grinned at him. "Well, I read it."

He moved to the edge of his seat, his eyes wide and inquisitive. "And?"

"And." She paused for affect. "I think it's brilliant."

He laughed and let out a long breath. "Really?"

"Yes, really."

He fell back against his seat. "Well, I can't say I'm disappointed you like it, Brooke. I was dreading the thought of having to break the bad news to Josh. How much of a bastard would I have felt?" Roy chortled, rocking back and forth in his leather chair.

Brooke rose to her feet. "Yes, I can imagine. Well I'm glad to have saved you from that horror. In all honestly, I think we're on to a winner here. It's a great read. Needs a few tweaks, but it's certainly going in the right direction."

"Good. That's what I like to hear. I'll give her a call and tell her the good news."

"Do you mind me asking what you would have done if I didn't like it?"

"Believe me, Brooke, if you'd have given it a thumbs down, all she would have received from me was a rejection letter and an extravagant wedding gift to ease my conscience."

Chapter Twenty-Nine

"Josh, Josh," Danni screamed, as she sprinted like a demented gazelle into the living room, slamming the door behind her. She stopped in her tracks, as she encountered a large bouquet of roses and a bottle of champagne in a wine cooler on the coffee table.

She looked down at the table and its delightful spoils. She hadn't even realised they owned a wine cooler. "Champagne and flowers are a bit overboard for a road sweeper's job aren't they?"

"Indeed they are, my darling fiancée, but we're not celebrating that."

Danni looked bewildered. "We're not?"

"Nope." He grabbed the bottle by its neck and popped the cork.

"So what *are* we celebrating, oh mysterious one? Not our impending marriage I hope!" She half joked.

"Not that either." Josh's hands were shaking as he poured two glasses of champagne and handed one to Danni. He raised his glass triumphantly towards heaven. "To your impending success."

"My *what*? What are you talking about?" She put the glass on the side. "Oh no, not this again, Josh. I'm not writing another book, I told you."

"You don't have to my little talented genius – you just need to finish the one you started." He whipped his phone from his back pocket and handed it to her. "You, Miss Gardener are now a – no have a listen yourself."

She snatched the phone from him, clutching it against her ear. "Josh, this is your dad."

He smiled. "I know. He called while you were out, he said he couldn't reach you on your mobile so he left me a message with the good news."

Danni jumped up and down on the spot. "I can't believe it, I can't believe it," she squealed excitedly. But within seconds her elation had faded to doubt. "Josh, you don't think he's doing this because he thinks I'm your fiancée?"

"I'm sorry to have to tell you this, Danni, as much as you like to think the worst of yourself – people can actually see you're a good writer. Oh, and by the way, my dad didn't give it the green light, he deliberately kept out of it."

"Then who did?"

"Brooke. And before you imagine she just did it to be nice, let me tell you that woman is known to be one of the best editors in the business. She is brutally honest, that's why my dad hired her. Her reputation rests on making wise choices, she's not going to put that on the line, however cute you are."

Danni's face lit up.

"So she liked it, she really liked it!"

"Apparently so. The contract is being drawn up as we speak," Josh shouted, unable to hide his utter joy for his friend.

"Oh my God, I can't believe it. I'm going to be published! I'm going to bloody well be published! Josh

– thank you. Thank you for everything. I still can't believe this."

Josh beamed as Danni showered him with hugs and kisses.

It was a bittersweet moment for her. The elusive dream of being published was now within her grasp but, wasn't there always a *but*. The contract wasn't for the book she wanted and Brooke wasn't there to celebrate with her.

Josh laughed. "Believe it, Danni. I told you you'd do it. My dad wants you to go to his office tomorrow to discuss book business."

"Really? Ah, I feel all shy and weird. Will you come with me?"

"Of course I will. Anything for my fiancée," Josh said with a half curtsy.

"Oh my God. What are we going to do about the big lie?"

"I've been doing a lot of thinking, Danni. It's like you said in your book, about people's expectations of one another and I feel ready now. By the time your book is published I'm going to tell him I'm gay."

"Josh, I'm proud of you. It's the right thing to do. Speaking of parents, I've got to share the news with my mum," Danni said pressing her mum's number on her mobile as she rushed to her bedroom. She stood by the window, waiting for her to answer.

"Hello darling," her mum's soft voice floated through the phone.

Danni cleared her throat as a trickle of excitement

made its way down her spine. "Mum, I've got some good news."

Her mum's voice took on a sympathetic tone. "I have no doubt you got the job, Danni, but I think you're making a mistake. I've always told you to follow your dream, not to give up. This is just a blip."

Danni raised her voice to drown out her mother's, "Mum, I got that job but that's not why I'm calling. I got a publishing contact."

"What! You did? Why didn't you tell me instead of letting me prattle on?"

Danni laughed. "I was trying."

"Oh, Danni. I'm so happy for you."

"Thanks, Mum."

"Will your picture be on the cover? Oh wait until I tell the ladies down the club. I told you someone out there would love your book."

"Um, it's not that book that's being published."

Her mum's voice took on a confused tone. "Oh not that book? So which then?"

Danni took a deep breath. "I wrote another one, a self-help book," she said quickly. She could just picture her mother's green eyes widening in surprise and her slender hand massaging her scalp as she took in the unexpected news.

"I see … I think, well that's good isn't it. A self-help book, maybe you could lend it to your dad and his new wife, they could use some advice!" she said laughing.

Danni let out a chuckle. She couldn't blame her

mum for being somewhat surprised; she had difficulty seeing herself as a lifestyle guru. "It's a long story how it came about but Josh's dad liked it enough to offer me a contract."

"That's brilliant, Danni. At least you've got your foot on the ladder. Wait 'til I tell your nan."

Danni nodded to herself as she strode across the room and began to unbutton her shirt. "That's exactly what I thought."

"So does this mean you're not going to take the job as a road sweeper?"

Danni cradled the phone awkwardly as she slipped out of her shirt and pulled a "It's a girl thing" T-shirt out of the cupboard. "Environmental officer mum not road sweeper."

"Oh right,"

"And yes, I'm still taking the job," she said before moving the phone away from her head whilst she pulled the T-shirt on.

"I was speaking to your nan about it yesterday and she has decided to give you your inheritance now, rather than wait until she passes."

Danni sighed rubbing her forehead. "Oh mum, she doesn't have to do that. There's nothing wrong with being a road ... Environmental ... Oh, whatever they're called. It's not forever, it's just until the book starts making money." She slipped out of her trousers and kicked them to the side before putting a pair of jeans on that were hung over the cupboard door.

"I never said there was. I'm proud of your work

ethic and I know a job's a job but you have such talent darling, and a degree. Your talent needs to be nurtured. And your nan wants to help."

"I'm very grateful but …" She looked out the window to the street below watching as the rain pelted down on the pedestrians. She imagined herself down there, a victim of the winter elements, broom in hand, at six o'clock in the morning. She then eyed her bed. It took less than a second for her to reach a decision.

"Tell Nan I said thank you and I'll dedicate the book to her."

"Good girl. Look, I've got to run, I've got a yoga class in fifteen minutes."

Danni smiled to herself. She didn't know where her mum got the energy to be as active as she was. If it wasn't yoga, it was rock climbing or running. Danni could only hope that by the time she reached forty-five she'd be doing the same. "Okay, thanks again. Give Nan a kiss for me."

"Will do. I'll come down for the weekend in a few weeks."

"Great, can't wait. Love you."

"Love you too, darling."

Danni moved to her desk. There was no point in procrastinating. She'd better phone Mr Jenkins and give him the bad news.

Chapter Thirty

"Danni, my dear girl. It's so wonderful to see you again," Roy gushed as he rose up from behind his desk, and marched enthusiastically over to Danni. He embraced her warmly, kissing her on both cheeks – the left, then the right. Danni always had trouble with the whole kissing malarkey. Some people did two, some just the one, while some keen ones went for three. Just plain greedy. Whatever the style, Danni invariably ended up with her nose in someone's eye or worse still, went the wrong way resulting in the embarrassing "face clash". Today, however, the kissing Gods were on her side and she came out unscathed. One kiss each on both cheeks – textbook.

Watching Roy in his own environment, Danni saw him through new eyes. Roy was every inch the handsome older man; dignified with an air of authority, strong but not overly intimidating. He seemed positively charming – at least to her. His physical appearance was less extreme than at the previous functions – no vibrant pink waistcoat – although the flamboyance was definitely still there, that certain "exuberance" that some unmarried male actors possess, though turned down a notch. Today he had opted for a somewhat Bohemian look: creased linen jacket, black T-shirt, jeans, and barefoot. Around his neck was a leather string with the silver emblem of Buddha. Once again he simply didn't strike her as a homophobe.

Danni smiled warmly. "And it's lovely to see you too, Roy."

Roy smiled then turned to Josh, patting his shoulder. "Hello, son."

Danni took a sharp intake of breath as she caught sight of Brooke sitting with her legs-crossed on a chair at the heavy oak table.

Damn, I didn't know she was going to be here!

Roy gestured for them to take a seat, then walked back to his own.

"Well, I hope my son has been treating you well," Roy said winking at Josh.

"Oh yes, of course – you know Josh." Danni grinned.

"Ha, well yes and no. He can be a mysterious one, that boy. I mean, he kept you a secret."

Josh rolled his eyes.

Danni smiled nervously, catching Brooke's eye. She was so uncomfortable about the whole fiancée thing. To lie in front of one person was hard enough – but Brooke as well.

"Yes, well, anyway. You've been causing quite a bit of excitement around here I can tell you," Roy continued. "You know Brooke."

"Hi, Brooke," Danni said hardly able to speak. The two women smiled warmly at one another for a moment before both breaking eye contact and looking down.

"Brooke has a lot of confidence in your work, as

do I after reading it for myself. You have quite an original approach, Danni. It's refreshing. Truly refreshing."

Danni briefly lowered her eyes modestly, and gave a nod to Brooke to acknowledge her further. "Thank you for saying so, Roy. It's my first effort in this genre so it was quite an experiment. I'm glad you enjoyed it."

"No, thank you. And I just want to put your mind at rest. Your relationship with my son has absolutely nothing with our decision to develop your work – none whatsoever. I'm a businessman, Danni. Great writing is one thing, but it needs to sell. I'm sure you can understand."

A smile broke across Danni's face. "I'm relieved to hear that. I wouldn't want to be given any favours. I want to be successful on my own merits."

"Well, a young person with integrity – quite a rarity these days." Roy smiled, flicking dust from the collar of his jacket in a rather theatrical way. He produced a rather thin contract and laid it in front of her. Her heart started to pound. So this was it? This was what she had been dreaming of her entire life. This was why she had endured – and been fired from – the dullest of jobs. This was her moment.

She picked up the stapled sheets of paper, flicking through them briefly. What the hell should she say? Luckily, she was rescued by Roy.

"This is a one book deal, Danni. That's how we work with new talent. When I first started this company, I was determined not to tie authors into lengthy contracts. If we get on and you like how I run things, I'm sure you'll offer us first refusal on your next book. But if we don't live up to your expectations or you get a better offer, who are we to stand in your way? The contract is pretty straight forward – but I think you should take it home with you and have a good read through before signing it."

Danni nodded. "I will."

"So let's talk money. I'm sure you're itching to know what happens next."

She nodded eagerly. If Danni was honest she would have given the rights away for free – just to have received a letter telling her they believed in her.

"We are offering you a small advance. We don't normally offer advances unless the book is really special. In this case I think it is. You'll receive the balance once the book is finished of course. All the other details about royalties and such are covered in your contract. We're planning to release the book about a year after you deliver us the completed version. Is that okay with you? It will be in e-book format to begin with and a paperback version will follow."

"Sounds perfect."

"Good. You'll be working with Brooke here. She'll walk you through the finer details, timelines and such."

Danni turned to smile at Brooke and once again lost herself in the depths of Brooke's eyes.

Roy leaned on the desk, pushing himself to his feet. "So, I'll leave it with you ladies. I'm afraid I have another meeting. Congratulations again, Danni. I look forward to seeing a final draft. Josh can I have a quick word?"

As Danni and Brooke exited the office, Brooke turned her head sideways. "Have you got time for a quick chat?"

An involuntary shiver ran through Danni. "Yes of course," she said following Brooke along a corridor and into a small windowless office.

Brooke cleared a pile of papers from a chair and indicated for Danni to sit there. "First I'd like to say congratulations. You must be so happy. And more importantly, we are very happy to be working with you, Danni. You really do have quite a talent."

Danni lowered herself onto the seat, maintaining eye contact with Brooke the whole time. How was it possible to have such intense feelings about someone that she hadn't even kissed yet? *Yet?* Was she going crazy to think that such a thing could ever happen? "Thank you Brooke, if it wasn't for you–"

"–Nonsense. Your book stood on its own merit. If we didn't pick it up some other publisher would. I didn't do you any favours. Your talent and hard work did."

Leaning forward slightly Danni said, "Thanks all the same."

Brooke leaned back in her chair and crossed her legs. "So this is your first time being published. How does it feel?"

"Like I'm in a dream and someone is going to come and wake me up and tell me to clear some dishes."

Brooke laughed. "I can imagine. Have you ever worked with an editor before?"

Frowning, Danni said, "No, I've never been able to afford one."

"Okay, if you decide to come on board, it's a pretty straight forward process. From what I've read first time round it doesn't look like it needs any major rewrites just a few sentences tightened up here and there. Obviously I'm here to help with the development of the rest of the book. So feel free to contact me with any problems."

"Great, thanks."

"Do you have a timeline for when you think you will be able to complete it?"

"I think within three months. Well, that's what I'm hoping for, anyway."

"Okay, that's fantastic. As I said, any problems just let me know. We can put a more detailed timeline together later, to make sure we stay on track for release."

"That's wonderful, thanks again for your help," Danni said rising from her seat.

"No problem."

There was a knock on the door. It creaked open and both women looked to see Josh appear. Danni strode over to the door.

Brooke turned her chair to face them. "Hopefully, I'll be speaking to you soon, Danni."

"You can count on it."

***

Danni looped her arm through Josh's and half skipped half walked beside him. "I can't freaking believe it, Josh. It's really happening, isn't it?"

He gave her a sideway glance. "Yep. I'm so happy for you, Danni, I really am."

Swinging around in front of him and walking backwards she asked. "By the way, what did your dad want?"

"Oh just more details about when we'll be setting the date."

Danni slowed down, before coming to a halt in the middle of the pavement. "What did you tell him?"

"That you wanted to concentrate on your writing for now."

She swallowed hard. "And he was all right with that?"

Josh shrugged. "Seemed to be. Anyway enough of my dad, what do you want to do now Miss Author?"

Danni giggled like a school girl. She was giddy and on a high. Brooke and a publishing deal, could the day get any better? "I dunno – celebrate?" She grabbed onto Josh's arm and pulled him towards her.

"Your wish is my command. My dad gave me some money to take you out and treat you."

"Oooh, really? Spoil me all you want, I was born for it." She laughed.

"Yep and what's more I'm going to treat our flat to a makeover. That's unless you're planning to move into some lesbian love palace with Brooke now you're about to be rich and famous?"

Danni slapped him on the shoulder. "Joooooshh!" Then she frowned. "Do you really think it's wise taking money from your dad like that?"

Josh lifted his eyebrows. "Yes. It's more like an advance on my wages. I'm going to work for him in the accounts department. I worked there a few years ago, they're a good bunch – for accountants!"

"Accounts, really? What's with the change of heart?"

"It's nearly winter and you see these hands," he said waving them at her. "I'd like them just the way they are."

"I always knew you were a wuss. Bloody builder my arse," she said laughing.

Chapter Thirty-One

The Chinese restaurant was full to capacity with a queue which snaked out into the street. May Ling's was famous for its chef's specials. Colourfully decorated with red ribbons and statues of dragons, it was a picture of vibrancy. The Peking duck was like no other Brooke had ever tasted, not to mention the dim sum. She was pleased that the chatter from the surrounding tables made their lack of conversation less conspicuous.

She watched as Megan navigated the sticky rice onto her chopsticks and into her mouth.

"You're very quiet today," Megan said between bites.

"Am I?"

"Yes. In fact you've been a bit off for a while now."

Brooke took a sip of her green tea and winced at its bitterness. "I don't know what you're talking about."

Megan let out a laugh. "You're joking right. I can't remember the last time we had sex."

"Shhh," Brooke hissed as she glanced around the room. There was a very good reason for that. Since their last argument, her attraction to Megan had faded to practically nothing, despite promising herself to make another go of their relationship. Danni was all Brooke could think about. From the time Danni had come onto the scene, the contrast between the two had astounded her. She felt guilty wishing it was Danni who was lying beside her at night. That it was Danni whom she shared her days with, and all of her dreams and desires.

Brooke forked pieces of shredded duck onto a pancake and folded it over. "I've been tired. I've had a lot on."

"Maybe if you stopped bringing your work home ..."

Brooke held the food inches from her mouth. "Let's not go through this again, Megan."

Megan leaned forward over the table and hissed in a low voice. "So now the tables have turned. Now it's you who doesn't like all the nagging, is that it?"

It was strange. Brooke thought she would be pleased that Megan had stopped doing overnight flights for the past few weeks. Megan had kept her promises and became a permanent fixture rather than a fleeting one. But instead of enjoying Megan's company, Brooke had found it suffocating, almost to the point where she had been praying for her to take a long distance trip.

Brooke bit a chunk of the duck pancake and chewed on it for a few seconds to buy herself time, hoping Megan would take her suggestion gracefully. Brooke looked at her for a long time. Nothing. Not one physical reaction to the woman who at one time could render her dizzy with passion with just a single glance. "Look, maybe you should, you know, go back to your normal shifts."

Megan let out a less than humorous laugh. "Ahh, so you're trying to get rid of me now," she said pointing a chopstick in the air.

"Don't be silly. I've just got a lot of work to get through before Christmas and I don't want to feel guilty about not spending time with you." Brooke prayed her words sounded sincere.

Megan looked at her suspiciously. "And that's the only reason?"

"Of course. What else could there be?"

Megan shrugged her shoulders. "If you say so, I'll let my boss know when I go in tomorrow."

"Good," Brooke said smiling as a weight lifted from her shoulders.

"So seeing as I'm not going to be around for a while, shall we have an early night tonight?" Megan asked, keeping her stare fixed on Brooke as she filled her own glass with red wine.

Brooke popped a piece of shredded beef in her mouth. "I can't. I have some work I need to finish up."

Megan raised her eyebrows suggestively and said in a low voice, "It doesn't have to be an all-nighter."

Brooke cast her eyes downwards and forced a smile. "Sorry. My head's just not in the right place at the moment."

Megan threw her napkin on the table. "Oh sod you then. Play your fucking mind games," she hissed.

Brooke's pulse began to race. "What are you talking about?"

Megan narrowed her eyes and glared at her. "Oh please. Do you think I don't know why you've been walking around like a lost puppy?"

Brooke blinked rapidly. "Sorry?"

"Oh, you heard me." Megan leaned over the table. "It's that Danni, isn't it? This seems to be your normal routine, bouncing from one woman to the next," she said disdainfully.

Brooke opened her mouth to protest but Megan stopped her with a deadly look.

"Listen to me, you'd better figure out what you want because I'm not going to play second fiddle to anyone. You're making a complete idiot of yourself, trying to hit on a straight woman for God's sake." She shook her head in disgust. "You think you're so noble don't you? But you don't give a shit about her fiancé."

"I–"

"Save it, Brooke." Megan caught the attention of a waitress. Brooke smiled awkwardly as she came to their table. "Can I have the bill please?" Megan said.

The waitress looked down at the plates still filled with food. "Is there something wrong Madam?"

"Oh no, the food is fine thank you. It's just that there's been an emergency at home."

"Oh I'm sorry. I'll be as quick as I can," the waitress said backing away.

Brooke tried to get Megan's attention. "Megan! Why are you behaving like this?"

Megan ignored her and glanced around the restaurant instead.

"Megan, please talk to me." Brooke felt like she was losing her mind. She immediately started to have doubts. Was she really going to put their relationship on the line for something she could never have?

As the waitress placed the bill on the table, Megan reached into her bag and withdrew some money. Standing, she threw it on the table, turned and walked towards the exit.

Brooke stared at Megan as she hurried from the restaurant. Who was it that said the older you get the more sense life makes? Whoever it was had better have a rethink. She was more confused than ever.

Less than three months ago, though her life wasn't perfect she knew where she fit into it. She was a highly respected editor. She had a partner who she thought the world of, but who was reluctant to commit. Not perfect, but manageable. Now a few months on, things had really taken an unexpected turn. Something had happened that she could never have anticipated – falling hard for a woman she barely knew. Who would have imagined that her life would be turned upside down so easily. But that's exactly what had happened.

Chapter Thirty-Two

Danni sat with her feet up on the leather foot-stool and glanced around their newly decorated flat. It was amazing what a lick of paint and a trip to IKEA could do. It had taken a few weeks but who'd have thought that a flat-pack could bring a girl such joy? She let out a contented sigh – everything was on the up and up. She couldn't believe that only a month ago her life seemed to be at a dead end – she had nothing and was going nowhere. But now look at her – she was going to be published – *her!* Danni Gardener! Un-freakin-believable! On top of that, she was going to have money in the bank. Okay, so she wasn't going to be rich … just yet … but if she didn't dine out at Harvey Nick's oyster bar every day, she would manage fine on her advance and her nan's money. What's more, she was even considering writing another self-help book.

Danni's thoughts of global stardom were rudely interrupted by the ringing of her phone. She picked it up without looking at the screen – figuring it was most likely Josh checking up on her now that she was a real lady of leisure.

"Well, hello dahling," she said mimicking the voice of Zsa Zsa Gabor.

"Hello?"

Danni jerked up into an upright position as she recognized Brooke's voice. "Oh shit, sorry."

"Danni?"

"Yes, sorry. I thought you were Josh. Embarrassing!"

Brooke laughed. "If you ever give up writing, you would make a great Gabor impressionist."

Danni's cheeks burned. *Note to self – always check who's bloody calling me.*

"Thanks," she said awkwardly.

Brooke was the last person she expected to hear from – most of their correspondence so far had been via email.

"Is everything okay with the book?"

"Yes, it's more than fine. I would like to meet up for a coffee to go over some points."

"Points?"

"Yes. There are a few places where I'd like to rearrange some sections and rather than going back and forth via email, I thought it would be easier if we just met and went through it in one go."

"Over coffee?"

"Yes. But if you'd prefer not to–"

"No, no of course I'd love … like to meet up. Entice me with a latte and chocolate chip muffin and I'm anybody's. Uhh, not literally, I'm not easy. Uhh." She clumsily joked.

Brooke laughed. "That's good to know. So, are you free today? Say one o'clock?"

"Yep, I'm free all day. One sounds good. Where?"

"Do you know Banjo's on Islington High Street?"

"Yep, it's that coffee house where all the yummy mummys go, isn't it? I always feel left out because I don't have a pram!" Danni retorted.

"Ha! Don't worry I'll try and hire one! Right, I'll see you then," Brooke said with laughter in her voice.

"See you then," Danni gushed cheerfully.

Danni placed her phone on the coffee table, and wiped her clammy hands on her jeans. *Don't overthink it; it's only a latte, not a marriage proposal.*

Now, what should she wear?

Chapter Thirty-Three

Brooke was acutely aware that she could have gone through the editorial changes with Danni over the phone, but she had the overwhelming urge to see her again. What she really wanted from their meeting could never be a reality, and yet she couldn't help herself. The need was so urgent it eclipsed her common sense.

Brooke arrived early at the café, hoping to grab a seat before the afternoon onslaught of mums with prams began. Too late. A row of robust three-wheel buggies were parked along the back wall like some kind of Pimp My Pram convention. As she walked through the heavy glass door, a tall stick insect of a man shouting into his phone brushed past her, knocking her with his elbow. *Arsehole.* She eyed the room and, not seeing any chairs available, started to feel uncomfortable at the thought of conducting her meeting with Danni standing up. Talk about awkward!

Luckily, a choice spot became available. Brooke swiftly threw her jacket over one of the chairs to stake her claim. She joined the back of the small queue that was forming around the counter and minutes later, was served by a lanky teenage boy whose face was covered in red pimples. "It's a ten minute wait for coffees, we're having problems with the machine," he said in a half-man half-boy voice.

"No problem, I'll just pay now. I'll have two lattes," she said as her gaze fell upon a tray of freshly baked chocolate chip muffins. "... and couple of those muffins, too, please," she grinned as she handed him the cash.

She made her way over to her table at the back. It was rather intimate with two old leather seats which would work well for poring over a manuscript. Brooke sunk down into the worn leather and removed her phone and IPad from her bag. As she clicked on the screen, Danni dropped into the seat opposite her with a wide smile on her face.

"Oh hi. Good timing. I've ordered some coffees to be brought over," Brooke said as Danni took her jacket off.

"Great and chocolate chip muffins?" Danni laughed.

"Of course."

Brooke's eyes followed Danni's hand as she flicked her hair behind her ear. "So how have you been Ms Soon-To-Be-Published Author?"

Danni spread her hands over the edge of her seat. "Never better. I'm still having to pinch myself to make sure I'm not dreaming."

"I can assure you, you're not. Listen, I wanted to say something about that night we bumped into you and Josh at the bar."

Danni opened her mouth to speak and Brooke held up her hand. "No please. Let me say what I have to say. I didn't want to say anything in front of Josh at the meeting with Roy, but I'm really sorry if Megan came across as a bit rude."

"Don't be silly, it was fine."

Brooke's features hardened. "No, it wasn't. She was rude and there was no need for it."

"Well, just a bit. But it's okay. Is she normally like that?"

"Rude?" The frown lines on Brooke's face smoothed out as she laughed. "She's all right most of the time. She has her moments. You know. Sometimes it just feels like we're not on the same page."

"Sometimes?"

Brooke rubbed the back of her neck. "Okay, most of the time. Anyway, I don't want to bore you with that."

"It's fine," Danni said reassuringly.

Before Brooke could say any more, a young girl appeared at their table and laid down two coffees and a white plate adorned with two delicious-looking chocolate chip muffins. Brooke and Danni both looked up and thanked her in unison.

Danni picked up her muffin and took a pinch out of it. "You were saying?"

"I think what it all boils down to is that we both want different things out of life," Brooke answered, sipping her latte before placing it back on the table.

Should I really be telling her this much about myself? For some reason, Brooke just felt so at ease with Danni. She didn't feel judged.

Brooke pushed back a strand of wayward hair. "I guess some couples have that shared sense of where they are going. I'm sure you do with Josh."

A momentary look of discomfort crossed Danni's face. Brooke saw it and, for a second wondered whether she had got it all wrong about Danni and Josh. Perhaps they were having problems as well? Is that why they hadn't set a date yet?

"Everyone's relationships are different," Danni answered. "I get on so well with Josh because we are best friends first."

"I can tell that."

Danni nodded her head, picked up her coffee with both hands and took a sip.

"So, how many frogs did you have to kiss before you finally met your prince?" Brooke asked.

"Not that many thankfully. I've never been in a serious relationship before, just fleeting ones." She leaned forward. "Not that I'm, you know – promiscuous," she added quickly.

Brooke laughed. "Don't worry, I know what you mean. So, I guess you're getting all the questions about having children? I bet Roy has been on at you."

Danni choked on her coffee. "Uh … children. To be honest we haven't really discussed it. How about yourself?"

"Probably not wise at the moment – the way things are going. Wouldn't be the best environment for a new arrival." She picked up her coffee. "Anyway I didn't get you down here to be my relationship counsellor."

"Brooke, I honestly don't mind. I know we have only met a few times, but sometimes it's good to speak to someone you don't know that well. I'm very trustworthy and I promise not to tell anyone – unless of course you have murdered someone, in which case I would feel duty bound to turn you in." She smiled, lightening the mood. Brooke burst into laughter.

"Anyway, I'm here if you want to talk."

"Thank you, I will remind you of that when I call you at three a.m." Brooke grinned, sipping her coffee. Nodding towards her phone she said, "Now, do you mind if I use the recorder on my phone – it will just be easier when I'm working on your book."

Danni shook her head and settled back into her seat. "Not at all. I feel like I'm being interviewed. Fame at last. Go right ahead."

For the next couple of hours, the two women discussed, philosophised, and guzzled several coffees – and a rather unhealthy intake of muffins of the chocolate variety. Danni spoke about her book with such passion that Brooke couldn't help but be moved by her conviction. She was making her question her own life and the expectations she placed on others, namely Megan. Was she expecting too much of her? Was she holding the bar so high Megan didn't have a chance of ever reaching it? Maybe. But maybe not. Perhaps Megan had been taking her for a fool and *expecting* her to put up with it.

It had been a productive meeting, fascinating, and when Brooke noticed the time, she immediately pressed stop on the recorder and hurriedly put it back into her bag. As much as she would have loved to sit there all day with Danni, work beckoned.

"Thanks so much for meeting me, I think we've made some great progress," Brooke said beaming with enthusiasm.

Danni held her gaze as she slipped into her jacket. "Anytime. It's been so good to go through it like this – better than a dry old email any day. Though my waistline might not agree." Danni laughed, looking at the empty plate before them.

"So what are you up to for the rest of the day?" Brooke asked checking her bag to make sure she had everything.

"Most probably do a bit of window shopping before Josh gets home. Are you going back to the office?"

"Afraid so. I have a meeting at four."

Danni picked up her bag and swung it over her shoulder. "So, do you fancy coming round to mine for a drink some time? Not to discuss the book, just to chill out, put the world to rights."

Before Brooke could respond, a frazzled looking woman and her wailing child appeared beside them. "Sorry, are you leaving?"

"Oh yes, we are," Brooke answered, gathering her belongings and slipping past the woman and screaming infant.

Danni came to stand beside her.

Brooke shivered inwardly as the two touched shoulders. "Yes. I'd like that very much."

"How about this weekend, Saturday perhaps?"

Danni asked, moving out the way to make room for a man and buggy to pass by.

Brooke's nails dug into the softness of her flesh. "Saturday, sure."

"Brilliant. I thought we could have a girly night. You know cocktails, something to eat and lots of chat. I can't resist a mojito."

The skin on the back of Brooke's neck prickled at the idea of spending an evening alone with Danni. "Sounds like just what I need."

"Good. Saturday it is then."

They walked to the exit together. Once outside the two women stood for a minute rather awkwardly before saying a quick goodbye and heading in the opposite direction.

What the hell was she doing? She couldn't help but get drawn closer and closer to her. She knew all this, she knew it was perhaps folly, but still the urge to walk this path was too strong. Brooke had to follow it, wherever it might lead.

Chapter Thirty-Four

"I'm packed and ready to go," Megan called out from the bedroom.

Brooke eased herself to her feet slowly. For the first time in their relationship she didn't feel a sense of dread at Megan's impending departure. In fact, she was glad to be having some space.

The past few days had been tense – not because Megan hadn't been trying her hardest to be attentive and affectionate, but because Brooke had more than enough distractions on her mind. Editing Danni's book as well as meeting up with her had intensified Brooke's feelings to an almost unbearable level.

Hearing the sound of the suitcase being dragged towards the front door, Brooke exited the living room and went out to see Megan. As Megan rummaged through her bag, she looked up as Brooke neared.

"Found it," she said with relief as she withdrew her ID pass and hung it around her neck.

Brooke smiled. Megan was forever misplacing her ID, it was a miracle she found anything in her bag considering it was filled with so much junk.

"So I'll see you in a couple of weeks, have a safe trip, say hi to your mum for me and have a lovely Christmas," Brooke said feigning a sad smile she didn't feel.

Megan moved around her case and pulled Brooke into an embrace. "I will, and don't work yourself too hard." She pulled back and looked Brooke straight in the eye. "I'm going to miss you."

Brooke's body stiffened. "Me too."

Megan leaned her face forward and kissed Brooke on the lips. To her surprise Brooke felt nothing. It was as if the link that had once held them together had been broken. Not that it could all be laid on Danni's doorstep, their demise had been a long time coming. Meeting Danni had provided the catalyst Brooke needed to put things into perspective.

"Well, I'd better get off. Don't want to miss my flight," Megan said.

"No, of course not."

Megan stopped in the open doorway and turned to Brooke. "This time apart will do us good. We will really get things back on track when I return. We'll have a brilliant New Year's Eve."

"Let's just see how we feel when you get back," Brooke answered truthfully. Megan bowed her head and headed down the communal hallway.

Brooke gently shut the door and slowly walked back to the living room. What was she going to do? Maybe she would use the time to sort her head out – really figure out what she wanted.

The problem was – she already knew.

***

The Captain's authoritative voice resonated through the taxiing aircraft.

"Flight time to Tenerife today will be five hours

and twenty minutes. Weather along the route looks good so we are looking at a nice, smooth flight. Please sit back, relax, and enjoy your time with us."

Megan's body tensed as the plane increased its speed along the runway. This was the most exciting part of the journey for her. The speed, the anticipation, the exhilaration of leaving the ground and everything behind each time. It was her escape. Her freedom.

She smiled at the sight of the young couple in front of her, hands tightly entwined as the plane steadily climbed in altitude. Megan's petite, auburn-haired work colleague Jackie nudged her, drawing her attention away from the couple. "So, you told Brooke you were going to visit your mum in the US for two weeks. What if she calls her house and asks to speak to you?" she asked, as if getting some vicarious thrill from hearing her friend's tales of deceit.

Megan turned to face her. Jackie was the only person who knew about her double life. She was her accomplice even. Without Jackie covering her shifts when she needed to be with one or the other, Megan would never have got away with it.

"Nah. Brooke wouldn't do that. She doesn't even have her number – I'm not that stupid. Plus I told her ages ago my mum wasn't exactly over the moon with my sexual orientation. There's no way she would ever call her house."

This was in part true. After Megan's mother discovered she was gay, it was as if her daughter had almost ceased to exist. Gone was the woman who sang

Megan's praises to the neighbours, boasting of her "jet set" career. She was now indifferent to Megan's accomplishments and took little if any interest in her everyday life. Not that Megan cared anymore, self-preservation had kicked in and she had long since given up trying to win her mother's approval. She simply accepted that was how it was.

"God Megan. You're walking on such thin ice. I don't know where you get the energy to maintain a double life."

"Neither do I. But what's a girl to do?" She smirked, proud of her morally dubious abilities.

"Choose one," Jackie said, patting the top of her hair into place.

"If it was that easy, don't you think I would have already? They both have qualities I want in a partner – just not in the same body."

Jackie gave a short shake of her head. "Like what for instance?"

"I dunno. They're like chalk and cheese." She leaned into her, lowering her voice. "The sex with Alison is mind-blowing."

"And she has the child you said you wanted," Jackie reminded her.

Megan forced a grin and said through gritted teeth, "Yeah and there's that."

"So why isn't she enough?"

"Oh because she wants too much from me. She keeps going on about me leaving this job, and that isn't going to happen for anyone."

Megan was cabin-crew through and through. She lived and breathed it, and she was damn good too. She loved the freedom it gave her. Seeing places she had only dreamt of. Besides the romance of the job, in a practical sense, it was also the perfect cover when it came to splitting her time between Brooke and Alison. Up until now neither of them had suspected a thing.

"She wants you to give up your job? That's ridiculous?" Jackie said defiantly.

"Brooke doesn't put that kind of pressure on me. In fact, lately she's even come around to the idea of thinking it's best I work the hours I want."

"Well there you go. Dump Alison and commit yourself to Brooke. Save yourself the worry and me, too. Your life makes me anxious; God knows what it does to you."

Megan let out a long sigh and turned to look out the small window, watching as London became a spec on the horizon. "Pick one? You make it sound so easy."

"Megan, babe you can't keep juggling both women. Sooner or later it's going to all come crashing down around you and you might be left with nothing."

Megan twirled the loose strand of hair on her neck with her finger. "Yeah, maybe you're right. Anyway, I might have my decision made for me anyway."

"How so?"

Megan paused for a moment. Brooke hadn't actually *said* anything but her whole demeanour was different. It was as if she had been replaced by a walk-in. Like that movie *Invasion of the Body Snatchers*. She was physically the same, but the look in her eyes was different.

Megan stared ahead at the passengers in the front row, aware of them but not actually seeing them. "I think she has the hots for a new writer that's just joined her firm."

Jackie let out a short laugh. "No way! Brooke loves you, why I don't know, but she does. I can't see her looking out for someone else."

"You know, a few months ago I would have believed that but recently …"

"What?"

The intercom beside her sounded in Megan's ear. Picking it up she listened for a few seconds, hung up then unclipped her seatbelt and stood.

"Ah forget it. It's not important. Let's get to work." The less she thought about the Brooke situation the easier the next two weeks would be.

Chapter Thirty-Five

Rain and hailstones splattered against the living room window with great urgency. The early morning sky was bleak and dark.

"I can't do it, I can't do it," Danni repeated to herself as she struggled to complete her morning workout which consisted of forty press-ups. Although she was just twenty-four, the last thing she wanted was bingo wings – never a good look.

"You can't do what?" Josh asked entering the room wearing a blue tracksuit, a bowl of steaming porridge in his right hand.

Danni rolled onto her side and looked up to face him, wiping away an imaginary speck of sweat. "I'm sorry, Josh. I want to break our engagement."

"But why?" he asked taking a spoonful of food into his mouth.

Danni bit her lip and rolled up into a sitting position. "Why, hmmm let's think – how about," she jumped up onto her feet, "'cause I'm not really your fiancée and it's messing up my chances of getting a date."

He raised his eyebrows. "A date in general or a date with Brooke?"

Danni reached over to the sofa, picked up a cushion and threw it at him. Josh crouched protectively over his bowl. "Come on, babe, it's not that bad is it?" he said laughing.

"Don't babe me, and yes it bloody well is." She flopped down on the sofa, lifting her legs in the air. "I really like her and this lie is like kryptonite to my chances of getting any further with her."

Josh spoke between mouthfuls of food. "Err, ok, Superwoman. Do I have to remind you that Brooke's in a relationship already? So that in itself is a substantial stumbling block, is it not?"

Danni sighed. "How can I forget? But it doesn't look like things are going that great between them at the moment. She's coming over for a drink tonight."

"Really?" He remained silent for a moment as he rubbed his chin. "So, how do you see this ending? You tell her you're gay, and what do you think she's going to do? Fall into your open arms and within a week you move in together and buy a cat. Please don't tell me you're that naive?"

She frowned. "Oh shit, was my cunning plan that obvious? Of course I don't bloody expect that, besides I'm more of a dog person. Look, I just don't like lying to her, that's all. What's worse is she thinks *our* relationship is a match made in heaven."

Josh gave a slight shake of his head as he let out a squeal of laughter. "Well, you are lucky being engaged to me, D. I am quite a catch."

Danni bent forward and held her face in the palms of her hands. "Come on, Josh, I'm serious. How are we going to untangle ourselves from this mess? Christmas is coming up as well and I'm sure your Dad will expect us round again at some point. I just can't keep up this charade any longer."

"I know, Danni. You really do like her, don't you?" he asked sliding to sit beside her and placing his bowl on the coffee table. "Jesus, I didn't realise it you had it this bad."

She lifted her head and turned to face him. "I wish I didn't. I've never felt like this about anybody before. It's great that I've met her but then again it sucks big time, not being able to have her I mean. Plus, it doesn't help that she seems to have Lucifer's sister as a girlfriend."

"Danni, I hope all these feelings aren't coming about because you think you should rescue her from the She-Devil. Brooke's a grown woman. She doesn't need a knightess in shining hotpants."

Danni rolled her eyes. "And I don't want to be one. I can't explain it. Something about her. It just feels right, like she's worth all the heartache."

"Oh my God." Josh slid to the floor onto his knees and grabbed Danni's hands. "Where's Danni? Please bring back the old Danni. I think Barbra Cartland has come back from the dead and taken up residence in your body."

Danni looked down at him with a smirk. "Okay, mock me all you like but one day when you fall in love …"

Josh fell backwards onto the floor and held his hand to his chest in true am-dram style. "Love," he croaked. "Did Danni mention the word love?"

Oh my God she had. How on earth had those words

slipped out? "I don't mean love as in I *love* her. I meant love as in when you really like someone … fall in love, you know."

He rolled up into a sitting position. "Quit digging, D, I know exactly what you meant. So do you want to tell her tonight?"

Danni nodded. "Well I do think it's best all round if she knows the truth. I'm sorry, Josh. I'll tell her not to say anything to your dad. It won't affect things with him."

"Hey, don't worry. It doesn't matter. He's going to find out soon anyway."

"I'm sure he'll be fine with it. I mean he looks like–" She stopped herself in time. Now was not the time to tell Josh she thought his father may be hiding a secret of his own. "–he's an understanding kind of man. It'll be fine. Hey, I know, why don't you invite him over for dinner and we'll break the news together? Yeah. That's it! He won't be so hard on you if I'm there."

"I'll think about it. Anyway I'd better be off to the gym. I'll be out late tonight – I'm going to see about getting that tattoo."

"Okay. And Josh, I'm really sorry."

"Don't be silly. You have nothing to be sorry about. You played your part perfectly and I've got some great memories of you in that outfit. I might even post your pictures on Facebook," he said as he pushed himself up and ran towards the door to avoid a slap.

"You wouldn't dare," Danni screamed, giving chase. But Josh was too quick; he'd managed to escape out the front door. Danni heard his laughter echoing down the stairwell. So it seemed had Mick from next door. She heard the chain rattling, then the door slowly opening. It would look rude if she rushed back inside, so she waited.

"You alright Dan?" Mick said, when he finally made an appearance. Today he was sporting pyjamas and slippers that reminded her of the ones her granddad used to wear.

"Yeah, I'm good Mick. How about you?"

"Yeah, yeah. All cool."

An awkward silence ensued as they stood in the hall eyeballing each other.

"Do you want a smoke?"

"Bit early for me Mick, got a lot on my plate today."

"Yeah, I hear you're gonna be one of them novels."

Danni's face creased in confusion. "Aye?"

"You know a novel – one of them people that writes books."

Danni smiled. "Ahh, a novelist. Yes, kind of, and if it wasn't for you, I would never have come up with the idea, so thank you."

"Me?"

"Yes, remember when we were in McDonald's that time …" She stopped. Mick had a pained expression on his face as if his brain was booting up after years of inactivity. To be honest, the guy probably couldn't even remember yesterday, let alone weeks ago.

"Never mind, Mick, but thanks anyway. You were a great help."

He looked at her blankly, as if he had forgotten what they were even talking about.

"It's all good. All good."

"Right anyway, better get on," Danni said cheerfully.

He nodded, slowly closing his door.

She wandered back into her flat, her thoughts firmly fixed on the impending evening. She had forgotten to ask Brooke what kind of food she liked, but was quietly confident that her fridge stuffed with the full Marks and Sparks's range would save the day.

Everything was set; all she had to do now was calm her nerves which were getting worse by the minute. She'd always expected that getting older meant those pesky nerves would become a thing of the past, but no such luck. It was as if the entire cast of Cirque Du Soleil were rehearsing in her stomach. The very same feeling she had when she was waiting to go on her first date – with Nicola. What a date that was. She had babbled her way through the first hour, been catatonic for the second and nearly thrown up during the third, just at the point when Nicola's squid hands darted up her top. How very dare she!

No, thinking about first dates was not one of the best ideas, besides, this was not a date. It was simply drinks and dinner with her editor. Oohh she liked the way that rolled off her tongue, *my editor*.

She turned to the sink, opened the cupboard underneath, and withdrew four bottles of cleaning detergent – when Danni was nervous there was only one thing to do – clean.

By six o'clock the flat looked like a showroom, and Danni, like a bedraggled mess. The kitchen appliances sparkled, the floorboards shone, the skirting boards were pristine. Even her nan would dub her efforts "eat off the floor clean".

It was time to rinse away all of that hard-work grime with a nice, hot shower. Danni had little time to transform herself into the hottest dish on tonight's menu.

Chapter Thirty-Six

The aroma of freshly baked bread emanating from the kitchen made Megan's mouth water as she reclined on the sofa in the lounge. Alison and Kelly were baking her a treat after what had turned out to be a gruelling flight back to the U.K with a number of unruly passengers. She pulled the fleece blanket covering her legs up to her chest and turned to her side, flicking on the TV. She snorted as Jeremy Kyle's condescending voice filled the air. She quickly changed the channel – that's the last thing she needed to hear about; other people's drama.

The door flung open and Kelly bounded in like an excited puppy, holding a slab of bread in her hand, a yellow river of melted butter sliding down her little wrist.

"Look what I made!" she said excitedly, climbing onto Megan's stomach and pushing the bread up to her nose.

Megan sniffed the air, then smiled. "Mm … smells good enough to eat," she said, quickly leaning forward and taking a bite.

Kelly giggled and attempted to move back. Grabbing her, Megan wrapped her in her arms and tickled her stomach. The little girl yelped and squealed as she writhed about in Megan's arms, begging her to stop, and when she did, pleading with her to carry on.

Stifling a yawn, Megan released Kelly, who slid to

the floor, still gripping her piece of bread. She ran from the room screeching as if she was being chased by an imaginary wolf. Megan shook her head – *that kid's going to be a handful when she grows up*.

Megan tolerated Kelly more than loved her. She could honestly say that she would be much happier if she didn't exist. Although the ready-made family seemed like a good idea at the time, it was fast becoming a drag.

Megan still wanted to stay with Alison and make things work, even with her child, but she just couldn't let go of Brooke. The very thought of someone else possessing her, actually made her feel sick. To think of another woman touching the most intimate parts of her body, the beautiful body that belonged to Megan, enraged her. It was never going to happen – at least not if she had anything to say about it.

Megan sunk deeper in thought. She knew she didn't want to lose Brooke, but what was she going to do about the recent disharmony? She could feel her grip on Brooke loosening. She was no longer as clingy as she had been, and that was concerning.

She had tolerated Brooke questioning her every move for the first couple of months of their relationship because she had wanted her so badly. Even though her sex life with Alison was all consuming, the need to own Brooke had overwhelmed her. Brooke was such a straight-laced woman who kept her emotions bound up so tightly that she had been shocked by the passion and ferocity she exuded when they made love or fought. She became addicted to flicking the switch on her, turning her from calm into a ball of fire in mere minutes. But, sadly, the enjoyment had soon worn off, though the buzz from the power she held over her, hadn't. It was like a drug. She loved that a successful, intelligent woman like Brooke wanted, no *needed*, her so desperately that she would turn a blind eye to all of her wrong doings – and there were plenty of those. She had always been able to play Brooke's emotions so easily, and she felt a perverse sense of pleasure in that knowledge.

Swinging her legs onto the floor, Megan dug into her back pocket to check her phone. Switching it on, she was surprised to see there were only messages from Jackie and a few other friends – nothing from Brooke. A deep frown creased her forehead. What the fuck was going on? Was Brooke playing games with her? She shook her head.

She really doesn't want to go down that road with me. Anger seethed within her. She'd never considered Brooke the cheating type but the recent change in her and the emergence of Danni was really starting to worry her.

She began to type a message on her phone, but then deleted it – if Brooke wanted to play games, so be it – she was still quietly confident Brooke would make the first move. She switched her phone off and pushed it down the back of the seat, deciding that was where it was going to stay until she went back. *Trying to fuck with me Brooke? Not a chance in hell.*

With a determined look, she headed to the kitchen. Alison was bending over the oven, putting a tray back in. Damn, Alison was so sexy when all flushed and sweaty. Megan moved swiftly to her side, brushed up against her, then whispered in her ear. "So, do you want to put *Frozen* on for Kelly?" She leaned back and arched her eyebrows. "And then you and me can go make our own private movie?"

Alison laughed. "No. How about you do some painting with Kelly for half an hour, then she can have a nap."

"And then I can get what I want?"

"Don't you always?"

Megan pretended to think about it. Her expression turned serious. "Only because you know what's best for you."

"Oh please," Alison said wriggling out of her arms and taking a step back. "If you know what's best for *you*, don't even think about talking to me like that. I'm not one of these women who are at your beck and call. No man or woman's got ties on me. You remember *that*."

Megan held her hands up in surrender. "Okay, okay, I was only kidding."

Alison put her hands on her hips and eyed her from the bottom upwards.

"Yeah well, do you see me laughing?"

Megan turned and leaned against the worktop. "No, and I'm sorry."

Kelly looked up from her painting, confusion on

her beautifully freckled face. "What's wrong Mummy?"

Alison smiled. "Nothing sweetheart. Mummy M is just trying to be funny."

Megan started towards the door. "And failing miserably," she said in a sarcastic tone, as she stepped out into the hall and slammed the door behind her.

Chapter Thirty-Seven

Danni emerged from her bedroom looking like a new woman. Hallelujah! The ugly duckling had become a swan, and in record time too. It was eight o'clock and this girl was hot to trot, ready to roll, though not too much as she didn't want to crease the clothes she had just struggled to iron. She had opted for the sexy, understated look – skinny jeans and a vest, her hair pulled up into a pony tail. She quickly applied a dash of perfume, lipstick and deodorant and… badabing!

"Sorted," she said, winking at herself in the bathroom mirror.

As she turned to leave the room, her inner calm was quickly shattered by the chime of the door bell. She immediately stopped in her tracks. *Oh my God she's here, she's actually here.*

This was it. This was her moment. She quietly tip-toed to the front door and peeked through the spy hole where she saw a spoon-faced Brooke looking towards the door. It always amused Danni how strange people looked through a spy hole – their faces distorted in that way that faces do after you've had a few too many Jager-bombs. She couldn't just leave her standing there, what if her hemp-happy neighbour Mick appeared on the scene with a big, fat dooby? Now that wouldn't be a good look.

Without further procrastination, Danni quickly opened the door and put on what she hoped was a confident but casual smile.

"Brooke," she said warmly, taking in the beauty on her doorstep.

Brooke really did look stunning. Jeans, suede ankle boots, and a fitted leather jacket that hugged her figure perfectly. Something Danni couldn't wait to do. She wished they could just skip drinks and head straight to the bedroom. If only…

Brooke stepped across the threshold and handed her the small bouquet of flowers she was clutching.

"Wow, thank you. That's so kind," Danni said. Nerves aside, the gesture made her feel a bit teary. "No-one has ever given me flowers before – except for Josh and that one time at primary school when my fish died. And on that occasion, I got a wilted dandelion to lay on the match box I had buried little Moby in. So you win. Anyway, come in, come in."

Stop babbling Danni.

Brooke stepped into the flat and followed Danni into the lounge. "What can I get you to drink?" Danni asked.

"A coffee would be great."

"Coffee? Sure. Be back in a jiffy. I'll pop these into some water too. Thanks again, they are lovely," she said as she started for the kitchen.

Minutes later, Danni was back with two steaming coffees in a pair of Royal Dalton mugs, courtesy of a car boot sale. She loved a bargain and what a find those had been that day. She handed one to Brooke and slid down onto a red bean bag.

"Take a seat. If you're anything like me, you're exhausted after that trek up the stairs. In fact, I'm petitioning the block to get a Stannah stair lift installed, but so far, no luck!" Danni laughed.

"Hahaha. It wasn't that bad, my stamina's quite good." Brooke smiled, glancing down.

Danni choked on the coffee halfway down her throat. The comment was innocent enough, but for some reason everything Brooke uttered seemed to take on a whole new meaning for Danni. She was becoming a walking *Carry On* film, possessed by the spirit of the late Sid James.

"Are you okay?" Brooke smiled

Danni grinned and nodded. "Yes sorry, I drank that a bit too quickly," she said, clutching at her throat.

Brooke took a seat and placed her bag at her side, waiting until Danni signalled she was okay.

"So. You've got a nice place here," Brooke said glancing around. "Very chic."

Danni was quietly proud that Brooke had commented on her efforts and hugely relieved that she hadn't seen the place a week ago.

"Thank you. Though I can't take all the credit. I owe a lot to my dear Swedish friend, IKEA."

Brooke smiled and sipped her coffee. She cleared her throat. "So, about your book. I was really impressed with the last chapters you sent."

Though Danni fought to keep her voice calm and her whole body for that matter, she trembled with excitement. She hoped Brooke didn't notice.

"Thanks. You know I don't think I'll ever get used to hearing it being called 'my book' – it seems so strange."

"I can imagine, but enjoy it! You should be proud of yourself, Danni."

Danni beamed. "Thank you. That means a lot to me."

"I'm only being honest. Don't worry, I'll be just as honest if and when I don't like something." Brooke raised a brow. "Do you know, it always amazes me when really good writers are filled with self doubt?"

Danni blushed slightly. "So when you're not turning manuscripts into master pieces, what do you do for fun? Cinema, running, break-dancing? Don't tell me, theatre?" she asked hazarding a guess. Brooke didn't strike her as a ten-pin bowling sort of girl.

"Me? Well to be honest, I'm not a huge theatre-goer. Saying that, I really want to see…" She paused.

"What? Go on." Danni cocked her head. "*The Woman in White?*"

Brooke pulled a face. "Nope. that's not quite my cup of tea. Oh God, this is embarrassing. I'll give you a clue. It's aimed more at the children's market."

Danni thought for a second. "Gosh I don't know – *Dora the Explorer Goes to Rehab? Postman Pat Does Bangkok?* "

Brook shook her head, giggling.

"Okay. I give up," Danni said, throwing her hands in the air.

"Do you normally give up so easily?"

Danni lowered her eyes. "No, especially not on things I want."

Oh my God, what is wrong with my voice? It had gone all seductive and sultry.

"Okay. It's … *The Snowman*," Brooke said clasping her hands together and laying them on her lap.

"What, you want to build one?" Danni asked frowning. "Sorry, we'd have to pop over to the Alps for that."

Brooke laughed. "No, I want to go and see *The Snowman* – the production."

Danni pinched her bottom lip, twisting it with her fingers. "Riiiiight. Very festive – what with Christmas only a few weeks away."

"It wouldn't be Christmas without *The Snowman* animation. I think I must have watched it a hundred times."

"So why don't you go and see it?"

"I wouldn't go to the show without a child," Brooke retorted.

"Are you joking? Is that the only reason?"

Brooke shook her head before taking a sip of her drink. "Come on, how sad would that look? A lone woman sitting amongst a load of kids. Weird."

"Won't your partner go with you?"

"Megan? Oh no, she hates kids. She gets a rash being within two feet of them."

"Really?" Not that Danni was surprised to hear that. That woman looked like she could curdle the milk of human kindness.

"So, tell me. How did you meet her then? Megan, I mean?" Danni asked.

Brooke looked lost in thought, reliving those first moments. The honeymoon days.

"Well, it's funny but I actually met her on a flight coming back from Japan. She's an airhostess."

Danni felt a pang of jealousy. Love at thirty thousand feet. That Megan was one jammy cow.

"Hmmm. I thought that was against the rules, picking up passengers?"

Brooke leaned back on the sofa and stretched her legs out in front of her. "It wasn't as crude as that – she slipped me her number on a napkin. The rest, as they say, is history."

"Sounds very romantic." For some reason, she couldn't picture Megan in the role of a trolley dolly – weren't airhostesses meant to be friendly people? Who knows, maybe she was more pleasant at higher altitudes. The thin air can have that effect.

"So, anyway, about you and Josh," Brooke said in a matter-of-fact way.

Danni put her mug on the floor and got on her knees. "Yes, me and Josh, about that, you see–"

Brooke leaned forward, holding her attention. "Sorry to interrupt, but can I just say, you guys are really sweet together. He's a great guy. Decent, you know."

Danni looked at her trying to ascertain how exactly she was going to tell her the truth.

"People like that are pretty rare. Good, kind people I mean. Honesty is everything, don't you think? I can't bear lies." Brooke leaned back into the sofa.

"Uh huh, yeah, me too."

Cue the vodka.

"Do you want something stronger to drink?"

Brooke picked her cup up off the floor. "No thanks. I could do with another coffee though if you don't mind. I'm a bit of a caffeine freak."

Danni pushed herself up onto her feet. "There are worse things to be addicted to. At least it's not crack!" she said taking the cup from her.

Whoops – was that inappropriate?

" Ummm. Do you want something to eat? I've cleared out the local branch of M and S. I wasn't sure what you liked. Rest assured I got a few bags of Percy Pigs should we not be able to decide."

Brooke shook her head. "No thanks, I'm fine for now. Just a coffee will do."

"Well let me know when you get peckish."

Danni wandered into the kitchen, flipped the kettle on, then reached for the freezer door, grabbing the bottle of vodka by the neck she poured herself a large measure. Freaking great. Now what was she going to do? After that little speech, how was she going to go back in there and shatter her dreams of honesty and perfect love? Damn this situation. Damn Brooke, too, for being so hot. *And while I'm at it, damn Josh and his bloody dad who was responsible for this whole stinking mess. Life is so unfair.*

She downed the vodka, wincing as it burnt its way down her throat. Dutch courage, that's what she needed – or Russian anyway. She filled up a tall glass with the vodka and dropped a couple of ice cubes into it. If Joan Crawford could (*allegedly*) get away with disguising vodka as water, then so could she – after all, she was an actress of some sorts.

Turning back to the boiled kettle, she quickly finished making Brooke's coffee and entered the lounge feeling less stressed about the whole situation. It was amazing what a snifter of alcohol could do.

Easing herself down onto the bean bag, she watched as Brooke sipped her coffee. She loved looking at her lips and the way they puckered forward. Oh God, the way her tongue slowly moved along the top of her lip to lick away the froth was sending shivers of excitement through her whole body. Even the sight of her slender fingers gripped around the handle was making her ache. *Down girl!*

"Sorry, Danni, you were about to say something before I interrupted you."

She loved the effect Brooke had on her. Those eyes could jump start a corpse, they were so intense.

"Was I? I can't remember. It couldn't have been that important."

"So where's Josh today?"

"He's gone to look at some designs for a tattoo. He's got this idea he needs to get one before he reaches thirty."

Forgetting for a minute it was vodka in her glass;

Danni took a mouthful of her drink and nearly spurted it all out. She would make a dire alcoholic.

"Oh okay. Hopefully I'll see him before I leave."

"He might be home late, but stay as long as you like." Danni was growing braver as the warmth of the booze mingled with her blood. "I like your company."

"And I like yours too." Brooke smiled

Danni ran her fingers through her ponytail, twisting the ends around her finger. "I'm glad to hear it."

Brooke stared wordlessly at her for a few seconds before she said. "So, Josh is thinking about getting inked then. And you? Do you have any tattoos?"

Danni pulled her face as if she had just sucked on a lemon. "Oh no. Not my thing really. I always imagine how it will look when I'm all wrinkly. Do you have any?"

Brooke nodded. "Yes. Just the one."

Danni cleared her throat, slightly embarrassed. "Oh well, that's nice. I mean I do like tattoos if they're nicely done. It's the big dark scary ones I don't like."

She quickly took another sip of her vodka-water.

"I know what you mean. I had mine done when I was eighteen and thought I was rebelling against the world."

Danni started to get up. "Can I have a peek?"

"Err sure. But I have to warn you, it's on my breast."

She halted midway and gulped. "On your … breast?"

"Yes. You know, on one of the two things you have."

That may very well be the case. But Danni's breasts weren't Brooke's breasts. Oh boy. She moved onto the sofa and sat beside Brooke. Danni watched while Brooke removed her jacket and unbuttoned her shirt. Droplets of sweat trickled down Danni's back, her mouth suddenly dry as her gaze moved over Brooke's chest, up the graceful line of her neck, the soft outline of her jaw, the fullness of her lips. She had never wanted to kiss someone so badly in her life. She slowly blinked, lost in a daze of what it would be like to feel Brooke's skin pressed against her own, her nakedness against her body. To touch her. Danni was breathless, dreaming about all the things she ached to do to Brooke. Danni desired Brooke more than any woman she had ever known.

"Here it is," Brooke said raising her breast upwards to reveal a tattoo of two white doves in a heart.

Brooke's voice broke Danni's trance. Danni swallowed hard. "Wow – that's pretty nice as tattoos go."

Brooke's dark long eyelashes slowly flickered as she stared back at Danni.

Tentatively, Danni raised her eyes to meet Brooke's, willing her own heart rate to slow down before it exploded inside of her chest.

"In fact, it's beautiful, like you."

Danni couldn't tear her eyes away from Brooke,

she was so lost in the moment. Brooke's long thick hair hung restlessly against her chest, her blue eyes, though fully dilated, were guarded, and held a hint of anxiety.

"Dan …"

Danni put her finger to Brooke's lips and smiled, before pushing back Brooke's hair behind her ear. She half expected Brooke to rear backwards, to tell her to stop, to back off, but she didn't. Instead, Brooke cast her eyes downwards, focusing on Danni's mouth. Surely this wasn't her imagination. The chemistry between them was now undeniable. Danni's heart fluttered wildly as she leaned her head forward. She was so close now, the faint scent of Brooke's perfume enveloped her senses. Danni's insides trembled like a blob of jelly as she raised her hand to Brooke's cheek, gently brushing the back of her hand against the smoothness of her skin – the mere feel of her sent tremors through every fibre of her being. This was it. A few more seconds and there was no going back – the moment could never be undone.

Suddenly, she caught her breath as Brooke pre-empted her move and brought her face to meet Danni's, their lips finally making contact. Electricity surged through her as Brooke's eager tongue gently parted her lips. She was punch drunk, but she knew it wasn't the alcohol that was responsible for the way she was feeling. It was the amazing woman she was now holding in her arms.

"Hi honey, I'm home." The sound of Josh's voice

jolted them apart. The moment was shattered. Fear and panic flared in Brooke's eyes as she fumbled with the buttons on her shirt. Danni desperately wanted to say something to her but before she had the time, Brooke was standing, bag in hand. As she reached the door, Josh appeared.

"Hey Brooke, good to see you," he said, leaning down to kiss her cheek.

"You too, Josh. Look, I'm really sorry to be rude, but I have to go."

"You're kidding. I've only popped back to get changed. I'm going straight back out again," he answered with a hint of bewilderment in his voice.

"No really. I have work to do at home. It was nice to see you both again."

Danni rose from the sofa and willed herself to say something. *Anything.* But before she could Brooke had hurried out the room and Josh stared at Danni in puzzlement as the front door banged shut.

"Errr, did I interrupt something?"

"What do you think?"

"Did something happen? Did you tell her about us?"

"Oh God. No, I didn't tell her about us. "

"Then what the hell was the swift exit all about?"

Danni sunk down into the sofa, running her hands through her hair.

"Oh Josh, you came at the worst possible moment. I thought you were going to call before you came back."

"Bloody hell, Danni. She was only here an hour. I didn't think you'd make a move that quick."

"It seems like she was barely here for five minutes. I only wanted to see her tattoo and things sort of like got intense. Do you think she'll tell your dad?"

"I doubt it. Why would she?"

"Dunno. I don't know anything anymore. Oh bloody hell. What a mess."

"Come on, it's no big deal. So you had a little moment with the woman you fancy the pants off, so what?"

"So what? Well it kind of blows our cover of being the perfect couple doesn't it? We had the status of Brangelina."

"Look, don't panic. We'll have to talk later. I need a shower and a quick change. Most importantly, do not freak out about this. Go and read a book – take your mind off things."

Yeah right, like that was going to happen.

Chapter Thirty-Eight

Sitting in the back of a black cab, Brooke's hands were shaking so badly she had to trap them underneath her legs to calm them down. What on earth had she done? Just because *her* relationship was in trouble, it didn't mean she had to drag Danni and Josh down with her. She dreaded to think what would have happened if Josh had walked in on them and seen her with her shirt unbuttoned, kissing his fiancée. She felt like a complete slimebag, an utter fool. Not to mention an unprofessional one. What had taken place at Danni's could have a serious impact on their working relationship, not to mention the guilt she felt about Megan. What had she been thinking half undressing like that to show off her tattoo? She couldn't even blame it on alcohol. Whatever had come over her?

The cab came to a halt jolting Brooke out of her thoughts. Brooke paid the driver, exited the cab and quickly made her way to Ethan's flat. After ringing the bell twice, Ethan pulled open the door and ushered her inside.

"You what!?" Ethan asked as he stood in the centre of his light airy living room wearing jogging bottoms and a T-shirt.

"I know. I can't believe it myself," Brooke said as she shook off her jacket, laid it on the edge of the white leather sofa and sat down.

Ethan's shocked expression changed to one of

concern as he looked down at her. "Does Megan know about this?"

"Are you crazy? You're the only one I've told."

"Well, at least you haven't completely lost your marbles." He moved to the window and sat down on a single leather armchair. "Brooke, you can't just go around kissing straight women. You know you'll just get hurt in the end."

She gave her head a short shake. "Don't you think I know that? But I can't help the way I feel about her."

Ethan was on his feet again. "So why did you go round there knowing how you felt?"

"I don't know. I just wanted to see her again. I need a drink." Not her usual concoction of cocoa and cream with two lumps of sugar, but a stiff one.

He rubbed his hand over his face. "I think I'll join you."

Ethan left the room and Brooke listened to him pottering about in the kitchen. It had been a mistake going to Danni's, she realised that as soon as she had seen Danni and felt the undeniable pull towards her. She placed her face against her palms. From personal experience she knew that life could change in a matter of seconds. That things you took for granted could vanish into thin air. But this connection she had with Danni was something that caught her off guard.

Ethan re-entered the room holding two glass tumblers full of a dark liquid and a bottle of brandy tucked securely under his arm.

He handed Brooke a drink and knocked his own back in one gulp. "You know, any sane woman would have made an excuse not to attend tonight, but not you. You walked straight into it with your eyes wide open knowing full well what the consequences could be." He refilled his own glass.

"I know. I'm an idiot." Brooke slipped off her shoes and tucked her feet underneath her. She took the first sip of her drink, savouring the heat as it burned down her throat and spread throughout the rest of her body. The booze seemed to have the same affect on her as Danni did.

Ethan walked over to his IPod station and turned it on. Soothing sounds of jazz soon filled the air as he returned to his chair. "I don't know what to tell you Brooke. I really don't. I thought you would have learnt your lesson after Penny."

Though his words stung her, she knew he was right. Why she always felt she needed a woman in her life she didn't know. It wasn't as if she'd been brought up in an insecure home or she was neglected by abusive parents. No, far from it. Her childhood had been as much near to perfect as it could be. Even her mother had noticed her pattern of behaviour when it came to relationships and had discreetly suggested Brooke was a rescuer, always trying to save someone.

Her mother, as usual, was right. Brooke had tried so hard with Penny, her lover of two years, right up until the day Penny left her and returned to her abusive ex-husband. Despite all the allowances Brooke made for her, in the end they just weren't enough. Penny's excuse was she couldn't bring her children up with the stigma of having a lesbian mother.

"I never thought I could feel like this about someone," she said, more to herself than Ethan.

"It doesn't matter what you think or feel, Brooke. She's engaged to your boss' son. There can't be a happily ever after with this sorry tale."

Brooke looked down at her drink and noticed it was finished. She hadn't even realised she had drunk it. At least now there was an excuse for her imagination running wild.

***

Brooke arrived home later that evening still feeling like the worst person in the world. She didn't bother turning the lights on in the flat. She needed the darkness to enshroud her, the light would only expose her for what she was – a lousy friend and a cheat. There she had been giving Megan the third degree about her comings and goings, when in reality it was Brooke herself who needed to be watched carefully. It was Brooke who had been unfaithful. She was the one who couldn't be trusted.

Kicking off her shoes in the passage she headed straight to her bedroom and stripped down naked, slipping in between the cold cotton sheets. Poor unsuspecting Josh. Would Danni tell him? If she did, would he then tell his dad? She wouldn't blame him. How could she have been so stupid, so careless –

though some might have said it was only a kiss – Brooke didn't look at it like that. There had been intent behind that kiss – a longing to be intimate with another woman. She was torn between guilt and pleasure. She was now one of those women she read about in problem pages, whose relationships were torn apart by a moment of weakness.

Tossing and turning, her mind just wouldn't settle. Should she unburden herself and confess to Megan what had transpired? Call Danni and apologise? Leaning over the edge of the bed she retrieved her mobile phone from her pocket and checked her messages – there were none. It had seemed like an age since she had last spoken to Megan – maybe that's why things had happened with Danni. Because Megan wasn't around. She pressed Megan's number and waited a few seconds before hearing the familiar message "Please try again later". Maybe it was for the best that she couldn't get through to her. What was there to say?

As her eyes closed she went through the evening's events over and over and concluded that the only real option was to refrain from seeing Danni again – at least on a one-to-one level. As much as the thought pained her, she knew this was the right thing to do – for Danni's and Josh's sake as well as her own.

Chapter Thirty-Nine

The delicious smell of pork and apple sausages wafted from the kitchen and into the living room where Danni sat. She had promised herself that she wouldn't devour them just yet, not until she had done the one thing she had been putting off all morning – call Brooke. Four days had passed since she had last laid her lips, *ahem*, eyes on Brooke. Every look, every feeling, every touch that had passed between them that night had been stored and logged in her memory bank.

Lana Del Rey blasted from her IPod as she reviewed the changes to her manuscript. Her only contact with Brooke had been via email – and very curt emails at that. Danni had responded in kind, making the suggested changes to the manuscript and attempting to draw Brooke out with humour, but, alas, nothing had worked. There had been no mention of the "incident". It seemed that the kiss had really sealed their fate. Maybe it was enough to make Brooke realise she really did love Megan after all. Or maybe it had thrown her into turmoil. Danni hated the thought of Brooke fretting as much as she hated the thought of never seeing her again.

They were both adults; surely there was no reason why they couldn't still be friends. There was only one thing to do – she would act. If the mountain wouldn't come to Mohammed …

With a new-found determination, she googled

"The Snowman" and waited for the results to load. Clicking on the link to the Peacock theatre, she followed the instructions to purchase two tickets. If Brooke turned down the offer, she could always go with Josh instead. He was a big kid at heart and could easily be bribed with a Cornetto when he got there.

Buying the tickets was the easy part, now all she had to do was call Brooke.

Not giving herself the opportunity to back out, Danni picked up her phone and dialled the number. She was genuinely surprised when Brooke answered the phone after two rings, so much so, that she was at a loss for words.

"Hello? Hello?"

Danni took a deep breath and prepared herself for the rejection she thought would soon follow. "Uh, Brooke. Hi, it's Danni."

"Hey there, Danni. How are you?"

So far so good. Brooke's voice sounded friendly enough. "Yeah, things are great."

"That's good. Very good. So are you calling about your book? Did you get all the amendments?"

Danni stood up, and began pacing the floor. "Uh yes. I." Her mouth hung open, the words catching in her throat. "I've got two tickets going spare to see *The Snowman.*"

Brooke's soft laughter echoed through the phone. "*Going spare?*"

Danni cleared her throat. "Yeah, for this Saturday."

"So, you just happen to have tickets to a

children's show, a show I've wanted to see for ages? What are the chances of that?" She laughed.

Hearing the humour in her voice, Danni flopped down on the sofa with a smile stuck to her face. "Okay, okay you got me. I bought the tickets to take you. You know, to make things right." She looked towards her computer where an email Brooke had sent earlier was open on the screen. "I hate only speaking to you via email Brooke. I don't want to cut you out of my life, just because of–"

"–I know what you're saying," Brooke said wistfully. "But what happened was wrong."

Danni faltered for a second, her mouth twitching with nervous tension. "I know, but–"

"There's no but Danni. We both have partners. I've been feeling terrible about the whole thing."

Brooke's words caused an instant tightening in Danni's stomach. "So what you're saying is we can't be friends, is that it?"

"I didn't say that. As long as we don't overstep any boundaries, I don't think there's any harm seeing each other."

Danni held her breath. "So is that a yes to *The Snowman*?"

"Um, well I guess so. Yes."

Danni slowly released her breath. "Fantastic. So I'll meet you at Holborn station, Saturday at two?"

"Okay. Sounds good. And Danni?"

"Yes?"

"Thanks for thinking of me. It's really nice

hearing from you again."

Danni gripped her phone tightly as she said goodbye.

Was this for real?

Brooke had just agreed to go to the theatre with her. Ironically, it took a Snowman to bring about the big thaw between them. Now she really was in the mood to celebrate – with a sausage baguette smothered in onions. Oh and a healthy dollop of ketchup.

Chapter Forty

Brooke placed her mobile gently back on the desk, and resumed concentration on her computer screen. That had been one tough conversation. How she'd managed to keep her cool she didn't know, but she had said what needed to be said, even if it had frazzled her nerves. Her first instinct had been to ignore the call. But she couldn't do it. She missed Danni too much and had been aching to hear her voice again. She had come to the realisation that she wanted Danni in her life, no matter what her feelings for her were. It was up to her to have some discipline, to control herself. She knew what she had to do and it didn't involve cheating or getting herself involved in a love triangle.

Her eyes darted to the side as a flying paper clip landed on her desk with a ping sound. She tilted her head in the direction it had come from – Ethan. He was grinning like a schoolboy, rocking back and forth on his chair. Brooke raised her eyebrows inquiringly. "You called?"

"I want to know what's got in to you, Ms Brooke! One minute you look like you've lost a pound and found a penny, the next like a cat that's got the cream."

A smile spread across Brooke's face. "Do I?"

Ethan ran his hand over the top of his head and let out a heavy sigh. "Yes, you do. I'll never understand women as long as I live. You all seem to blow hot and cold at the drop of a hat."

"Oooh, having problems with Helen are we?"

"Nah, I'm not actually. It's you. You've been miserable for days and after one phone call you're all happy again. Who was it, dare I ask?"

Brooke tapped the side of her nose with the tip of her finger. "Nobody you know."

He shrugged his shoulders and shuffled some papers on his desk. "Oh, you want to play it like that. I thought we didn't keep secrets from each other."

Brooke could have lied and put her mood swings down to relationship problems, but that couldn't be further than the truth. Her life with Megan no longer had an effect on her. She had felt herself becoming more and more detached from their dysfunctional relationship.

"Okay, but when I tell you I don't want any snarky remarks or funny looks."

He pointed a finger at himself. "Huh, from moi?"

Brooke laughed shaking her head. Despite his annoying ways, she trusted Ethan. He had always been a good, loyal friend.

"Okay, that was Danni."

His eyes widened. "Thought so. And?"

"And nothing. All that stuff before was just a childish crush."

His gaze lingered a fraction, his eyes studying her face. "Riiiiiight …"

Brooke turned her attention back to the computer screen. "This is why I didn't want to tell you.

I knew you'd react like this," she said without looking up.

"Like what?"

"All suspicious. Like something's going on between us."

"And is there? From what you were saying the other night, it isn't the most outlandish suggestion is it?"

She snapped her head round to stare at him. If he hadn't been so close to the truth she might have laughed his comment off. Instead she looked him directly in the eye. "Forget about the other night. There's nothing to worry about. She's just a client and a friend."

Ethan broke their exchange and looked down to his own computer, tapping away at the keys as he said, "If you say so. If I started smiling like that after one of my friends called, I think they'd be very worried."

"That's because your friends are Neanderthals, Ethan."

His head jerked up. "No need to insult the poor guys. Just because they can't get a handle on why some chicks prefer chicks, doesn't mean they're backward thinkers."

"No, but asking if they can watch goes a little bit too far Ethan. They are hardly enlightened are they?"

She knew she was being a bit harsh, but she'd had the unfortunate experience of spending an evening with his caveman buddies once at a work function Ethan had brought them to. To say they had been the most condescending sexist men she had ever come across was an understatement. She couldn't quite grasp how Ethan hung out with them seeing as he seemed to be the total opposite.

"Come on Brooke, I've apologised a million times about their behaviour, they were pissed. They're really nice blokes ... when they're sober ... or asleep." He laughed.

Brooke smiled and nodded, deciding she would let it go. After all, she had spent far too long discussing a group of men who were partial to drinking their own urine. Today was a day for her to be happy. She was going to see Danni again, and *The Snowman*!

Chapter Forty-One

Kelly stood in front of the long mirror hung on the hotel wall. Her tiny hands were trying with little success to tie a pink bow in her hair. Megan grabbed her arm.

"Come on, Kelly. Let's put your jacket on, otherwise we're going to be late for your surprise!" Megan coaxed. Kelly's face crumpled.

"Noooooo. I want to wear my bow."

Megan held her firmly. "Jesus, well put your coat on first, then you can put the stupid thing in your hair."

Alison glared at Megan. "You're such a natural with children, aren't you?"

Megan looked up at her then opened her mouth to speak before slamming it shut. The pair of them were really annoying her. What with Kelly whining all morning, dictating what she did and didn't want and Alison indulging her every whim. She let out a sigh as she pushed herself up in to a standing position. "What? Look, I just don't want to be late and miss half the show."

"I thought this outing was about Kelly, not you."

"It is. Oh, forget I said anything. Jeez, I can't put a foot right lately."

Alison turned to her daughter. "Come on darling, get your coat on and I'll tie your bow. After the show we can get some ice cream. How would you like that?"

"Yeahhhhhh."

Megan narrowed her eyes as she watched them both. All Alison ever seemed to do lately was bitch at her, and little Kelly had turned into a whiney demanding little diva. She didn't know how much longer she was going to be able to put up with them. A pang of regret struck her. Instead of being here, she could have been at Brooke's place, relaxing, having "Megan time" in a relatively stress-free environment. But no, she was here playing servant to a five-year old Mussolini. The time for change was nigh. No amount of sex or respectability was worth this much hell.

Alison smiled at Kelly, before glancing up at Megan with an I-told-you-so look on her face. "Right we're ready. It didn't take that long, did it?"

"Whatever," Megan said zipping up her coat. She was not looking forward to spending the next hour listening to a boy sing about a bloody snowman. This was what she detested the most about being with a parent. The child outings. When it was just Alison and her, things were ideal. They had plenty of fun and Alison's attention was focused on her and her alone. When the brat was around, that's all they seemed to talk about, as if she were the centre of the Universe. Well she may have been to Alison, but she certainly wasn't to her.

The taxi ride was as frost cold as the weather outside. Megan sat huddled in the corner of the cab while Alison wrapped her arm protectively around Kelly's shoulder.

"Sorry about the cold, the heater will get going in a minute," the cab driver called out to nobody in particular.

Megan studied them from the corner of her eye. *Maybe it really was time to move on; make her decision.* She was starting to feel more and more claustrophobic and trapped, and those were feelings she didn't appreciate one little bit.

The cab pulled up outside the buzzing theatre and Alison slid out with Kelly, leaving Megan behind to pay the fare.

"We're here!" Alison said excitedly, the little girl's eyes beaming as she saw the queue of children.

"Can you read what it says? *The Snowman!* Isn't this just the best surprise?"

Kelly's eyes lit up and she jumped up and down chanting, "Snowman! Snowman!" excitedly.

Seconds later Megan joined them in the queue.

Alison turned to look at Megan who stood stony-faced beside her. "Is this how's it's going to be all day? If it is, I'd rather you just went back to the hotel."

Megan ignored her, staring straight ahead.

"Megan, did you hear what I said?"

The woman in front with two small children turned and eyed them both. In an instant Megan bent down to Kelly. "Hey sweetheart, how about I get us some sweets for the show?" She glanced up again to see the woman smiling down at her.

Kelly looked at Megan with caution. "Can I have some popcorn?"

"You can have whatever you want," she said planting a kiss on her braided hair, before standing back up again.

"She's adorable," the woman said.

"We think so too," Megan replied with a wide smile as she playfully nudged Alison.

Alison's face was fixed in a scowl as the woman glanced from Alison to Megan. Megan gave her a small smile and a this-is-what-I-have-to-put-up-with look then shrugged, happy when she saw the sympathetic look in the stranger's eyes.

Finally, they negotiated the crowds and arrived in the lobby of the theatre. Kelly grabbed hold of Megan's hand and pulled her towards the counter. "Look popcorn, Mummy M."

Megan forced a laugh. "Hold your horses, sweetheart. Let me see if Mummy wants anything." She released Kelly's hand, letting her run off by herself. Turning to Alison she said, "Come on, let's make up. I forgive you."

Alison's mouth flew open. "You …"

Megan reached out and held her shoulder. "Look, let's not make a scene. You don't want to spoil Kelly's day, do you?"

No response.

Megan laughed good-naturedly. "Good, let's go and get some sweets then."

Megan slipped her arm around Alison's waist and pulled her close. "Hopefully Kelly will sleep through the whole night if we tire her out enough today," she said pulling Alison into an embrace and kissing her on the mouth, ignoring the stares of passersby.

"Mummy M, Mummy M, I'm over here," Kelly called from in front of the counter, waving her little arm, with a bag of popcorn in her hand.

"Come on, let's go and have some fun," Megan said, taking Alison by the hand and leading her towards Kelly.

***

The sound of children's laughter filled the theatre as Brooke and Danni made their way down the aisle to their seats. Brooke was grateful Danni had booked seats in the dress circle which meant they had a perfect view of the stage and no bobbing heads obscuring them.

"I can't believe I'm actually going to see this show at last," Brooke said smiling, not even attempting to conceal her child-like excitement as she leant over the balcony to look beneath her. As she scanned the crowd, the intense anticipation soon turned to confusion as she narrowed her eyes, squinting as her vision honed in on a familiar figure. Megan! She would recognise that white fur-hooded jacket anywhere. *How could it be?* Brooke watched as Megan's arm casually encircled the woman sat beside her, a small child on her lap. Her mind veered between shock and disbelief. What on earth was she doing here, in London with another woman?

"Hey don't lean too far over, I'd hate to traumatise all these kids if you fell over," Danni joked, gently enclosing Brooke's wrist with her hand and giving it a small tug.

Brooke barely heard her. Her mind was too busy concentrating on the scene playing out beneath her – they looked like a perfect family of three. Reluctantly, Brooke eased back into her seat as the lights dimmed and the stage curtain parted.

She felt Danni's cheek brush her ear, the sweet scent of perfume assailing her senses. "Are you okay?"

Brooke turned to her and held her gaze. She opened her mouth to speak, but no words came out. She was too stunned, too shocked to utter a sound. Instead, she nodded dumbly and slowly looked back to the stage as a little boy in pyjamas appeared, dwarfed by the stage props. She sat paralysed, trying her hardest to concentrate on the figure through blurred vision. Maybe there was a simple explanation for Megan being here, perhaps she had told her but Brooke had forgotten. Yes that was it – what other reason could there be? The alternative was just too painful.

"So is this how you would have imagined it?" Danni whispered into her ear, the warmth of her body emanating through her thin jumper.

"Yes," she said flatly as she moved to the edge of her seat and gazed downwards again. The little girl was laughing with glee and clapping her little hands as the white blob of the Snowman appeared and the music began. The woman's head turned to face Megan and Brooke's heart leapt into her mouth as she beheld the two of them looking at each other in a way that revealed they were more than just friends. She stared in horror as Megan's face buried itself in the woman's neck.

Brooke's hands gripped the rail; trembling, sweaty. She jerked back a little when she felt Danni's hand cover hers.

Danni stared at her with a puzzled expression. "Brooke, you look like you've seen a ghost," Danni whispered as the song tempered off.

Brooke inhaled deeply and shook her head. "I'm afraid it's a lot worse than that."

***

As they left the theatre hall, Megan pulled Alison to one side. She smiled warmly. "About earlier, I hope we can put it aside and enjoy the rest of the day."

"Of course we can. It was such a lovely performance, I don't want to fight anymore."

Megan lifted her hand to stroke Alison's face, then half-turned towards Kelly with a smile. Suddenly, she froze, her hand stiffening, before dropping limply to her side. Standing barely six feet away was the last person she expected to see now – Brooke!

Adrenaline coursed through her veins as she saw Brooke's eyes skipping rapidly over the crowd as if looking for something, something she was desperate to find. Suddenly, she caught sight of Megan.

Brooke stood rigid, her piercing eyes boring into

hers. Megan felt the blood rush from her face.

"Megan? Are you okay?" Alison shook her shoulder.

"I ..."

Megan watched in slow motion as Brooke straightened her back, tilted her chin up and headed in her direction.

Alison shook her arm. "Megan, I asked if you're all right?"

"What?" Megan replied, bracing herself as Brooke made a beeline towards them. Megan glanced to the exit. Should she just run? Too late. Brooke was in front of her, her face full of bewilderment and disgust. "Megan! What the hell? Aren't you meant to be in America?"

"I am. I was."

"So what are you doing here? Why haven't you called?" Brooke glanced at Alison. "And who's your friend?"

"I'm Alison," she said taking a step forward. "Megan's *partner*."

"Partner?" Brooke flicked a look of revulsion at Megan, her suspicions confirmed with those two small words. "Is she your partner, Megan?" she demanded, raising her voice as she took a step forward.

"Listen Brooke ..."

"And who exactly are you?" Alison said, her face a sea of confusion.

Brooke's eyes widened. "Me? Well, I *was* Megan's partner until thirty seconds ago."

"What the hell is she talking about, Megan?" Alison snapped.

Megan's hands trembled, the shock of what was happening finally penetrating her brain. The day of reckoning was here. She had been caught. She thought desperately of a way to diffuse the situation. Shaking her head in hopeless resignation she said, "Nothing. Look ladies, there's been a misunderstanding here."

Brooke rested her hands on her hips. "Really? A misunderstanding? Well let's hear it then. Come on, I'm sure Alison would be interested to know how the last time you left our bed, you said you were going to see your mum for two weeks."

"What. Your mum's alive? But … but you told me she was dead."

Megan swung her head towards Alison. "I can explain that. I was talking about my step mum. She's dead."

Megan noticed that they were beginning to attract attention. The woman she had met in the line earlier glanced at her, refusing to make eye contact, as if embarrassed by the scene.

"So this is what all the cloak-and-dagger behaviour was about. Another woman," Brooke said.

Kelly pushed her way past Danni, who remained silent throughout the encounter, and tugged on Megan's coat. "Mummy M, the lady wants the money for my ice cream."

This was all she fucking needed, the brat on top of all of this.

Megan looked down at Kelly, rage boiling inside her. She was trapped, caught like an animal in a snare. Unable to contain the emotion, she snapped at the little girl with utter vitriol, "Just leave me the fuck alone, will you? You little brat." Almost immediately, Megan clamped her hand to her mouth.

Kelly's angelic face froze. Within seconds she lowered her chin down to her chest, her bottom lip quivering, her little body racked with sobs, as tears streamed from her eyes.

Alison's face was thunderous as she spun Megan around by the shoulder, and with one swift movement, struck her cheek with full force, leaving a white handprint. "Don't you ever talk to my daughter like that. Ever!"

Brooke's face twisted into a mask of incredulity as she looked down at the crying child. She shook her head in absolute disbelief.

A nervous tick pulled at the corner of Megan's mouth. "Oh Ali, I'm sorry. Kelly I'm so, so," Megan said desperately, reaching out for the child.

"Don't touch her!" Alison said, scooping Kelly into her arms protectively.

Megan was lost. Beaten. "Look, this is all a misunderstanding. I–"

An elderly man with short grey hair and baggy eyes approached the group.

"Excuse me ladies, is there a problem here?"

They all turned to him.

"No," Brooke said calmly. "There's no problem.

It's all been sorted. Sorry to have caused a disturbance. Come on, Danni. Let's go. I think we've seen quite enough."

Megan stood rooted to the spot, watching Brooke's retreating back. She turned back to Alison, making a last pathetic plea.

"Alison, I'm so sorry about that. I can explain. Brooke was an old girlfriend. She's got a bit of a problem letting go. Look, let's forget about it and go back to the hotel. We don't want to spoil things for Kelly. This is her day, like we planned," she said, breaking into a nervous smile and putting her hand on Alison's shoulder.

Alison brushed Megan's hand away, shaking with rage. She lowered Kelly to the floor, fumbled in her pocket for some money and gave it to her. "Here sweetheart, go and pay for your ice cream, I'll be there in a minute." She bent over and lovingly kissed the top of her head.

When Kelly was out of earshot, she turned to face Megan, her eyes blazing, her lips trembling. "You listen to me and listen good. Don't let me ever see you near me, or my daughter again, do you hear me?"

Megan nodded and bowed her head.

Alison leaned in and whispered in her ear. "I swear to god, you show your face again, you're gonna live to regret it."

Megan rubbed her cheek with her hand as she watched Alison spin around and go in search of Kelly.

She was left standing alone, defeated. Bitter.

She attempted to shrug it off, reassuring herself with her usual arrogant banter. *They're no big loss.* She was planning on getting rid of them anyway. *Let Alison find out the hard way. Women aren't going to be knocking down her door, not for a single mum with a brat.*

Megan turned quickly as if suddenly invigorated by a glimmer of hope. Maybe she still had time to find Brooke. Perhaps all wasn't lost yet, surely she would be able to talk her round.

On the pavement outside the theatre, she looked from left to right but there was no sign of her. Oh well, she'd wait for her at her flat. Maybe prepare her a nice meal, a candlelit bath. A smile broke out on her face. In spite of everything, she was still sure of her ability to make things right. Such was the depth of her delusion.

Chapter Forty-Two

"Whoa, Brooke! Slow down, I can't keep up with you," Danni implored, jogging alongside her visibly shaken friend. She grabbed Brooke's arm in an effort to halt her progress. Brooke reluctantly stopped, head bowed, and ran her hands through her waves of thick brown hair.

"Hey, listen. Are you ok? Jesus Christ, that was insane."

"Tell me about it," Brooke answered abruptly.

"Brooke, I'm so sorry you had to find out that way. God, that poor child. Do you know who they were?" Danni asked.

Brooke shook her head. "Never seen them before in my life. I thought Megan hated kids." She shrugged her shoulders. "Just goes to show how much I know. Do you know what the worst thing is?" Brooke's deep blue eyes welled up. "I don't even care about the cheating. Yes, it hurts but it's more the fact she's been lying all this time, making me think it was all in my head – that I was being unreasonable. God, how could I have been so dumb? I knew it. I bloody knew it."

"Don't be hard on yourself, Brooke. You were giving her the benefit of the doubt, that's all. What do you want to do now? Go back to yours, maybe pick up some things?"

"That's the last place I want to go. If I know Megan, that's the first place she'll go to try and talk me round." The frown on Brooke's face deepened. "No, I just want to be far away. Some place where I don't have to face anyone. Some place where I can drink lots of wine and feel bloody sorry for myself. Just for a while."

"You can come over to mine?"

"Won't Josh be there? No, I don't want to be any trouble. I'll just check myself into a hotel; I can shut out the world and have a good think."

"Okay. Well, at least let me take you to one, get you checked in. I don't want to leave you like this, so upset."

"Thanks Danni. I can't think straight at the moment so it probably wouldn't be a bad idea. I'm so sorry to put you out. Bloody drama. I wish you hadn't been dragged into all this."

Danni stood by the kerb and hailed a cab. Half an hour later, Brooke had checked into a suite, with roll-top bath and garden views in a nearby hotel. Ironically, it was a popular choice as a wedding venue, with its beautiful old world charm and heavy stone walls. She felt a little extravagant, but the thought of being crammed into some pokey hotel room was too much to bear, not after everything that had happened.

Danni took a bottle of chilled white wine from the ice bucket, poured Brooke a large glass and handed it to her where she sat on the bed.

"Aren't you having one?" Brooke asked, gesturing towards a second glass.

"Oh … yes. I didn't know whether you wanted to

be by yourself."

Brooke gave a choked, desperate laugh. "No, it's fine. Besides, I can't be sitting here drinking alone. That really would be tragic." She swallowed the despair in her throat, closing her eyes as she sipped the first mouthful. "What a mess," she said in a low, tormented voice. She was assailed by a terrible sense of bitterness. "How could I have been so stupid?"

A raw and primitive grief overwhelmed Brooke as she stood up, glass in hand and walked slowly to the window as if under water. Conflicting emotions followed one another in quick succession. Anger, hurt, relief, and more than anything else, shock. Why had she ignored the signs? Was it because she couldn't bear to face the truth? Was she afraid of losing Megan or was it fear of being alone? Brooke floundered in an agonising maelstrom. For the past few months she had been living like a bird in a cage, and now, even when the door was left wide open, she felt afraid to fly through it. Such was the hurt. But now the difficult decision to move on had been made for her, though it had been done in the cruellest possible way. She bowed her head and wept, deep sobs racking her body as she cried hopeless empty tears.

Well it was all over now. No more guessing games, no more waiting for phone calls that never came, no more … Megan. Feeling the pressure of Danni's comforting hand on her shoulder, she raised her face with all the dignity she could muster. With her other hand, Danni drew Brooke's head onto her own shoulder, rubbing her back in a circular motion as she shushed her in a low soothing tone.

"I know there's nothing I can say to make you feel better, but for what it's worth I think she's a bloody idiot," Danni whispered with quiet emphasis. "If you were my partner, I'd ..."

Brooke drew back and looked at her, her eyes shining with tears. "You'd what?"

Danni blinked, remaining silent for a long moment. Hesitation flashed in her eyes as they travelled over Brooke's face. "I'd never let you go." A huskiness lingered in her tone.

They stood staring at one another for a few seconds before Brooke smiled and touched Danni's cheek softly with her hand.

"You're a good person, Danni. Josh is a lucky man."

Heavy with melancholy, Brooke leant her head forward so it rested on the base of Danni's neck.

Brooke let out a long sigh and remained motionless for a while.

"Why don't you have a lay down?" Danni said, raising her hand to touch Brooke's head, stroking it softly.

Brooke tried to gather her wits, to say something but only managed a mute nod in response. Danni released Brooke from her embrace and guided her towards the bed.

As Brooke lay down, weariness enveloped her as she attempted to concentrate on the anonymous hotel painting of flowers in a field. As tension ebbed away, Brooke sank into an exhausted sleep.

***

The room was darker than before. Opening her eyes, Brooke felt as if she'd been thrown from a nightmare. Her first reaction was panic. *Where was she?* She shifted, as though to rise to her feet, but realised there was a warm hand wrapped around her waist. Unconsciously, it tightened its hold on her at her movement. Brooke turned her head to look over her shoulder. Seeing Danni, she relaxed. *Right, the hotel…*

Settling back down on the pillow, she leaned over and flipped the switch on the lamp next to her. Looking down towards her feet, she noticed her shoes had been removed and the duvet pulled up around her. Now, though, it rested across her hips. She shivered as a cold breeze blew in through the open window. Grabbing the duvet, she moved to tug it higher. It caught and when she pulled again, she could see the problem. Danni had slept on top of the covers. Her body weight now had the duvet held fast. Turning to face her, she paused to study her features. Her soft skin, her cheekbones, the delicacy of her features and for the first time, she noticed a small beauty spot just by the base of her ear.

Brooke reached forward and pushed a loose strand of hair away from Danni's eye and lingered, letting her finger trail down to her perfectly proportioned lips.

It was supposed to be a gentle, soft caress.

Brooke didn't expect Danni to wake. When Danni opened her mouth, her eyes sprang open, too. She was watching her, sleepiness instantly gone.

"Brooke?"

Brooke jerked back. "Sorry I didn't mean to wake you," Brooke whispered.

Danni smiled lazily. "Don't worry. I'm a light sleeper plus I liked what you were doing."

Brooke looked confused.

"You look surprised," Danni said.

"I am, considering you're not–"

Sitting up on her elbow, Danni leaned over her. "What? I'm not gay?"

"That and because you're engaged."

Danni stammered, "Not any more. Look, well, Josh and I, we're not together anymore. I'm not engaged."

"What? Why didn't you tell me? Oh God, look at us both. This really is Heartbreak Hotel."

"I didn't get a chance to say anything after what happened today – there didn't seem to be an appropriate moment."

"I'm so sorry, Danni. So sorry."

"It's okay. Look, I really don't want to talk about it now. Can we just focus on you? How are you feeling?" she said leaning up on her elbow.

"Better. Much better." She couldn't believe it but she actually did. It was as if by releasing Megan, she had somehow been given a new lease of life. She now realised that loving Megan had been a curse rather than the blessing it should be.

"I can't wait to start making new changes in my life. I feel ready to be me again."

"Good for you, Brooke. What's your first mission?"

"To be more bold, more impulsive."

"Hmm, that could get you in a lot of trouble."

"I don't care. Being careful up until now hasn't exactly made my life a bundle of joy. I want to be more like you. Carefree and fun loving."

"I like you just the way you are, Brooke. Don't change a thing. She cheated on you because she has a problem. It has nothing to do with you. You're everything anybody could wish for in a woman."

Danni cupped Brooke's face with her free hand. The two women stared at one other intently. There was a closeness between them now that seemed to make them completely unafraid to expose their vulnerabilities. Two souls meeting, sharing one precious moment. With assumed tranquillity, but an inward tremor, Brooke leaned forward and pressed her lips against the nape of Danni's neck.

An electrifying shudder reverberated through her as she moved her mouth over Danni's with a hunger that belied her outward calm. Their kiss was a glorious embrace of tongues, a mimic of intercourse; all heat, moisture, thrusting, and writhing. When they came up for air, both panting heavily, Brooke saw how dark Danni's eyes had become and knew hers were probably the same. Danni wanted her. Desired her.

And Brooke felt the same heady lust.

Brooke's fingers moved down Danni's neck, leading the way for her tongue and lips. Danni arched to allow her full access and took advantage of Brooke's preoccupation to slip button after button free from her shirt. Each unbuttoning exposed more of her womanly attributes. As Brooke nipped at the curve where Danni's shoulder and neck met, she snaked her hand into the front of her jeans. She worked the zipper down then, anxious to touch her. *How would she feel?*

Danni's fingers grasped Brookes and pulled them away. Holding them, she pressed their palms together.

"Are you sure about this?" Danni asked.

"More than anything," Brooke answered, using her hands to emphasise the point. Running them down Danni's sides, she placed her hands possessively on her breasts. She paused to trace the toned muscles of her stomach, then slid her fingers to her hipbones and down the sleekness of her thighs. Despite the layer of clothing between her palms and her skin, the heated warmth of Danni enticed her. Danni was on fire. *For her.*

Neither said a word as Brooke straddled Danni's waist, the weight of her body pressing Danni down into the bed beneath her. Consumed with passion, she took hold of Danni's wrists and pinned them above her head. Leaning over her, eyeing her flushed face with a look of burning intent, the thrill of desire coursed through her veins as she lowered her mouth onto Danni's. Rocking back and forth on her knees, her hot wet tongue glided around the outline of Danni's soft lips.

Brooke's breathing deepened, quickened as she smiled down at her playmate. What she saw in Danni's eyes was the look of total surrender. Intoxicated by the moment, Brooke teased Danni's lips apart, darting her tongue in and out with a mixture of light and forceful strokes until at last their tongues met again in a long passionate kiss. Danni attempted to free her hands from Brooke's grip.

"You're too impatient," Brooke said.

"But I've waited for this for so long."

Brooke released her grip on Danni, sat back on her heels and moved her hands to her shirt, slowly releasing it one button at a time. Brooke's shirt fell from her body, revealing a toned body with firm breasts half-covered by a black bra. Danni let out a moan as she reached out to touch them.

Brooke laughed. "Soon." She then slid from the bed and slipped out of the confines of her tight jeans, knickers, and bra. Danni lifted herself off the bed and stood before Brooke. Leaning down, Danni's tongue caressed Brooke's sensitive swollen nipple with tantalising possessiveness. The thrill from her touch sent the pit of her stomach into a wild whirl. Adrenaline raced through Brooke's body. She tore at Danni's clothes with wild impatience until they were both naked. Her senses went into a spin. *Is this really happening?*

Brooke's lips pressed hard against Danni's mouth

until they both fell back onto the bed, hands roaming restlessly over each other's body. Her skin tingled as her hand squeezed Danni's breast firmly, rolling her erect nipple between her fingertips.

Brooke slipped her hand down Danni's body, parting her thighs for a gentle exploration of her womanhood. Danni rolled over onto her back, moaning softly as Brooke slid her fingers inside her. Danni arched her back in anticipation of every thrust, her breathing increasing, faster and deeper as Brooke felt Danni's muscles contract every time she entered her.

Brooke's heartbeat throbbed against her ear as she enjoyed the warmth of Danni's juices. *She is so wet.*

Brooke closed her mouth over Danni's nipple, the tip of her tongue caressing, licking it as excitement steadily rose in her own body. Manoeuvring herself back on top of Danni, Brooke rubbed herself over Danni's engorged clitoris. Brooke teased Danni with firm strokes. Danni groaned louder, lifting her hips off the bed as she clamped her hands over Brooke's backside, pressing her down harder, grinding in rhythm with her. Brooke lifted her face back to Danni's, her tongue finding renewed pleasure in the warmth of her lover's mouth.

With a fevered groan, Danni buried her face in Brooke's neck. "Oh my … God, Brooke!"

Brooke felt Danni convulse in pleasure as she was hurtled to the point of no return, still rhythmically moving her hips to prolong the moment.

Danni pulled Brooke's knees apart enabling Brooke to straddle her. With her hand underneath her, Danni stroked Brooke's clit whilst teasing her nipple with her tongue. For Brooke it was too much to bear, she grabbed Danni's hand and forced her fingers inside her. Brooke rode Danni hard, all of the hurt and anger towards Megan melted away as Brooke was drawn to a height of passion she had never known before. She collapsed forward, Danni still inside her, and pressed her lips to Danni's, savouring her softness.

All she wanted in her life now was Danni – her body and her mind – all of her.

Chapter Forty-Three

A dull grey light edged around the break in the curtain, the hypnotic sound of heavy rain and forceful winds sounded outside the window. Brooke wasn't in any rush to get up. She wasn't ready for reality to intrude on what was an incredible moment. She wanted to savour it for as long as she could. For the past hour, Brooke had been watching Danni while she slept.

Brooke felt a sense of freedom and gratitude for the lucky escape she'd had when she woke that morning. If she hadn't found out about the other woman, how long would Megan have strung her along for? In her heart she knew the answer. For as long as she could without getting caught.

Danni stirred beside her, opening her eyes, a lazy smile stretched along her lips.

"Good morning," Brooke said tracing her finger along Danni's collar bone, her nerves ignited by just one touch.

Danni smiled. "Yes it is isn't it? Unless you're going to say you regret anything."

"No. No, I'm not."

"Good. I thought I was going to wake up this morning and realise it had all been a dream."

"Believe me, that was no dream. I've got the scratches to prove it."

Danni buried her face in the pillow. "Oh no. I'm sorry about that. I got a bit, you know, carried away."

Brooke laughed. "Did you hear me complaining?"

Danni peeked up at her. "Actually no, I didn't." She blushed.

Brooke leaned over and burrowed her face into her chest, caressing her breast with her cheek. "I remember. I was there after all."

Danni kissed the top of her head. "Listen, if you have any further improper intentions, I'm going to have to take a shower first."

Brooke rolled over onto her back. "I'll go in after you. I'll order breakfast now. What do you fancy?"

"You, with ketchup, in a baguette," Danni joked, as she climbed over Brooke, jumped down onto the floor, and headed for the bathroom.

Just as she reached the door, Brooke said, "You never did tell me about you and Josh splitting up last night."

"Ahh yes. About that." She walked back towards the bed.

Brooke's mobile rang and she glanced at it on the bedside table. "Shit. Sorry. It's Roy. I emailed him to tell him I wouldn't be in for a few days. He's probably pissed off with me." She reached across and grabbed it.

"Oh no. I'll go and have a quick shower then tell you about it over breakfast."

As Danni strode back towards the bathroom and shut the door behind her, Brooke slid open her phone.

"Hi Roy, I…"

"Are you alone?"

Brooke jerked up into a sitting position, alerted by the sound of his voice. "Um, yes. Is everything okay?"

"No, not really."

She frowned. Was there something wrong with one of her edits? Was he having problems with an author? "What's happened?"

Roy was silent for a few seconds before letting out a long breath. "It seems my son has made a fool out of me."

"Josh?"

"Yes, Josh. Apparently he thought it would be funny to pull the wool over my eyes."

Brooke swung her legs over the side of the bed and scanned the floor for her hair band. All the while holding the phone between her head and shoulder. Upon finding it she quickly pulled her hair into a bunch on top of her head, "I'm sorry Roy. I'm not following you."

"Let's just say there won't be any wedding, no grandchildren. Nothing. Ever."

Was that why they had broken up? Josh had met someone else? If this was the case, poor Danni, it seemed was in the same boat as her. "Oh Roy. I'm sorry to hear that. But he'll meet someone else. He's only young yet. He'll meet another lucky lady."

"That's the point Brooke. He won't because he's GAY!"

The words just didn't make sense. "He's what?"

"You heard me. Gay and so is his make-believe wife."

The revelation hit Brooke full force. "Danni's gay?"

"Yes. Apparently so."

She hung her head between her legs, unable to comprehend what she was being told. "Are you sure you don't mean bisexual, that—"

"—I know the difference Brooke, and no, my son has no interest in women whatsoever. Danni is the one who has an eye for the ladies not Josh."

So that was why Danni seemed so experienced in bed last night. She felt humiliated, lied to – again.

"But why Roy? Why would they do this? I don't understand?"

"I wish I knew. I got an email from Josh last night, but I only just read it this morning."

"And he didn't say why?"

"Not exactly. He said some odd things in the email. Anyway, I'll be finding out this morning when I pay them both a visit. I really hope that boy has a good excuse for pulling this little stunt."

Brooke's heart was heavy with shock and disappointment. Why had Danni lied to her? Why didn't she tell her the truth before they had slept together? She fought to hide her own turmoil.

"I'll see you when I come in, Roy. I'm sorry."

"It's okay, Brooke. Sounds like you've got your own problems. I read your email about Megan. I'm so sorry my dear. Take a few days off and get your head together."

"Thanks, Roy. I appreciate your understanding

and I hope you sort things out with Josh."

"Thanks, Brooke. I just wish I understood why he lied. Anyway, I'll see you soon."

Brooke dropped back on the bed and threw her phone down.

Danni was gay. She could barely believe it. What the fuck was wrong with the world? Didn't anyone tell the truth anymore? Rising once more, she gathered her clothes together, putting them on in a rush. She must be the biggest fool going – first Megan and now Danni. She had trusted Danni. She thought she was a genuine person. But she wasn't. She was just like Megan.

Danni emerged from the bathroom smiling as she rubbed her head with a fluffy white towel. She looked startled when she saw Brooke getting dressed.

"Hey, I thought we were going hang out here some more, before you went home."

"Was that before or after you told me about Josh?"

Danni walked to her side and rubbed her arm. "Oh, please don't worry about that. It was amicable. I will tell you all about it later."

Brooke shrugged it off, pulling her jumper roughly over her head. "You mean it was never on in the first place."

Danni's face creased with confusion, her cheeks pale. "Sorry?"

"Don't play coy with me Danni. Your stupid game is up," she said, choking on her own words.

Shock lit up in Danni's eyes. "Game? I don't see–
"

Brooke ran her hand over her face trying to quell her anger. She could feel the blood racing to her cheeks.

"Oh God. Are you kidding me? Are you going to continue to lie even though your stupid little secret is out in the open? I know about you and Josh, Danni. You and your fake engagement."

She started for the door and Danni went after her, grabbing her arm.

"Please. Brooke wait," she pleaded. "How? Who told you?"

"Does it matter? The most important thing here is that it wasn't you."

"Please Brooke, just sit down a minute and let me explain. I promise you'll understand when I tell you. It wasn't supposed to hurt anyone."

Brooke was drained. "Well it has."

Danni opened her mouth to speak but before she could Brooke said, "Do you know what? Just save it. I don't want to know. I have had it with being made a fool out of. What is wrong with people and their games, stupid bloody games!"

She opened the door, stepped outside and headed down the hallway.

Danni stood at the doorway in a towel, calling after her. "Please Brooke, believe me when I say this had nothing to do with how I feel about you. It's not a game. I really care about you. I'm falling in love with you."

Brooke stopped in her tracks and slowly turned around. "Love? Don't make me laugh. Do you even know the meaning of the word? If you did, you'd know how important trust is."

Before Danni could respond, Brooke turned to the fire escape and disappeared through the door.

Chapter Forty-Four

Danni staggered around the hotel room in a daze, attempting to get dressed.

What the hell had just happened? How had Brooke found out about her and Josh? Pangs of regret tore at her heart.

She chastised herself. Why hadn't she told her the truth last night? This morning? *Because you're a bloody idiot that's why.* Always putting things off, thinking they could get done another day. Why oh why hadn't she gone with her gut instinct? She knew no good could come from lying. Her good intentions to help a friend had gone horrifically wrong.

This was a mess of her own making.

She slipped into her jeans, tied her wet hair into a ponytail and left the room.

She sifted through events in her mind. Perhaps Megan had somehow managed to uncover their secret, she wondered as she jumped into a cab outside the hotel. No, she was just getting paranoid now. The only person who could have told her was Josh and, for some reason, he wasn't answering his phone.

Racing through her front door, she burst into his bedroom without knocking.

"Josh, Josh wake up," she called, shaking his shoulder until he roused. The stench of alcohol was overwhelming.

"Not so loud Danni, my head's killing me," he

said quietly.

She dashed from the room and minutes later returned carrying a glass of Alka Seltzer fizzing away in a tall stem glass.

"Josh, drink this. You're not going to believe what's happened."

He rolled over onto his back and she supported his head while he drank the medicine.

"Josh, Brooke knows about us. Your dad knows about us."

He flopped back on his pillow with a groan. "I know."

Danni tilted her head, unsure she'd heard him correctly. "What do you mean, you know?"

"I told him last night. Well, I emailed him. I was trying to get hold of you to tell you, but your phone was switched off. I drank a bottle of vodka and I emailed him to tell him the truth."

She didn't know what to do. Kiss him and congratulate him or slap him.

"God, I wish you'd have waited until I'd spoken to Brooke. I didn't get the chance to tell her the truth. I guess your dad did that this morning. Now she thinks I'm a fraud."

Josh's hand flew to his mouth. "Danni, I'm so sorry. I told him so you could stop lying to Brooke," he said, his voice choking as he continued. "Oh God, I've really put my foot in it haven't I?"

"It's okay. I know you didn't mean for this to happen," she said flopping down onto his bed.

"If I've messed this up for you I'll never forgive myself."

"It's okay. There's no point in us falling out as well. What a mess. I just need to explain to Brooke properly, tell her it wasn't meant to hurt anyone. Oh God." She tried to muster a smile. "Hey, I'm really proud of you for telling your dad, even if you were as high as a kite."

Josh looked up at her with sorrowful eyes.

"I would hug you and all but." She looked down at his bare chest. "Oh what the hell, come here," she said pulling Josh into an embrace.

Leaning back Danni said, "So, have you spoken to your dad this morning?"

Josh shook his head, blinking quickly to release the tears.

"Well he obviously read it. And he called Brooke."

"Did he sound angry?" he asked, his voice still choked with emotion.

"I don't know. But Brooke sure was."

He sniffed a little and looked at her sheepishly. "What were you doing with Brooke? Did you spend the night with her?"

Danni glanced downwards. "No comment"

"Did you?"

"Yep," she whispered.

"And this morning she found out … about us?"

"Yep."

"Oh my God, it just gets worse!" Tears formed in

his eyes again.

"It's fine, Josh. How were you to know? At the end of the day it's my own damn fault. I should have come clean with her before I slept with her."

"Oh, D. I'm so sorry. What are you going to do about it?"

"There's nothing I can do. I lied to her."

Chapter Forty-Five

As soon as Brooke entered her flat, she heard movement in the kitchen. She braced herself. She wasn't in the mood to hear any more crap from anyone. She just wanted Megan to leave her key and never show her face again.

Megan breezed out of the kitchen with a mug in her hand. She looked at Brooke as if she had just stepped out for milk.

"Hi, babe, where've you been?"

Brooke frowned. Was she serious? "Pardon?"

"I thought we could go for breakfast this morning and talk about yesterday. Clear up any misunderstandings."

Brooke brushed past her and walked into the living room, Megan fast on her heels. "Are you on drugs, Megan?"

Megan looked surprised at the question which led Brooke to begin to really start questioning Megan's sanity.

"No why?" she replied, sitting on the edge of an armchair, slurping her drink like it was any other carefree Sunday.

Despite how down she felt, Brooke let out a genuine shriek of laughter. "I suppose you're going to deny that was you yesterday at the theatre."

"No, that was me. It just wasn't what it looked like. Alison was–"

Brooke shook her head in amusement. "Oh, so she dumped your arse?"

Megan smirked. "No, she didn't. Like I was saying, Alison is an old school friend of mine. Yes, I won't deny it, we've had a fling in the past, but that was way before I met you," she said in a calm reasonable voice.

"So her saying you were her partner was in her imagination was it?"

"No, not at all. It's a little game we play. She thought you were an ex and she was pretending to be my partner so you'd leave me alone. Anyway, I think I'm the one who should be angry with you. I caught you sneaking around with that Danni woma–"

Brooke held her hands up in the air. "You caught me? Oh God, Megan, just stop this bullshit. I want you out of my flat. Take all your crap and go."

"I don't know why you're getting so hysterical Brooke – I was out with a friend. Her daughter wanted to see *The Snowman* so I said I'd accompany them."

"Despite the fact that you're meant to be in America with your mum?"

"I got back yesterday. I was coming home and I bumped into her."

"And I suppose the little girl calling you Mummy M doesn't stand for Mummy Megan. Do you know something? I think you're insane. You really think I'm going to buy that bullshit?"

"It's the truth."

"So why haven't I been able to get in touch with

you since you left?"

"The phone lines were down, and I lost my mobile."

"Hmm, I see. Okay let me see your passport."

Megan looked flustered. "My passport? What for?"

Brooke held out her hand, palm upwards. "Just let me see it. If you're telling the truth your passport will be stamped with your arrival into the States."

"I don't know where it is. I think I left it in my bag at work."

"You know what? I hope you'll both be very happy together." Brooke breezed past Megan, walked to the front door and opened it.

Megan followed her again. "Let's talk about this Brooke – don't do anything you're gonna regret." Her voice held a sharp edge to it.

"It's too late for that. I already have for way too long."

"Please, Brooke, let me explain."

"It doesn't matter anymore, Megan. You could be sleeping with the whole of London for all I care. I really couldn't give a toss. It's over. I just want you out of my life. Now get out!"

Megan glared at her as she stormed out of the flat, Brooke slamming the door behind her.

Chapter Forty-Six

Danni sat on one end of the sofa, Josh at the other, his head bowed like a naughty schoolboy. Roy had the floor. If he didn't stop pacing, he'd wear a patch in their new rug.

"*Why* is what I keep asking myself? Why would my own son, my own flesh and blood lie to me like this?"

Danni jumped up to defend Josh. "Because you–"

Josh stood as well and slowly walked over to stand in front of his dad. "–It's okay Danni."

Danni couldn't help but notice how mature Josh suddenly looked for his age.

Josh stared his dad straight in the eye. "Do you remember last year, when I told you about my friend Adam and how we wanted to buy a house together?"

Roy looked perplexed. "You mean that rather strange boy you were hanging out with?"

Josh's features hardened. "Yes that one – that 'strange' gay boy. The way you behaved about him made me feel too ashamed to tell you who I really was." He shook his head in disgust. "You made me feel like I was nothing."

Roy looked like someone had punched him in the guts as he took a step back. "Is that what you think Josh, *I'm homophobic*?"

Josh puffed his chest out and narrowed his eyes. "Yes I do. *That's* why I didn't tell you I was gay!"

Roy looked defeated, like the stuffing had been knocked out of him.

"Josh, I was just concerned for you, I didn't want you to rush in and buy a flat with someone like Adam. Your mum was ill. I thought you were in turmoil. My dislike of that young man had nothing to do with his sexuality, I just thought he was irresponsible, the way he lived his life – drugs, no ambition. I was concerned he would just drag you down," he said, his voice slightly shaking. Roy's eyes welled up. "I'm sorry, son. I'm sorry and ashamed that I made you feel that way," he said, his eyes dropping to the floor.

Josh rubbed his hand over his face, suddenly looking very weary.

"Come here," Roy said engulfing him in a hug. "There's nothing on this earth you could do to make me ashamed of you. When your mum was alive you were the apple of her eye and you're still mine. You're my son and I'm proud of you, whichever way you swing," he said with a wink.

Danni's eyes welled up. She was going to cry. It was like having the Jerry Springer show right there in her front room.

Roy patted Josh's back. "And dragging your friend into your mess as well. Whatever must you have thought of me, Danni?" he said turning his attention to her.

The corner of her mouth curved up into a wide grin.

"Well I did think it was a bit odd, you being … I mean being so nice and easy-going." She glanced down at her chest and said with a nervous laugh, "On a side note, this isn't going to have a knock on affect with my book is? I mean, I don't have to give back the advance, do I?"

Roy roared with laughter. "Of course not. I meant it when I said your relationship had no bearing on my decision to publish your book."

Her head shot up. "Phew, that's a relief."

Chapter Forty-Seven

The Boeing 747 soared over the Pacific Ocean like a bird, leaving a white mist trailing behind it. The passengers in the first class compartment had been fed and watered and were settling down for the remaining four hours left to London. Megan was going to have to go flat hunting again. Just the thought of it depressed her. Rental prices in London were astronomical, even for a studio flat. Thankfully, Jackie had invited her stay until she found somewhere else. In all seriousness, she could not believe Brooke had asked her to leave. She needn't have bothered though, Megan assured herself, as she had already made up her mind to leave anyway. She could do without the hassle of both Brooke and Alison, it was time to strike out on her own. Megan had returned to Edinburgh that night to collect her belongings from Alison's and had left without a second glance.

She would never make the mistake of dating a parent again, regardless of how "respectable" it made one look.

The bell rang and she rose to her feet, making the short walk to the passenger. Megan smiled down at the woman whose glass she had been refilling with champagne every twenty minutes. Nervous flyer but very attractive. She was in her early thirties, slim build, dark hair, and impeccably dressed. The lady oozed money.

"Don't worry, not long to go now," Megan said handing her a glass whilst making sure her fingers brushed against the woman's. The woman looked up at her, a knowing look in her eyes.

"Thank you." She eyed her name tag. "Megan."

"Anytime. If you need anything and I mean anything, just let me know."

The woman's smile acknowledged she understood the intent behind the words. Megan quickly scribbled her number on a napkin and handed it to the woman. She looked giddy with excitement as she slipped it into her bag. *As easy as that!* Maybe she wouldn't need to crash at Jackie's after all.

Chapter Forty-Eight

The beeping sound of the recycling lorry abruptly broke into Danni's sleep. She looked towards the window through one slit eye and groaned at the invasion.

Bastards.

She rolled onto her back and stared up into the darkness. *What kind of time is this?*

The noisy buggers had just interrupted a wonderful dream in which she was touring the US with her new book. The public and media had been lapping her up – personal appearances, talk-shows. There had only been standing room at the many bookshops she had visited. But the best part of the dream had been the woman who had stood beside her through it all – Brooke. For some reason her subconscious had conveniently managed to forget that Brooke wasn't actually speaking to her.

Christmas had come and gone all too soon. The only contact she'd had with her since had been work related. A couple of brief emails were the extent of it.

She decided there was no point in trying to go back to sleep. No doubt as soon as the recycling lorry disappeared, drilling from the building site a few doors down would start, followed by kids making noise on their way to school. No, she'd get up, do something useful like have a chocolate muffin and cup of coffee, while she updated her twitter with the latest about her book.

She had been surprised to find she actually had twenty followers on her page. Okay maybe not twenty exactly, after you subtracted family, friends, and pets – it was more like four. But four was better than none and by God she needed something positive to cling on to.

She took a shower and dressed before making the coffee and scoffing a couple of chocolate chip muffins. Now she was ready for the day. She made her way to the living room and settled down with her computer on her lap. Booting it up, she went straight to her twitter page – The Self-Help Diva.

One new notification.

"When's your book coming out Diva? I can't wait to read it!" From Twitter handle: @downtrodden20.

"Hi downtrodden – the e-book will be out at the end of the year with the paperback to follow a few months after."

Wow, look at her with her very own paperback book.

The door creaked open and Josh strutted over the threshold sporting black boxer shorts, a six pack, and hair that stood to attention like Ms Dias' in that scene from *Something About Mary*. He rubbed his eyes. "What are you doing up so early?" he asked.

"I don't know how you sleep through the bloody racket from those recycling lorries. I was making my way down to the earthquake shelter until I realised we don't own one."

Josh flopped down on the sofa beside her. "My dad woke me. He's invited us to a launch of some author's book tomorrow. I said we'd go. I think he wants to get back to normal, you know, put it all behind us."

"Okay cool. That's exactly what I want to do too."

She cleared her throat. "Do you think Brooke's going to be there?"

"I should think so." He covered his face with his hands. "I don't want to go to work today."

"Why not? It's the first day of your new job."

"Working in accounts is sooo boring."

"Considering you ended up staying on as a labourer throughout December, I thought you'd be glad to get out of the freezing cold."

"Yeah I s'pose."

"Go on, get to work. You'd just spend the day on Grindr again. Yuk," she said giving him a nudge.

He swung his legs off the sofa and stood, rubbing his toned stomach. "Okay, I'm going. There's someone I need to speak to today anyway."

"Who's that?" she asked, as he walked out of the living room.

"Never you mind."

Chapter Forty-Nine

Brooke removed her glasses, folded them shut, and laid them on her desk. She had just finished re-reading Danni's manuscript and was pleased with the end result. It was a good book, in spite of everything that had happened.

The past week had had been testing to say the least, but hopefully now she had finished editing it, she could put both Danni and Megan out of her mind and move on. It was for the best after all.

She caught sight of Josh walking along through the office. He waved, and the next minute he was standing by her desk.

He looked down at her with a nervous grin.

"Hey Brooke, I'm sorry to barge in like this, but have you got a minute?"

"Do I really have a choice?"

His face dropped. "Of course you have. If you want me to leave, just say."

She drew out a chair and indicated for him to sit.

"It's okay. I don't mean to be rude. What can I do for you?"

He slid onto the chair and pulled his beanie hat off his head. "Well, it's not for me. I need to talk to you about Danni."

Brooke pushed her chair away from the desk and stood up. "Josh, I don't mean to sound impolite but I really don't want to discuss the matter. What's done is done."

"Please," he implored.

His expression was that of a desperate man. She sighed with irritation.

"You've got a minute, tops. Then I've got to get back to work," she said.

"Okay, okay." He took a deep breath. "Brooke, I don't want you to punish Danni for something I pushed her into doing. I begged her not to tell you because of your close working relationship with my dad. I thought he would disown me if he found out I was gay. It was a stupid thing to do – pretend we were engaged but you must understand it wasn't meant to hurt anyone. I was afraid. Can you see that?"

"I sympathise Josh, I really do, but at what point was Danni going to tell me exactly? She said she wanted to come clean, but she didn't. Does she do everything you ask of her?"

"Yes, she does and I do the same for her. I'm not denying the whole pretending things was a stupid idea, it was. But it's not Danni's fault – it's mine. She's my best friend, Brooke and I would do anything for her. I'm the one who begged her to pretend to be my fiancée and I even talked her into writing a bloody self-help book She didn't want to do that either. Seems I'm not such a good friend after all."

He dug his hand into his jacket and withdrew a memory stick.

"Here," he said handing it to her. "This is the real Danni. This is what she really wants to write about –

and she's bloody good at it. She isn't a liar or a cheat or any of the other things you think she is. She's a loyal, decent person and I'm proud to her call my friend."

He stood and pushed the chair in.

"That's all I've got to say."

Josh turned and walked back through the office.

Brooke looked down at the memory stick in her hand.

She didn't doubt Josh's sincerity. She believed every word he said. Maybe if things hadn't happened with Megan she could have found forgiveness in her heart. But for now, it was all still too raw.

Chapter Fifty

Danni woke up with a start. She was surprised she had managed to fall asleep, such was her anxiety. Today was the first time she was going to attend an author's launch event, but more importantly, Brooke would be there. Seeing her face-to-face, she was determined to make her listen. Make her understand.

Danni glanced at the time on her phone. It was too early to wake Josh, besides whenever she was feeling nervous, she preferred to be alone. She needed to figure out what she wanted to say to Brooke without coming across as insincere or taking what she had done lightly.

She remained in bed for another hour fretting and turning scenarios over in her mind, until finally she heard the running of the shower – Josh was up. It was time to get the show on the road. Throwing back the quilt, she leapt out of bed and selected her clothes before heading to the bathroom.

Two hours later they sat in the back of a cab making their way to the launch. Danni dug her nails into her palms and suppressed a yelp. She hadn't realised they had grown so long. Josh sat beside her in a smart grey suit.

"Do I look nervous?" she asked him.

"Hmm, let's see," he said taking her hands in his and turning them over, palm up. "Sweaty palms." He pressed a finger to her wrist. "Fast pulse rate." He eyed her forehead. "Film of perspiration. Yes, Danni. You look nervous."

She inhaled deeply and blew out a breath. "Crap. I thought I looked really poised and cool."

"Maybe the Danni in the parallel universe does but not you."

"Thanks, Josh. That's just what I needed to hear. Not!"

"Well, here we are," Josh said moving to the edge of the seat. "Let's go and knock Brooke dead. Not literally. You know what I mean."

The car pulled up at the publishing house. Roy was stood outside the building talking to a short man with a pink tie.

"Hi, Danni, Josh. This is Roger. He just wanted to pop out for a cigarette before we get started," Roy said as they got out of the cab.

Roger threw his cigarette to the ground a shook Danni's and then Josh's hand enthusiastically.

"Lovely to meet you both," he said. "Shall we go in?"

"Yes, of course," Roy replied as he led them into the building and the open lift, pressing the button to the second floor. They walked behind him in a single file along the corridor and into an oblong shaped conference room, filled to capacity with members of staff. A quick scan of the brightly lit place told her what she feared – Brooke was not going to show her face. So that was that then. No point crying over split milk.

"Ladies and gentlemen, boys and girls," Roy called out, drawing attention to himself at the head of the room. "Today it gives me great pleasure to tell you all Roger Holt's book has gone storming into the charts and is already in the top fifty as we speak."

The room erupted in applause as Roger made his way to stand next to Roy.

"That's gonna be you soon Danni," Josh whispered in her ear.

"Speech, speech, speech," the crowd called out.

Roy held his hand up to quieten them.

"Ahem, what can I say? First and foremost I would like to say a big thank you to Roy."

After ten minutes, he neared the end of his speech which consisted of numerous thanks and a funny anecdote about how his pet puppy got rather amorous with his laptop and he nearly lost the whole manuscript.

"Lastly, I'd like to say a big heartfelt to thank you to Brooke," he glanced around the room, searching for her, "For not only editing the book but for helping me express myself in a way I never thought possible."

"Brooke's here," someone yelled from the back of the room.

Danni squinted as she looked in the direction of the voice and true enough, Brooke was standing at the back with a gorgeous willowy blonde. They looked very friendly indeed. Brooke waved at Roger, then after he finished speaking, turned her attention back to the blonde.

Danni gulped back the warm white wine she held in a plastic cup. It looked like Brooke had moved on already. She watched them as they laughed easily with each other. They looked so comfortable, so relaxed, just how Brooke and herself had been not so long ago.

As if sensing her stare, Brooke glanced over at her. Their exchange lasted all of a few seconds before Brooke said something to the woman, then they both looked at her with a smile. Danni's inner voice told her that she must have totally misjudged Brooke. Was she sadistic? Why else would she be getting pleasure out of flirting with this woman right in front of Danni's eyes? Was this her payback? She wanted to cry. But that she would never do. Never in a million years would she give Brooke the satisfaction of knowing that she'd hurt her. Broke her heart even.

"What's the matter Danni?" Josh said.

Danni turned to him, blinking back the tears welling in her eyes. "Nothing. This was a bad idea, me coming here." She shoved the drink in his hand. "I'm going home. Please make an excuse to your dad."

"Hey," he said catching her by the arm. "I thought you were going to talk to Brooke."

"Yeah, so did I," she said shrugging off his hand. As she turned in the direction of the exit, she noticed Brooke coming towards her with the woman in tow. Now she really was taking the piss. Was she actually going to introduce her? Brooke stopped in the middle of the room and waited until Danni had to pass her.

"Danni–"

Danni slowed down momentarily, just long enough to say, "Sorry Brooke. I can't stop. I have to be somewhere in, like, ten minutes. Good to see you again." The words came out at lightning speed. Without waiting another second, she brushed past her and exited the room. Now this was why she couldn't be bothered with relationships. There was always way too much drama for her liking. Bypassing the lift she made her way down the seven flights of stairs and out onto the pavement. She would just have to accept the glorious night with Brooke for what it was – a one night stand. Though she knew she didn't have any claims on Brooke, that she was a free agent, it still hurt. She inhaled deeply as she looked up at the building. Good luck to them. She just hoped her new partner was better than Megan.

Tears blurred her vision as she stood on the edge of the pavement and caught sight of the familiar double-decker that would take her home. Her phone vibrated in her pocket. Withdrawing it, she looked down and took a life-changing step forward, the text was from Brooke. She never got a chance to read the message. The next few seconds seemed to happen in slow motion: the screeching of brakes. Josh shouting her name. The shocked face behind the windscreen of the Mini, his mouth forming a scream. There was going to be an unavoidable impact. Then there was. Danni somersaulted across the hood of the car, flew through the air and fell to the tarmac with a sickening thud.

Her eyes still closed, she heard Josh's frantic voice getting louder and louder until he was by her side, sobbing, calling her name repeatedly. *Why is he crying?* Danni wondered and then the world went black.

Chapter Fifty-One

St Thomas' hospital was as busy as the London underground during rush hour. Doctors and nurses darted along corridors, clipboards in hand. Patients walked around aimlessly, searching for signs to their particular department. Brooke sat with Josh in the Accident and Emergency waiting room, their faces bleached by the harsh florescent lights. Josh stared at the wall in front of him, both hands on his head, his voice so choked with tears and emotion Brooke had to strain to hear what he was saying.

"Why didn't she look where she was going? I tried to warn her."

Brooke laid her hand on his back and rubbed it. She was trying to hold it together for Josh's sake, despite wanting to break down herself. She couldn't believe this was happening. Barely an hour ago she was seconds away from talking to Danni and telling her that she understood why she had been less than truthful. That she realised there was no malice in her behaviour. But now Danni was lying in a hospital bed, her condition as yet unknown. This was something she could never have anticipated. Not to the woman she loved. *Yes, she loved her.* As much as she'd tried to quell her feelings and break free from Danni, she just couldn't. She didn't dare think about a life without her in it now.

As if on cue, the door swung open and a stocky

dark-haired doctor walked out with a stethoscope hung around his neck, his expression grim as he hurried into the waiting room. He shook his head as he neared, his eyes refusing to meet hers. Josh let out a wild animalistic scream and dropped to his knees. Brooke froze, she couldn't move. She waited. She wanted to hear it from the doctor's own mouth. She needed him to tell her that Danni was dead.

The doctor stopped in front of her. "Is your friend okay?" he asked, gesturing to Josh.

She looked at his name tag hanging from his grey shirt. Dr Patel. "Yes. He'll be fine."

She felt relieved as the doctor glanced down at Josh again and walked on, stopping to talk to a young couple a few feet away before ushering them into a side room.

"Josh, Josh!" Brooke whispered in a ragged breath, poking him in the ribs until he looked up at her.

He whimpered. "Danni's dead, she's dead."

Brooke tried to pull him up by his arm. "Josh she isn't. Listen to me. Look," she said twisting his head toward the couple being led away by the doctor.

Josh watched the closing door with a puzzled look on his tear stained face. "But ..."

Brooke shook her head. "He wasn't looking at us."

"Thank God," he said wiping his eyes with the back of his hands before using the chair to help him to his feet. "Sorry about that," he mumbled sheepishly.

"Don't worry about it. I had the exact thought when I saw him heading our way," she reassured him.

The doors to the unit swung open frequently as doctors, nurses, and visitors streamed through in endless cycles. But no-one came for Josh and Brooke. The waiting was endless. Brooke pushed up her sleeve and glanced at her watch. They'd been in the waiting room for over three agonising hours. She was just getting ready to make an enquiry when a small doctor with a pointy chin and a dainty button nose headed towards them, a faint smile on her face. "You're Miss Gardener's friends?"

Brooke felt an immediate adrenaline rush. "Yes. How is she?"

"Well considering. She has had a very lucky escape with just a few broken ribs, not to mention a very sore head. We'll be keeping her in overnight for observation, just to be on the safe side, but she should be fine. You must be Brooke I take it," she said smiling.

"Uh. Yes."

"I've been speaking with Danni, just to make sure her memory is sound. She's been talking about you non-stop."

Brooke's face flushed. "Can we see her?"

"Of course. She's in the first cubicle down the hall on the right. We'll be moving her onto a ward as soon as a bed becomes available. Try not to talk too much, she needs plenty of rest."

Brooke shook the doctor's hand. "Thank you so

much."

"No problem." The doctor nodded as she walked on.

Chapter Fifty-Two

The cubicle was sparse, with a single metal bed and a green plastic chair. Danni lay beneath a thin blue blanket, trying not to move her head or any other part of her body for that matter. Pain oozed through every muscle and every joint. *Bloody mini!*

She moved her eyes to the entrance of the cubical as Josh drew the curtain back and peeked his head through.

"Can I come in?" he asked with a big grin.

Danni wore a puzzled expression, her eyes glazed over. "Who are you?" She slurred. Seeing the terrified look on Josh's face she quickly retorted, "I'm kidding, Josh!"

He narrowed his eyes at her. "That's really not funny."

"Sorry."

He moved closer to the bed, gently taking her hand in his. "How are you feeling?"

She moved a little and let out a groan. "Oh ... just great. Bloody fantastic considering. Mind you, I have had a load of pain killers. I'm high as a kite!"

"I thought you were a goner Danni," Josh said, bowing his head as raw emotion caught in his throat.

Danni lifted her hand and rubbed the top of his head. "No chance. It takes more than a Mini to get rid of me. A Mercedes perhaps – but not a Mini."

Josh laughed. "I'm so glad you're all right. Now I

called your mum and she's on her way too. She knows you are ok. Your nan is knitting you a new scarf to make you feel better."

Danni grinned.

"I'm going to get us some drinks. You have another visitor who wants to see you," Josh said, getting up from the chair.

Danni took a breath. "Oh God. Please don't tell me it's Mick, he's probably heard about the drugs in this place. I'm feeling trippy enough as it is."

Josh smiled down at her and backed away. Danni closed her eyes.

Maybe if I pretend I'm asleep he'll go away.

Seconds later, a pair of soft, warm hands covered her own and her heart lifted. They didn't belong to Mick. She'd know those hands anywhere; they were Brooke's.

Danni opened her eyes and looked at Brooke, seeing only concern and sadness in her eyes.

"We thought we'd lost you," Brooke said softly.

Danni closed her eyes as a single tear slid from them. "Why would you care about losing something you didn't want?"

Brooke gently rested her face against her chest. "Danni. I've wanted you from the moment I laid eyes on you. I haven't stopped wanting you for a minute since."

Danni coughed, her mouth suddenly dry. "You could've fooled me. Let's not mention the blonde bimbo you seemed to be glued to."

"Polly? She's an old friend who really is straight and happily married to my cousin."

Danni snorted. "Yeah, right."

"Did you read my text?"

"Er no, I don't know if you noticed but I was too busy meeting a Mini! Besides, my phone no longer exists."

Brooke laughed. "You haven't lost your sense of humour then. I was texting you to ask you to come back so we could talk. I'll tell you what I wanted to say." She took hold of Danni's hand in her own. "I want to start again? A fresh start. No more lies, no more secrets."

Danni sensed her pulse quickening. Is that all it took these days to get forgiveness, three broken ribs? If she had realised that, she would have flung herself in front of a car weeks ago. "You do know I never set out to intentionally hurt you don't you?"

"Yes. I was too wrapped up with the crap I was going through with Megan to see clearly."

Danni shuddered at the mere mention of Megan's name. "So what happened with her then?"

"I'm happy to say she is well and truly out of my life, and my mind."

Danni grinned at the welcome news. "Good. I'm glad to hear it. So," she went on, "Shall we seal our new beginning with a kiss?" Danni said.

"It would be my pleasure," Brooke said as she gently pressed her lips against Danni's.

Chapter Fifty-Three

Four days had passed since Danni's release from hospital. The effects of the morphine now long gone, the ache in her body was only kept at bay with the aid of very strong painkillers. She braced herself as she sneezed for the fifth time that day. The living room resembled a florist. There were beautiful blooms everywhere, from Roy, Brooke, her family, and even Mick who had popped over with a bunch of wilted leaves that looked suspiciously like "da herb"! Perhaps she should get knocked over more often.

Josh stepped into the room with a big smile on his face. "Is there anything I can do for you?"

"No thanks," she said looking up at him. "You've been an absolute star, but I think I can manage turning the TV over now," she joked. Though the doctor had said to take things easy, she wasn't a total invalid. Josh had been running about catering to her every need for the past few days. It was time to give the poor man a break.

A contented smile spread across her face as Brooke walked into the blossoming room, carrying a tray of delights. The smell of chicken soup filled the air. "Mmmm, that smells delicious," Danni said as her stomach echoed her assessment of the delightful smell.

"It is. It's my mum's special recipe," Brooke said placing the tray on the coffee table. She knelt down beside her, kissing her on the mouth. "Have you missed me?"

Danni tentatively reached her arm around her neck, gently pulling Brooke's face close to her own. "Er … you've only been in the kitchen for an hour."

Josh cleared his throat loudly. "Hellooooo ladies, I'm still here if you hadn't noticed."

The two women laughed, kissing once again to truly annoy him.

"Have you told her the good news yet, Brooke?"

"Good news about what?" Danni asked looking expectantly from one to the other.

"I read your book," Brooke said standing up and looking down at her proudly.

Danni was confused. "Yes I know – you edited it. Maybe it's you that's got concussion."

"No, not *that* book! The one you were hiding from me – *'Good Girls Go to Heaven'*."

"But, er, but how, who?"

"I gave it to her," Josh said grinning.

Danni groaned inwardly. "So what did you think? Is it as bad as everyone seems to think," she asked, not really wanting to hear the answer.

"Are you kidding me? I absolutely loved it," Brooke gushed.

"You did? But all the rejection letters."

Brooke settled onto the space next to her. "They're idiots. They wouldn't know talent if it ran them over!"

Danni winced. "Ouch!"

"Oops sorry. Bad choice of words." Brooke

laughed. "But anyway, I took the liberty of sending it to a friend of mine who works in fiction at another publishing house. Thought it was well worth a punt. I do have an eye for a good thing you know. Well the good news is my friend just texted me to say they're interested in publishing it."

"What! Are you serious?"

"I've never been more serious in my life." Brooke fished out her mobile phone from her pocket and showed Danni the message.

Danni's eyes scanned the small screen, her heart pounding inside her chest. "I can't believe it. Oh my God, this is amazing. I can't thank you both enough." She looked up at Josh, her vision fuzzy with tears. "You are such a sneaky little weasel! Thank you. Thank you so much, Joshie."

"Well, someone has to make sure you're talent is shared with the world," he said winking. "Anyway, you two love birds, I'm off to meet my dad. You know, have some father-son time."

The pain in her ribcage prevented her from jumping up and hugging the life out of him for all the things he'd done for her. She could not have asked for a better friend. Instead, she reached out for his hand, squeezing it as he placed it in hers. She blinked away the tears. "Okay. Tell him I said hi, and thanks for the lovely flowers and card."

He bent down and planted a kiss firmly on her bruised forehead. "Will do."

Seconds later the front door slammed shut.

Brooke rested her hand on Danni's leg. "Are you up for a bit of celebrating?"

Danni arched her brows. "Depends what we're celebrating."

"How about the fact that you've achieved your dream of becoming a published author, oh and just that other small matter of surviving a car accident!"

"In that case yes. Be gentle with me though!" She laughed, reaching for the buttons on Brooke's shirt.

Brook gently swiped her hand away. "Oi. I was thinking more along the lines of chocolate chip muffins, as many lattes as your heart desires and ..." she reached down into her bag and produced a DVD, "... season one *and* two of Orange is the New Black."

Danni's eyes widened as a smile broke out on her face. "You truly are a girl after my own heart!"

Chapter Fifty-Four

The charred smoky aroma of meat sizzling on charcoal wafted through the restaurant as the party of five reclined on plush leather seats around a circular glass table. A waiter quickly refilled their empty glasses with champagne.

When Roy got wind of the fact that Danni's mum had come to stay with her, he had insisted they all share a family meal. Danni was more than happy to oblige, she loved a good old nosh-up! Everything seemed to have fallen into place for Danni and Josh. Since Josh had come out to his dad, their once strained relationship had gone from strength to strength. Josh finally had peace of mind and Danni had two publishing deals, three broken ribs and the woman of her dreams.

Danni listened in as Brooke, Roy and her mother debated the merits of self-help books and the effect they had on people's lives. She was surprised to realise that her mum knew so much about the authors Brooke and Roy were commenting on. She had always thought she was only into James Patterson-type books.

"Well, looks like your mum likes her future daughter-in-law," Josh teased as he took a sip of his drink.

Danni playfully nudged him. "Marriage is jumping the gun a bit, Josh. I'm just getting used to sharing my bed with someone else."

Josh arched an eyebrow. "You could have fooled me. You two look like you were made for each other."

She let out a long breath. "I know it sounds a bit corny but that's exactly how it feels. It's like she's the final piece to my puzzle."

"Which just leaves me now, all alone with no love to call my own," he said pretending to wipe a tear from his eye.

Danni looked at him in disbelief. "Oh stop it, Josh! If you wanted a relationship you could have one in an instant. You've got loads of men throwing themselves at your feet."

Josh smiled. "Yeah I know. But it's not the same, is it? Not when you're really in to someone and they feel the same way about you."

Danni felt for Brooke's leg under the table and rested her hand upon it. "S'pose. It will happen when you least expect it, Josh. Just like it happened to me."

Josh nodded as Roy clinked on his glass. All eyes turned to him.

Standing abruptly, he addressed the table and declared "I would like to make a toast! To Danni's success and most importantly, to family. It's been especially wonderful to meet Danni's mum, Cynthia. Though we may not all be related by blood, being here with you all tonight, it sure feels that way."

"To family," they all said in union as Roy sat down again.

Danni shot Josh a look, and he grinned.

"It seems our parents are getting very well. I've

never seen my dad so engrossed in a conversation with someone. He's hardly spoken to anyone else," he whispered.

Danni glanced over at Roy as he sipped his pina colada, then roared with laughter as her mum made a remark. Hmmm, maybe she had been wrong about him all along. She'd never had a fully functioning gaydar.

A short waiter with a pencil thin moustache and a mop of thick black hair came over to take their order.

"And for you madam?" The waiter asked Danni, peering down at her expectantly with beady brown eyes.

Danni looked up at him. "I'll have the steak please."

"And how would you like it cooked?" he asked, his ballpoint pen poised over his little writing pad.

Danni glanced at Roy, who was busily scanning the menu, before looking back at the waiter. She spoke in a whisper. "Cremated!"

His face remained expressionless. "Very good, madam," he said before moving around the table for more orders.

"Your mum's lovely," Brooke said turning to Danni.

"I know. It runs in the family."

Brooke smiled as her mouth hovered near Danni's ear. "Oh, I knew that already. Though I might need a few more nights of passion to be sure."

Danni's cheeks flushed as she giggled. "Oi, saucy. We're in public."

Josh leaned onto Danni's arm. "Oh God, not again. I don't know if I'm going to be able to stomach all this lovey-dovey stuff from you two for much longer."

Danni turned to face Brooke, her mouth softening into a wide smile. "Well you'd better get used to it, because I'm in it for the long run."

"Me too." Brooke smiled.

Epilogue

One year later.

At an elegant mews house in Islington N1, a wire-haired terrier barked as another reveller arrived at the gathering, bottle in hand.

"He's rather *friendly* isn't he?" Rodger Holt remarked as he hobbled into the lounge room with "Sparky" enthusiastically wrapped around his left leg.

Danni turned away from the guest she was talking to, her mouth agape.

"Sparky, get off! Naughty boy," she scolded as she desperately attempted to pull the dog's gyrating body from the man's limb.

"It's okay, I know how excited dogs get when there are lots of people around."

Danni blushed, finally managing to free Roger's leg from the amorous dog hug. She apologised, "Sorry, Roger. Josh has spoilt this dog rotten." She patted her pet as he attempted to grab a sandwich from her plate.

"Only because he needs a male role model," Josh interrupted. "Poor thing, living in a house full of women. Don't worry, I've taught him how to put the loo seat down!" Josh laughed, sliding up to Danni's side and planting a kiss on her flushed cheeks. He looked dashingly handsome in jeans and an open neck shirt.

"Ha ha. If I ever have a son, please remind me

not to let you ever babysit," Danni said touching his face affectionately.

"We'll see."

With that, the room was suddenly plunged into darkness, as a hush fell over the once lively crowd.

"Three cheers for Danni!" someone shouted enthusiastically as the door flung wide open. Cheers erupted at the sight of an elegant Brooke in the doorway, carrying a majestic three tier muffin cake. As if on cue, the room burst into song.

"For she's a jolly good fellow… for she's a jolly good fellow!"

Brooke laughed as she joined the inebriated group in what was a pretty tuneless, but thoroughly heart-warming rendition. Roy took the cake and placed it on the large antique dining table, leaving Brooke to stand proudly at Danni's side.

"Congratulations, darling," Brooke gushed, turning her face to Danni's and dropping a quick kiss on her lips.

"Thank you. Thank you everyone!" Danni shouted triumphantly, tears brimming in her eyes as she looked around at her wonderfully cheerful guests.

How had all this happened?

"*Unlocking The Door to Love*" had reached number one in the "Holistic Self-Help" charts, she'd been interviewed in *The Guardian;* and best of all, she had somehow managed not to spend every penny of her earnings! *Result!* There was so much to take in, not just the book but her life as it now was, with the four-bedroom house in Islington she had always dreamt of, the woman she loved and a cheeky little dog, who did strangely enough know how to put the toilet seat down.

So, okay, she wasn't known as the female Oscar Wilde quite yet, and Brooke had done little to advance her knowledge of muffin making, but it was pretty perfect from where she was standing.

"So, my love," Danni whispered to a rather jolly Brooke, "this must be how it feels to go from faking it to making it. All we need now is for you to train as a pastry chef!"

Who said dreams don't come true?

6978195R00193

Printed in Great Britain
by Amazon.co.uk, Ltd.,
Marston Gate.